Praise for the Base Branch Series

"Megan Mitcham's books arc well paced, well-plotted suspense novels edged with stunning sensual intensity. Her lovers are cold and deadly--except when they are skin-to-skin. I can't wait for the next book in the series!"

- **DELILAH DEVLIN**
New York Times and USA Today bestselling author

"A true gift from an exceptional storyteller."

- **Cristin Harber**
New York Times and USA Today bestselling author

"This is a fresh and exciting story with lots of great characters."

- **5 Star Amazon Review**

"Megan now joins my elite team of must read authors. I fell in love with her work in *Enemy Mine*, and it just gets better the more I read."

- **TNT Reviews**

BOOKS BY MEGAN MITCHAM

BASE BRANCH NOVELS
ENEMY MINE
JUSTICE MINE
STRANGER MINE
WARRIOR MINE
DANGER MINE
PRISONER MINE
VERSIONS
VIRTUES
VARIATIONS
NEVER MINE
RELENTLESSLY MINE
FURIOUSLY MINE
CAPTOR MINE

BUREAU NOVELS
FOR ALL TO SEE
PAINTED WALLS

ANTHOLOGIES
ANTICIPATION
CONQUESTS
ROGUES
SEX OBJECTS
COWBOY HEAT
HIGH OCTANE HEROES
WILD AT HEART VOLUME II
benefiting Turpentine Creek Wildlife Refuge

Captor Mine

Base Branch Novel #13

Megan Mitcham

Copyright Warning

Published by MM Publishing LLC

Edited by Jenny Sims

Proofread by Tina Rucci & Lynn Mullan

Cover Design by RBA Designs

Variations
All Rights Are Reserved. Copyright 2017 by Megan Mitcham

Publication: September 2017

Digital ISBN: 978-1-941899-30-4

Print ISBN: 978-1-941899-31-1

To the men and women of the armed services, who inspired these stories and protect freedoms on a daily basis, thank you. Our lives are possible because of your sacrifice. You are true heroes! We honor you today and always.

To the readers who've stuck with the men and women of the Base Branch through thirteen books, thank you. You are rockstars!

The characters of Base Branch, the 700,000 plus words I wrote, and you guys taught me so much over the past three years. I plan to take those lessons and put them to work on the Stalker Series, the Stronghold Series, the Strong Series, and hopefully many more to come.

I hope you hang around and help me grow with each book.

All the best,

Megan

Chapter One

"Katrin, my light."

"Dad?" Kat whirled from her patient sprawled unconscious across the operating table to the opulently carved door her father pushed through. Had she been in her operating room in her hospital, he wouldn't have gotten nearly this close to the sterile environment necessary for surgery. But here —in his makeshift operating room, in his house, and staffed with his people—so much was out of her hands. Another cubic centimeter of resentment syphoned itself to the already overflowing ventricles of her heart.

"You shouldn't be in here." Kat positioned herself between her patient and her father.

He waved away her concerns with his large hands. His skin, while always pale, held a waxy quality that gleamed in the bright lights. It struck a memory. She sat at a long oak table in the dining hall of her boarding school. Excitement brimmed her cheeks with the knowledge her father would join her for the first time since sending her away. Around her, parents embraced their children. None were the overly boisterous displays she'd recently observed in the States, but they'd been warm and endearing in their upper-crust modesty. Finally, her father strode confidently through the double doors. She reserved the urge to run to him, though her heart demanded it. Her feet tapped anxiously beneath her until he drew near, leaned down, and retrieved her hand. He placed it on the back of his cold, clammy hand, and patted it once. "My light, you're looking as brilliant as ever. I'm delighted to see you." His words, incongruous to his affections, echoed in her mind.

"Your care and abilities amaze me more than you know." His voice and proximity jarred her to the present. Dark eyes glistened with appreciation.

Unbidden, a smile stretched her lips. She should have tossed him from the room on his ass. Her patient was far from out of the woods. One bacteria could end the life she'd worked so tirelessly to save. Instead, Kat snapped up the token he offered like the insecure little girl she was, throwing away years of intense therapy.

"You know I treasure you, right?" He cupped the tops of her shoulders. A chill from his fingertips seeped through the thin fabric of her scrubs.

Maybe she should check his circulation or, at least, draw a blood panel on him. It could be anemia or Raynaud's disease.

"Do you have numbness in your fingertips or toes?"

The dark eyes that scared her as a child gleamed and narrowed. "Seems an odd answer to my question."

He'd asked a question? Kat gritted her teeth and searched her synapses for his last comment. No wonder she had zero friends. People liked attention, conversation, care, and concern. She liked solving problems. Once the problem had a sufficient answer, her interest zipped along to the next issue.

"I'm sorry." Kat peeled back her bloody gloves and folded them inside out, careful not to touch any bodily fluids. She clutched them in her hands like a talisman. If she could solo a seven-hour surgery, by all that was right in the world, then she could hold a proper conversation. "Occupational hazard." Shc grinned and then realized her mask still covered her face. "Your hands are cold. I was concerned you might have anemia or suppressed circulation."

"You're too good to me." He gave her shoulders the old one pat. "It's time I returned the favor." Her father turned her toward the door and carted her along with a robust frame that outweighed hers by a hundred pounds or more.

"What?" Her heartbeat soared in a mixture of excitement and dread. All she'd ever wanted was her father's time and attention. At long last, she was getting it, but at whose expense? The man she'd just cut open, toyed with for hours, and sewn back together needed her. There was no hospital staff to check his vitals, much less change the reservoir on his wound drain or the dressing at the surgical site.

She craned her neck to grab one last glimpse of the massive black man before her father ushered her around the corner into a long hallway. The machine she'd hooked her patient to before the surgery was the best in the business. If any of his markers dropped below norms, it would alert her.

"I can't go far. The most critical hours are those right after surgery."

"Wouldn't the most critical hours be during surgery?" Her father walked only as far as the next door on the same side of the hallway as the mock surgical wing and tossed the door wide.

"Well, yes." She nearly choked.

A mirror image of the bedroom next door glittered in its grandeur. Sculpted and gold leafed vines crowded two massive windows across the room as well as the bed on the far-left wall. Thick draperies and bedding with handwoven designs anchored the room while the beveled walls and ceilings gave the illusion of unstoppable height.

None of this magnificence made her tongue knot in the back of her throat.

Her luggage sat on the chaise. Her luggage from her Dunbar, Maryland, apartment only five blocks from Johns Hopkins University Hospital. Her hospital. The hospital she'd been taking a sabbatical from to study at Charité in Berlin for two months, which was approximately four thousand miles from where she and her father stood in his home outside Stockholm, Sweden.

"You've worked so hard, my light. Please, make yourself at home." He gently pushed her into the room and closed the door.

The echo of the heavy wood meeting its frame sent Kat into a spiral. Hadn't he wanted to spend time with her? Sweat slicked her palms. Wasn't that why she'd left her patient? The air inside her mask thickened to the consistency of syrup. Who was the man her father had fetched her all the way from Germany to save, and why did she have to be the one to save him?

Kat gripped the corner of the wall. The raised edges of beautifully stained wood threatened to close in on her. She ripped the mask from her face and teetered across the room and around her bags to an ornate mirror. Staring back was the face of a strong, intelligent, beautiful woman.

"You are no longer a girl. You are a strong, intelligent, beautiful woman worthy of love and devotion." As she spoke, the brilliant blue eyes staring back brimmed with tears. The woman's lips shook. A frown broke the façade.

Her well-constructed exterior shattered, hit the floor, and disintegrated as if never there.

Kat covered her face and sobbed silently as she had every day under her father's care. No matter how many times she told herself she was no longer the girl he'd ignored for so many years, when faced with the man on his own turf, the self-affirmations were a bald-faced lie. It wasn't her petite stature or his gigantic one that gave her pause. It wasn't that he'd ever beaten or abused her in any way.

For as long as she could remember, he simply, painfully dismissed her.

Tears rolled steadily down her cheeks. She wiped them away and glared at the woman she'd become. Her curly blonde hair held itself together in a knot atop her head beneath a surgical cap. One good tug and the disposable material and curls tumbled onto her shoulders. After years of taunts about her frizzy mane and no feminine help to speak of, she'd learned through much trial and error how to tame the mess. She'd picked her career of choice and the proper colleges to attend, which would aid in her success, at age ten. All without the guidance of a parent or guardian.

She looked past the reflection and addressed the terrified, lonely girl. "Above all that, you've succeeded."

Sure, she'd succeeded. Talking to herself in the mirror. It wasn't quite the landmark for achievement she'd hoped for, but she could get it if she refused to quit.

Kat turned away from her image more determined than ever to talk to her father and make him listen for the first time in her life. She dropped the gloves, which needed to be disposed of properly, the mask, and the cap onto the foot of the bed and hurried to the door. Her fingers wrapped around the gold lever and twisted. The metal gave way, bottoming out when it faced the intricately designed wood floor, but it didn't release the latch. Thinking that the latch hadn't caught in the first place, she pulled. The door remained closed. She pushed the lever up and pulled out. No change.

She stepped back and assessed the door. There were no obvious buttons, catches, or bolts. Her fingers balled into a fist and struck the door three times. "Hello? My door isn't opening. Hello? I need help, please."

No one answered.

Tamping down her irritation and confusion, Kat moved methodically through the room of seemingly endless doors. The first between the main entrance and the bed's sconced headboard gave freely into a palatial bathroom that echoed like a tomb. She backtracked and assessed the five remaining doors. "Don't know why I bother, but..." She rounded the bed and yanked on the handle between the bed and far wall of windows and French doors. It gave way to a cavernous closet.

Irritation mounted a horse and galloped hard and fast toward an unacknowledged fear. A fear she refused to voice.

She ran to the wall of windows and doors and pried at each without success. Her feet pounded faster through the room to the last door that stood opposite the foot of the bed. Both her hands gripped the handle and heaved. The door flew backward, knocking her off balance...in more ways than one.

Her patient lay on the operating table as she'd left him only minutes ago.

"I don't understand." She held tight to the handle to keep from hitting the ground physically. Metaphorically, she crashed into it from a much greater height. Her heart raced ahead of her feet and mind.

This room, like hers, had five doors. She tried the windows and French doors first. Kat burst through the closet door, expecting it to be empty like the one in "her" room, only this one had clothes. They didn't take up one tenth of the available space. She snatched a shirt from the nearest hanger and assessed the soft cotton. It could wrap around her twice and her father once, but he wouldn't be caught in the gym in such a casual ensemble. Next, she pulled a pair of pants off a hanger. The long tag swung wildly about. It was a size too short for her father. He towered over most men.

Kat turned and peered into the room at the man she'd been given no background information about—even after she'd asked repeatedly—yet ordered to save.

"What the hell?" Kat held the jeans to her chest but ripped a hanger from the nearest rack and slung it through the wide space. "What the hell?"

She bit back tears and debilitating fear and walked to the last door. The door she'd walked out of with her father not more than ten minutes ago. Her steady hands shook as she reached for the lever and twisted.

No change.

Panic threatened to rip free from her insides. Years of training in the field of trauma forced her to bank them. She walked to the man on the table. His large hands hung off either side of it. Thick forearms braced the rest of his muscular arms from dangling over the edge.

"Who are you?" She begged him to wake and answer, knowing he wouldn't. The swelling in his brain had forced her to place him in a medically induced coma. He'd been unconscious since she'd first seen him this morning. She wondered, not for the first time, how long he'd been in this state before she arrived.

"How were you hurt?" Had her father accidentally hurt the man and trusted only her to revive him without reprisal? Would he survive?

He didn't answer.

Neither did he code, which left her in this unfathomable predicament.

As a doctor, a surgeon, she was invested in a patient's health through duty and honor. Never before had she been a prisoner to a patient's prognosis. She stared at the large African American man whose pulse registered weakly through the beeping spikes of a monitor. A metaphorical chain linked her existence to every peak and valley, and she needed to know why.

Kat leaned over and secured her palm to his left palm. The warmth of his skin seared hers. His temperature was up, but it didn't surprise her. She'd measured it before and after the procedure, but the heat it generated shocked her. Everything else in her life was cold and unfeeling. Though his calm face didn't show it, this man was warm and frantic in his fight for life. She lifted his heavy arm and crossed it over his torso, moved to the other side and repeated the measure. Then she checked the monitor one more time, stalked to the door, and beat on it with all her might.

Seconds bled into minutes, which threatened to congeal into a half an hour. Before she knew it, her fight had decimated a significant chunk of time. Her knuckles cried with each additional strike. Her hands pulsed. Sweat dripped down her forehead and nape, soaking the collar of her scrubs. Still, no one answered.

Sadness and fear morphed into an uncontrollable rage. How dare her own blood keep her locked away like some misbegotten fairy-tale princess? By Maud Mary Chadburn, her surgical idol, someone would open the door and tend to her one way or the other. "Cover your ears, Maud," she whispered.

"If this man's life is in any way important to you, you will open this door and speak to me."

She hadn't threatened to harm her patient. Not exactly, but the impetus was there more than she was comfortable with. Kat couldn't be expected to become a prisoner on her father's whim. She'd done it before, but she'd had no choice. Now she had choices; too bad all of them sucked.

Kat ceased her tirade on the thick wood and waited silently.

The beeps of the monitor grew as with each passing second someone refused to answer her call. It reached a fevered pitch, pinging off her amygdala and forcing her to respond the only way she could to get her father's attention. She stopped next to the monitor.

"I'm sorry," she whispered and pulled the leads from the device.

Flatline sang loudly enough that it tried to wake its failing patient, at least in her mind. In reality, it only alerted medical professionals of their failures for the patient. In this case, neither scenario applied.

Twenty seconds after the call began, the door swung wide. Her father consumed the space in the threshold. "What's wrong?"

Gee, where to start? Um, how about imprisonment? That tact wouldn't work with her father. His emotions were so few as to be nonexistent. She'd have to speak in a way in which he could relate.

Kat plugged the lead back into the machine. Silence suffocated the room for three heartbeats. The monitor caught up to her patient's vitals and beeped in time.

Her father's wide chest puffed.

She stepped forward. "If I'm going to save this man's life, I need access to more medical equipment."

He gave her his back.

The triumph of moments ago plummeted. She couldn't be locked in this room with a man she knew nothing about—except the physical makeup of his impressive body and just as extraordinary injuries—until he died or reached recovery.

Kat moved to the end of the operating table and took two steps toward the door. When her father turned back and stepped into the room, she stalled. A man with a large gun strapped to his chest stepped into the space her father had occupied.

"Tell Aron what you need, and he'll get it for you." He pointed at the armed man who looked more clear-eyed sentinel than errand boy. Honestly, she'd never seen eyes such a light, translucent blue. They were eerie as hell.

"Do you understand?" her father asked.

"Not much of the past two days." Her teeth ground.

"I know you have questions. As do I, which is why you need to do everything in your power to make sure this man makes a full recovery."

What the hell did that mean?

"Who is he? How did he receive his injuries? Did you hit him while you were driving?" Her voice pitched higher with each unanswered question.

"My light." He sighed and stepped forward.

She'd always loved his pet name for her. It showed that, maybe more than anything else, he cared for her. As she grew up, though, Kat saw it as the placating tool he used before he handled her.

"All you need to know is that he is a very dangerous man. I need him alive to answer my questions." Kat opened her mouth, but her father lifted his hand. "Now, I must go away for a while. I trust my men to take care of you. I trust you to take care of him." His index finger stabbed in the direction of her patient. "When he wakes, let Aron know immediately." He patted her shoulder once and turned.

"I'm a prisoner." She couldn't keep the word from forming nor the hysterics from rattling her vocal cords.

"Hardly, my light. You're in the finest estate in the countryside with the most competent security and staff sworn to keep you safe so that you may fulfill your calling and heal this man."

Aron moved into the hallway and out of sight, allowing her father to exit. His hand rested on the handle. He looked at her, really examined her features, while she sneered at his sharp face and cool visage. "I know you'll make me proud."

"When will you be back?" She didn't know why she asked the insane question. After all, she was a scientist at heart. There were so many more important things to know. She was also the young, scared girl she'd tried time and again to leave behind.

The sentence she'd heard as many times as she'd posed the futile question was all he left to keep her chilled until his return.

"When my business is appeased."

Chapter Two

A clatter from behind sent Kat into the
stratosphere. Her feet dangled in space for several
seconds. Every extremity drew tight to her body
ready to defend an attack. What? Was she going to
blink her patient to death with her penlight? And
wouldn't that be counterproductive to the care
she'd administered to bring him back from the edge
of death? Her shoes found the floor again, and she
whipped around from her bag with the small tool in
hand to find the source of the noise.

He laid on his side just as she'd positioned
him twenty minutes ago. Not the source of the
noise.

The door chirped and then opened. Aron
stalked inside with a covered tray in his hand. It
hosted a fallen bottle of Creed Silver Mountain
water. He stalked across the room and placed it on
the coffee table between the foot of the large
hospital bed she'd had delivered four weeks ago
and an antique sofa.

"I told you I didn't need that fancy water."
She huffed and shoved her glasses up her nose.
Hell, people in so many countries didn't have
access to clean water. She didn't need or want a
bottle of water that cost more than her rent. No one
should.

After weeks of having the same one-sided conversation, she knew Aron wouldn't respond. During the first week, she'd thought him a mute until he'd been forced to ask her a question about her medical supply list. He was capable, just not willing.

When he headed for the exit she hadn't walked through in far too long, she tugged the hem of her scrubs and poked her tongue out at him. "Thank you." The door closed with a thunk. "For nothing," she added.

The door opened, and Aron stepped back inside with a scowl tattooed on his face.

"Yes?" Kat smiled sweetly.

"Any change?"

"Well, the skin at the site of the wound drain is healing nicely since removal, and his bowels are firming." Her inner badass, the one she wanted to wear on her sleeve like a spiked leather jacket, chuckled quietly, safely inside.

"Katrin," he snapped.

"What?"

"Has he woken?" Aron growled.

She pointed at the large, unconscious man— the dangerous man—and shrugged. "Powers of observation fail you?"

Aron's upper lip curled. She'd grown accustomed to his snarl by the fourth day. He wouldn't hurt her. He also wouldn't let her go. Father's orders.

"No," she relented. "No change."

The brute retreated.

"Thanks again," she purred. When the door closed, she added, "For nothing."

At least, they fed and clothed her.

Kat had heard horror stories from across the globe in and around emergency rooms for the past decade. If she knew better, she'd count her blessings, but how could she? Ever since she'd eliminated the sedatives from her patient's doses of medication, she'd been a real-life jack-in-the-box. Touch the lever and... Ka Pow! She launched into the air. How could she not?

The man could crush her without trying. He nearly succeeded every time she rolled him to keep his blood flowing evenly and his skin from breaking down and developing bedsores. Striated muscles stacked upon corded muscles stacked upon bulky muscles. An obviously powerful man—it would seem impossible to incapacitate him.

What had it taken to knock him down so thoroughly? A car. A bulldozer.

Since it was all for the best, the how didn't matter. His body needed to heal, and frankly, he scared the hell out of her. She shouldn't be afraid because the security here rivaled a small prison. The night and morning shifts rotated statue-imitating guards like a menstruating girl changed panties. During the day, however—the only time she asked for supplies—Aron stood watch.

Over the years, Kat had worked in busy emergency rooms with criminals of all varieties. She'd treated them all with the same care and compassion as she did a sweet old man or a little kid. Those criminals had been in handcuffs, though.

Her patient's massive hands lay crossed over his chest, unencumbered except for the coma. They could do damage, if desired.

Kat needed him to get better so she could get far from this prison and back to her life. More than that, she wanted him to get better. As lethal as he was, she shouldn't want him to, but it was in her blood. It had been from an early age. The need to fix people propelled her.

***

She removed the glasses she didn't really need and set them aside. The snaps on both sides of his hospital gown stuck. Kat wiped away at her eyes unimpeded and yanked harder. The sticky clasps finally gave way, and she pulled the gown down, front and back to the middle of his torso. Her fingers and forearms ached from the effort of shifting his weight to get the material down. The detailed striations over his muscular chest and arms had disappeared over the past several days, yet time and his sedentation had done little to minimize their bulk. Likely, the NG tube she'd inserted through his nose into his stomach—when it'd become apparent he wasn't waking—worked enough to maintain his body composition. A glow returned to his smooth chocolate skin. The delineation of his abdominal wall remained intact.

Kat cleared her throat and moved to the head of the bed where she'd prepped a shave station. "Mind in the game, Kat." If left in this state, it wouldn't be long before his condition began to deteriorate. She smoothed her soft pink scrubs, lathered his skull, and proceeded. The razor skimmed easily over the crown of his head and even the area above his ears. His nape was the hardest to get in his prone state. From the first time she'd seen the man, whose name she still didn't know, his hair had been tightly cropped to his head. "Sorry," she whispered.

In the second week after she'd removed the sedation and IV, skittishness had given way to resignation. Now, three weeks later, resignation rushed to concern, and she needed his head free of the soft tuft that had grown.

Kat eyed the line of MRIs she'd demanded her patient have the moment she'd first heard of his condition before she arrived as well as the ones she'd ordered since. Worry that she'd missed something stole her appetite over the past two days. When she'd ordered another scan, Aron had refused her and accused her of overreacting. Maybe she was. The body had a unique way of defending itself against trauma, sometimes shutting off for years before it returned to complete and normal function.

Each image showed a healthy brain free from lesions, tumors, and bleeds. Still, he remained unconscious, and she didn't have years to spare.

She'd assessed the body scans to no avail, which was why she rinsed away the shaving cream, set the grooming kit aside, and proceeded with a physical examination. Her fingers glided over the smooth surface of his bald head. Each rise and dip warranted extra exploration, but time and again, she found no softness in the bone. Her hands worked down to where his skull met his neck. Along his spine, small mountains of muscle held each vertebra in a precise column.

"Nothing." Kat withdrew her hands, braced her palms on either side of the bed, and groaned.

His blood panels were clear. His leg was healing nicely. He retained flexibility in his joints and muscles, thanks to daily stretching and hourly repositioning. His pulse and blood pressure were better than hers were. Why was he unconscious? Kat had no clue. Sequestered—who was she kidding—imprisoned as she was, she couldn't consult with other doctors or order more tests.

Desperation pinched her nape in a death grip. The walls threatened to crumble and trap her

in the collapse. She had to get out, which meant
she had to get him better.

Kat wrestled his gown back up and fastened
the snaps closed. She sat on the edge of the bed
and frowned at him. Coma specialist wasn't in her
bag of tricks, but she'd studied it dispassionately
when she attended university. Patients with even
partial brain function could hear while
unconscious. They also responded positively to
physical contact.

He needed a new doctor. Kat didn't do
touchy-feely. She didn't coddle. The one thing she
did do was freedom. Having an absentee father
taught her independence from an early age.
Freedom to roam the world and explore any and
everything kept her sane.

"Sir, can you hear me?" This was stupid,
worse than talking to yourself because this guy
wasn't going to answer. Kat would answer herself in
a Tokyo second. She repositioned, facing him.

"Sir, my name is Katrin Royan. I'm a doctor.
I've..." *Been taken prisoner and ordered to make you
well, so help me out.* If he could hear her, that
probably wouldn't help his condition. "I'm here to
care for you." The man's full lips, thick brows, and
stout chin remained still. "Can you help me out a
little? Wiggle something?" She assessed his body for
the slightest movement. "Anything?"

Wow, she sucked at this. Kat rolled her eyes
and headed for her lunch.

***

The door chirped. Kat released the hand
she'd been holding, jumped off the bed, and stood a
few comfortable feet away. Aron strolled in with the
same overpriced water and tray of opulent food.
Outside the row of windows and the door, daylight
dimmed. Another day. Another disappointment.

Add it to the stack of days and it equaled a month and a half of incarceration.

"I have to speak with my father," she announced. Where was her father's business, and what was so important that he would lock her up ever, but for so long without checking on her? At boarding school, she received monthly letters from him. Visits hadn't been so frequent. Yet now she was a prisoner in his house. Was he not here or just not seeing her?

Aron ignored her and placed the tray on the coffee table.

The impetus to do something drove her very likely to her death, but somewhere was better than nowhere. And Aron wouldn't hurt her. Her father wouldn't allow it.

"I'll take it in my room." She smiled at the ogre.

His scowl morphed into a sneer. Ghostly eyes rolled to the top of his head. The gesture warmed her aching heart. Knowing she irritated him was the only satisfaction she'd gotten in too long. Her gaze drifted to Coma Pete. She'd taken to calling him that last week. The nickname fit him about as well as incapacitation did—not at all—but she liked the endearment. It took off the sharp edge of his imposing size and sturdy features.

Aron rounded the corner into the room she'd been sleeping in for the past two weeks when her neck and nerves could take no more of the couch in Coma Pete's room. Really, she'd gone when she knew he wouldn't code in the middle of the night or wake and smother her in her sleep.

Kat sprinted for the only door that opened. Her hideous orthopedic clogs clapped against the hardwood, but she didn't care. Get her out of the room and give her open space. She'd stomp the big man in a run or die trying.

If she got away, she could send a specialist for Pete, and the police for her father as he'd clearly gone off the deep end.

"Katrin!" Aron's baritone shook the walls. It propelled her faster.

Her hand reached for the handle. Every time she'd tried the door, it'd been locked, but she'd never tried it when Aron was inside. Each time he entered, he left without entering a code or putting a key in the lock. Kat's fingers wrapped around the cold metal and wrenched.

The latch gave way, and Kat ripped the door back. The polished wood of the oak paneled hallway and lush carpet with its scrawled design filled her view.

"No, Katrin!" He was so close. His large frame cast a shadow over her.

She pushed forward, feeling the warmth of the hallway against her cheek. The scent of flowers knocked down the antiseptic one embedded in her skin.

Something hard and immovable clamped around the back of her neck. The hallway tilted and flipped. Kat's shoulder and hip landed with a thump that reverberated through her skeleton and organs. Aron's face appeared in front of her. His lips moved in wide, frantic movements she couldn't decipher. The rich copper of her blood seeped onto her tongue. Veins swelled in the guard's neck. Air refused entry to Kat's lungs. She tried to roll onto her side and stretch her neck, but nothing relieved the void.

Aron's face came so close that, for an instant, she thought he might kiss her. She'd always said if she were attacked, she'd fight, but she couldn't breathe, much less claw and kick. He belted another line of words that wouldn't compute and then tossed her away. She hadn't known she was off the floor. Its impact—the second with the ungiving surface—assured her that she'd been.

Kat rolled onto her side. Aron's boots retreated from the room. She wheezed air into her lungs, and little by little, their capacity returned until she panted. Her cheek pressed against the inlaid flower bud, which when lined up with its friends made a circle around her fetal-poisoned form. Rage bubbled to the surface. How dare he lay his hands on her? How dare her father leave her locked inside his house? How dare she lay here like a victim?

It took more effort than she'd admit to roll onto her hands and knees. Once there, she crawled to the end of the bed and pulled herself up. Coma Pete lay in all his resplendent perfection, his large eyes hidden by lids and pouty lips waiting for the words that weren't coming. She climbed onto the end of the bed and stared for a long time.

"Damnit, Pete, wake up. I really need you to wake up right now." Tears leaked from Kat's tear ducts for the first time in as long as she could remember. She lay her head on his powerful thigh and sobbed.

Chapter Three

If the *beep, beep, beep* didn't stop soon, Hunter would lose his ever-loving mind. For hours and days, months and years, or hell, maybe seconds and minutes, the incessant noise continued. Time had no bearing in the pitch of expansive black. It stretched apart and bound together, an erratic rubber band slinging him about so ambivalently he couldn't grasp the concept of progression. The unyielding *beep, beep, beep* trampled over the first string of thought he'd ever pieced together, it seemed. Damn the noise. He'd tried finding its source so many times to no avail. In the darkness, he couldn't see anything. Bleak nothingness went on like eternal night. He didn't mind blindness as much as the beeping. The dark was peaceful. It didn't hurt. Nothing hurt, but like the faintest hint of light on the horizon before the rise of the sun, a twinge spoke of agony to come.

Beep, be—

What was that?

Praise the good Lord. It broke through the constant shrill sound. *Beep, beep, beep. No!* He screamed and clawed against the darkness. At least, he tried. His arms were two massive, wet clumps of sand. Still, with all his might, he tossed them through the air, reaching and grabbing at nothing—but something—time and again. The reprieve fueled him. *Please, come back.* What the respite from the irritation of mind-chewing noise was, he didn't know. It didn't matter. It was different. It was new, and the first thing besides the *beep, beep, beep* in so long.

He couldn't find it. No matter how hard he fought, it remained just beyond his grasp. Defeat and the constant beeping sucked him beneath the viscous black.

Chapter Four

"You look like a domestic abuse case. A high-class couple," Kat assured herself. Men with money abused their women as much as the poor, maybe more. The thing that delineated the two castes of assholes—outside opinion. Poor men didn't care if their ladies sported black, blue, and busted faces. Rich men hid their barbarism with gut shots and severe spankings, but every now and then, their control slipped. Those missteps usually ended with busted lips or brows that required the careful hands of a plastic surgeon, not a lowly ER doctor.

Her blue eyes rolled in the reflection of the steam-rimmed mirror. At least, they weren't bloodshot anymore. Crying took it out of her. Even after a full day, she still felt a tickle in the back of her throat and the pressure in her sinuses. The cold compress and sleep helped her swollen mouth form a none too gruesome scab even if it ran the width of her lower and upper lips.

The door in the other room chirped.

Kat's pulse spiked, throbbing in her mucus-filled sinus cavities. She longed to slam the bathroom door, lock it, and hide from the man who'd forced her to confront the ugliness that had seeped into her life. Inequality, oppression, murder, rape, and worse existed in the world. Too many times, Kat witnessed its aftermath but always in someone else's life.

Aron revealed a fear and vulnerability she hadn't known existed inside herself. The uncertainty it stirred made her constantly queasy and made her hands shake. A surgeon couldn't have quivering hands, and a man couldn't hold this power over her.

She tightened her ponytail, hitched her scrub bottoms, and marched into Pete's room. The door to the outside, the world she'd been exiled from, remained open, wide and taunting. Aron stood in the center of the room, daring her. Screw him, but she stepped away from the one thing she wanted more than anything else; freedom.

He unceremoniously dropped the basket of linens he held to the floor, turned back to the gaping doorway, and walked through it without closing it. He reentered with her tray, and an evil smirk appeared where his scowl had been.

"Thank you." Kat forced the words through her airtight larynx.

Per usual, he didn't speak, just turned and left.

Kat walked to the window and peered outside at the expansive lawn to the trees in the distance. Between them—past the locked windows and doors —stood a solid brick wall at least ten feet tall. The ornamental texture of the façade gave her hope that it would provide footholds and enough hand grips for her to scale it. But first, she'd have to get past the guards. The larger of the two she'd catalogued was propped on a wrought-iron bench at the edge of the path that led to a small rose garden. It wouldn't be long now before he took his first of many afternoon naps. He and his slightly smaller counterpart patrolled the yard intermittently throughout the day and night. Over the past week, she'd learned that the smaller, more reliable one, made his rounds every hour on the hour. His lazy counterpart, however, didn't abide by a schedule. The fluctuating variable would make escape more difficult but not impossible, as long as she took her time.

At the very least, neither of them had a dog she'd have to outrun or more likely get eaten by.

What the hell were they patrolling for? Maybe the Finnish threatened invasion? Why the hell else would they need all this security?

Her gaze wandered back into the room to the basket Aron had left.

"About that time, huh, Pete?" She scooped the linens from the lined wicker and walked toward the only thing that kept her grounded in this madness—her patient, a very dangerous man. "The guard isn't sleeping yet, but it won't be long now." Kat shook her head. "You two need to exchange places. He's far more suited for your gig and you his. You'd do a much better job. Then again, if I actually had any viable hopes of escape, they'd be dashed with you out there."

She didn't know why she bothered to learn their schedules. The fear of getting shot in the back kept her prisoner as much as the glass and walls.

Like all the mornings before, nothing had changed. She patted his hand, and a smile replaced the dour expression she'd had since yesterday. Maybe some things were changing. Touching his hand had become second nature. His brawn no longer scared her, not even after Aron's manhandling. Actually, she'd grown to hate seeing such a capable man deteriorating before her eyes. Had he deserved this? Would he be the same person when he woke? What if he didn't remember anything about his old life?

"Pete," she whispered conspiratorially, "what did you do that was so terrible that you, unconscious and completely vulnerable, warrant so much security?" She put the fresh gown, towel, and washcloths on the table next to his bed and then filled a basin with near boiling water and a mild soap.

How was her father involved? Her brain played chess with the possibilities while she moved the basin to the side of the bed as she had done too many other times to count now.

"Did you steal something? Hurt someone?" Kat stripped the bed. Starting with the top corners, she rolled the material down under his large body and off the end.

He kept mum on the details, which was probably a good thing. It was bath day—a hell of an awkward time for him to come to. A foreign chuckle rumbled its way up her esophagus, expunging a little of the tightness cramping her throat. She pulled the covers off him and tossed them into a pile next to the basket.

"I should empty your wound drain onto them and make Aron cart those off. He'd vomit, and that would give me great joy. But you're all closed up." Kat patted his foot, moved to his shoulder, and unfastened the snaps of his gown. "You're ready to wake and take on the world, Pete. I mean...what a way to wake? Naked with a woman. There could be plenty worse ways."

Just because he was unconscious didn't mean Kat took liberties with her patient's body. As if he were awake—and incapable of washing his own broad chest, biceps, and abdomen—she started with his head and worked her way slowly down, scrubbing and wiping the soap and grime away, revealing only as much skin at a time as was necessary.

"Focus, Kat."

She turned his head from one side to the other, cleaning each side and stretching him at the same time. With his head turned away, she moved around the bed, grabbed a fresh cloth for his face and chest, and wet it.

Kat turned back. A gasp escaped her split lips.

Coma Pete faced her. His eyes were closed, but he'd definitely moved. It wasn't unheard of for coma patients, but it was a first for her.

"Pete?" Kat eased to the side of the bed and leaned close, searching for any sign of movement. "Pete, can you hear me? It's Kat, your doctor. You're safe here." Guilt gnawed at the back of her brain. Was he safe? She'd been ordered to care for him. So surely he was, but yesterday's attack forced her to face the ugly question. Was she safe here? Sure, she was. Her father wouldn't let anyone harm her, but where was he?

"Pete, if you can hear me, move the fingers on your left hand." Her gaze lasered onto the hand closest to her. Oxygen stalled in her lungs. Seconds passed. They turned to a minute and another.

Nothing.

"It's Kat. I'm your doctor. If you can hear me, blink."

Again, she waited for him to reveal the amber orbs she'd seen only during examinations when she forcibly peeled back his lids. Again, disappointment kneed her in the belly.

Would he have a scary, hollow gaze, or would he surprise her with kind eyes? The rich amber hue was so stunning and warm. What would they convey when they were awake?

"Would you hurt me?"

Chapter Five

He first noticed the change about sixty thousand beeps ago. The continuous, noisy intervals never ceased, but they irritated him less and less as the time passed. Hunter still couldn't tell the amount of time that had elapsed, but he'd latched onto the concept of them moving by, if only at a snail's pace. The beeps were the ruler that delineated the distance between the warmth on his hand, the intense darkness, and the brightening to gray. The blackness never truly receded, but something lightened it for about thirty-three thousand beeps at a time. He didn't count that high. Who the hell had the patience for that? Not him, but he could calculate like a beast. Something very important depended on his ability to destroy numbers in seconds. Those beeps were the best because the warmth came more frequently.

With increased frequency, things changed.

Change was good. Change had gotten him out of Brentwood, and the rat-packed house that had nothing to do with men singing and dancing in suits or actual rodents. There had been so many people, so close to him, on top of him, holding him down. They'd drowned him in proximity and loneliness.

A sound, separate and contrary to the insistency of his ruler, hummed on the far side of the gray. The soft melodic murmur—of what, he didn't know—soothed his fraying edges. He focused, ignoring the beeps, ignoring the house and the past, and allowed the murmurs to stroke his temper. The hypnotic sound shoved the beeps behind a thick curtain. They still helped him keep measure of this strange world, but they gave way to undiscovered lands. In this new land, the gray lightened several shades. In this land, there was more. In this land, something mattered.

If only he knew what that thing was.

Hunter hadn't a clue what drove him, yet a sudden urgency lit his brain on fire. What was it? The answer was so close. His fingers stretched, grasping through the cold dark toward the light and sound and new. It strained his flaming synapses, threatening to char them into a useless pyre. Hunter Masters wasn't a man who caved under pressure. Under incredible strain, he flexed and pushed; he dug in and moved forward and remembered.

He needed to find something.

What?

No damn clue.

Necessity propelled him. Whatever he needed to find was vital, and the soft, sweet sound could find it for him if only he reached a little further. He was Hunter Masters, a...

Well, shit. Another dead end. Whatever he was, he did not quit.

The soothing sounds receded. Gray thickened to a viscous black. It eased in around him, blocking his reach and pinning him to the nothingness.

Hunter roared. He crouched and pressed his boots into the blackened ground. Desperation to find the thing he sought but didn't remember propelled him. The tips of his boots ate into the dark one step at a time. Each strain drained and invigorated him. Hope, ever alive even in the most dire of circumstances, and the return of that sound increased the push and pace of his efforts until suddenly he crashed through the pitch of night to pure and encapsulating sunshine.

No, not sunshine. Sunshine was yellow and warm. This was blinding and cold.

Fucking great. He was dead.

He quit pushing ahead because screw this, he was more determined to find something than he was to die. Something required him to survive. So he would survive. He had to because Oliver needed him.

Ha!

Memories didn't flood back in a deluge of ah-ha, but one tenacious image dogged his heels. Oliver's bloody face haunted him like a kaleidoscope of Stephen King novels.

Hunter had to find his friend. He had to save his friend now.

The melodic sound returned, and warmth encapsulated his hand. As suddenly as he remembered Oliver's plight, the murmurs morphed into words. The words were inquisitive. They thrilled him even though he couldn't discern their meaning yet.

Chapter Six

The chilling, unrelenting beep of flatline ripped Kat from the silence of sleep and tossed her into the ruthless world. She landed on her feet. Her veins revved with one-hundred-proof adrenaline. Her pupils dilated in the dark of night. Her heart shot across the room, propelling her forward to accept the challenge of death's toll. As she ran, she struggled to calm her pulse with deep breaths and logic.

Pete's wounds had healed weeks ago. His vitals had been consistent over the past month—consistently better than most productive, non-comatose members of society. Maybe the power went out, causing the alert. She skidded through the doorway, held her breath, and sought the light switch. Brilliant, near blinding light filled the room. Her heart sank.

He lay on the bed unmoving. The flatline flipped her the proverbial bird. Maybe the lead had fallen from the machine. From her position, the line was clearly and firmly attached to the monitor, just as she'd left it when she'd gone to bed.

Kat shoved off the doorframe and rushed forward, ready for a bare-knuckle battle with death for this man's life. Years of training and the solitary gathering of knowledge prepared her for this one moment. The desire to save this man's life outweighed any patient in her past—the old, the young, the innocent. Although this man was far from innocent. He was dangerous. Guilt should have plagued her, but it remained cold and impassive. Kat wouldn't save him for her father. She'd save him for her own selfish needs; the need to be free, the need for a marathon session with her therapist.

She yanked the crash cart from a far corner, ready to beat him back to life for her own needs. The faintest layer of dust coated the machine she never expected to use, not after the first week of recovery.

What if he'd had a heart attack? Not possible with his blood panels. An aneurysm? There would be nothing she could do to bring him back. Kat refused to accept defeat before even lifting a fist or, in this case, a paddle.

"I'm going to fight for you, Pete. I thought you were a fighter. Fight, damnit. Fight if you want to live." She pulled the pillow from behind his head and tossed it to the floor.

His skin was warm, warmer than her father's after he came back from a run. Pete couldn't die, not with skin that reminded her of life...even as the toll of his passing continued to fill the room. The constant tone mocked her to the point of insanity. She ripped back his gown, exposing his massive heaving chest and froze.

Pete's heart beat against his sternum like an insistent fist. His ribs expanded and contracted in rapid form, revealing the perfect delineation of his abdominal wall.

Kat placed her hand atop his heart. It thudded against her palm. She held it in place for longer than she should've. This wasn't the

professional way to take someone's pulse, but she
wasn't a professional right now. At this moment,
she was a woman fighting for the life she'd known.
She needed reassurance more than five gold stars
above her name. A first, for sure. Nothing came
between her and her career. Not ever. Not until
she'd been held prisoner against her will. Not until
a man's life meant more than her life's mission.

Each bump of his heart against her hand
reassured her. It soothed the frazzled end of her
nerves and calmed her own frantic heartbeat. The
rhythm of his pulse mesmerized her, syncing with
hers for two beats.

She withdrew her hand as though his
warmth burned her, and he had. Something passed
between them, sealing her fate to this man's like
her father never could. Her fingers tingled. The
sensation shot up her arm, tickling her chest.
Every frenzied beat of her heart threatened to
launch it right out of her chest.

The flatline continued to scream inside the
room that seemed to close in around them. Why?
Kat moved around the other side of the bed. The
sensor that she'd taped to Pete's chest lay on the
floor. She picked up the sensor. The adhesive was
rolled back on one side and ripped on the other.
Her gaze slid to Pete. She hung the line over the
machine, disabled it, and eased onto the side of the
bed.

Clutched between his fingers was the NG
tube she'd installed to nourish him weeks ago. He'd
yanked it from his body.

"You are fighting," she whispered in the
renewed night silence.

Behind his lids, she watched as his eyes
rolled rapidly from one side to the other as though
he were looking for the way out of his unconscious.

Kat swallowed the spike of excitement that bubbled up. No matter how much she cared for him, no matter how much she wanted him to be well, this man wasn't her friend. She grabbed the hand she'd become too accustomed to holding and smoothed her palm over his darker one.

"Are you going to wake up tonight and tell me who you are?" She watched his eyes for any sign of movement. Nothing more than the search.

"Are you going to tell me about the no-good you've been up to, Pete?" Kat's eyes drifted to his full lips. Her cheeks flushed. The heat dove from her face downward. She swallowed again for an entirely different reason, a reason she didn't like at all. He was her patient. She shouldn't think about what his lips would feel like on her mouth...and other places.

Chapter Seven

Holy mother. Give him back the darkness. Light brought pain unequal to any he'd experienced. He'd had the life almost beaten from him twice—his smart mouth. He'd been shot—a little more than a flesh wound. He'd been burned—military training exercise gone awry. He'd been stabbed—mouth again. None of that shit came close to the all-encompassing, bone-deep ache that radiated from his left foot. Light also brought awareness, which Hunter clung to with both hands. It was the only thing keeping him from begging for death or, at the very least, unconsciousness. He remembered what he'd searched for in the dark.

Oliver.

His friend's safety eclipsed everything, even his own well-being. Oliver and Tyler were the brothers, hell, the only family he ever had, though neither DNA nor blood linked them. He didn't have to worry about Tyler. He was safe, but Oliver... He'd been searching for Oliver. The kid had gotten himself into some deep shit, and Hunter had been dogged about saving him and the woman he loved from the clutches of Tor Royan.

"Oliver?" Hunter's voice sounded like rocks being pulverized. It felt that way too. With each syllable, the flesh in his throat caught and the sides stuck together like taffy. He swallowed nothing and pressed on, holding firm to awareness. "Oliver? Marina?"

He peeled his eyelids open to search for his friends. Cobwebs created a blurred world. Several blinks pulled back the webbing and revealed a vibrant blue sky. No, not a sky. The sky had never been so bright and clear. At least, not in Hunter's neighborhood growing up or in the countries he'd visited as an adult. He allowed his vision to adjust to the brilliant blue. Dark pupils formed in the center of the sky, transforming them into striking eyes.

Awareness was a hand he crushed inside his own, despite the mind-numbing pain. His brain had taken all the vacation it would get. As the seconds passed, Hunter's vision smoothed. Blurred webs became smooth lines. Those lines became a pert nose, sharp cheekbones, a strong jaw, and gnawed red lips. She was gorgeous. The sight of her dulled the pain shooting up his leg and into his groin.

This nurse was a hell of a lot prettier than his last nurse. She'd had helmet hair and a brown, crooked tooth. There was something to be said for personality. A great one could transcend almost any perceived physical flaw. Old helmet hair had made him laugh so hard he'd busted his stitches. Sweat beaded across Hunter's forehead. Chills crawled up his arms and across his stomach. He could sure use some laughs right about now. He didn't know what was wrong with him, but his gut said he wouldn't like it.

The nurse lifted something to his lips. "Drink," she demanded.

Hunter fumbled with the straw. Her fingers grazed his dry, cracked lips. She steadied the plastic, and he gulped down cool water. His throat felt as though it hadn't worked in months. He

choked and hacked. Water slipped across his cheek
and down his chin. Still, what little water made it
down soothed his parched throat. Before
embarrassment could bubble up, his nurse wiped
away the mess with the back of her hand.

"Try again." She readjusted the straw. This
time, she didn't touch him.

Her crystal blue eyes narrowed to slits, and
her teeth pinned the corner of her bottom lip. With
her attention to detail, she did not touch him this
time. Too bad. Her skin was smooth and soft
against his cracked mouth. She didn't work like a
trained nurse. The stethoscope was missing from
around her neck. The scissors and bandage tape
were absent from her pocket. In fact, she didn't
dress like a nurse at all. Tousled curls hung wild
about the tops of her breasts, the mounds of which
crested the top of a pale pink cotton shirt with
white lace trim. She looked as though she'd been
yanked from a down and dirty dream.

Were his foot not threatening revolt against
his body, Hunter could have easily placed himself
in that fantasy and brought it to life for her. As his
luck would have it, though, shit never went to
script.

"Who are you?" Their simultaneous questions
collided in the static laced air between them. Her
sexy, sleepy laugh rolled over him, stealing the edge
off the blinding pain.

"I'm Kat." There was gusto behind that
dreamy voice. This woman had a backbone and a
nice rack.

"Short for Katherine, Kathleen, or Katie?"

Her head tilted and one sharp brow rose.
Maybe it was her command of the room or it could
have been his pain and vulnerability, but her

intensity revved the already frantic pace of his heart. Hunter shifted under her scrutiny.

Bad move!

Lightning bolts shot up his calf, through his thigh, into his groin, and ricocheted back down, ending in an explosion at his knee. Hunter doubled over in pain. His right hand shot out toward his leg to stem the ache. Katherine, Kathleen, or Katie's hand railroaded his. Their palms met, and her sleek, long fingers wrapped around the back of his hand.

"Hold on to me," she demanded.

Hunter tried to pull away. Her strong grip held him in place. "I don't want to hurt you."

"I'm not a waif like all the Katherines, Kathleens, and Katies you've known." Grit braided the strain in her voice, and her hold didn't waver.

He couldn't argue. His teeth melted together. Sweat dripped from his nose and down his chest.

"It will pass. Give it a minute."

Her promise seemed hollow in his ears, but he didn't have much choice. The eternal minute passed. The pain remained, though more bearable than before.

"It's that obvious," he wheezed, "that I've known my share of Katherines, Kathleens, and Katies, huh?"

"You fellas all have the same tell."

"What's that?"

"It's the look." Her red lips rubbed together, as though determining exactly how much information to reveal. "It's like y'all are staring at your next meal, and you haven't eaten in a while."

"How long has it been since I've eate—?" Another wave of agony crashed against him, stealing the last syllables from his mouth. He tried to be strong and unflappable, but he'd never experienced pain like this. It knotted his insides and assaulted his brain.

"You've been here nearly seven weeks."

The words stunned him almost as much as the shearing of his flesh from the bone. At least, it felt like that. As if he was being skinned alive, he crushed her hand in his. He couldn't stop himself. If she let go, he might fly off the bed to get away from the torture. "What the fuck is wrong with me?"

"Your body is going through the process."

"Of what? Am I turning into a werewolf?"

A small smile curved her mouth, creating the slightest of dimples in the hollows of her cheeks. "Not a werewolf, I'm afraid."

"Superpowers?" He joked because he knew this was bad.

"From where I'm standing, you already have them. Your body is healing from some pretty serious injuries." She pulled a cloth from somewhere and blotted it across his forehead and down his neck.

"Well, you sit here and let me stand there. From this vantage point, death would've been easier."

Her sweet, stern face drew close enough to kiss, but the stance almost threatened. Surprised at the sudden move, he reared back. A dark halo appeared around the room.

"You're not a guy who likes easy, are you?"

"Easy's relative." He huffed and struggled to focus on her words. On her mouth, too. "It's all been pretty easy until now."

"I'm not easy. This won't be either, but you'll make it through. A little at a time."   The room went blurry. He liked it. The pain receded. Her hand stayed.

Chapter Eight

Kat didn't know what to expect when he first woke, but that hadn't been it. The fear her father had instilled in her colored her outlook on this man for the first week. Back then, she hadn't expected to live past the encounter. Yet here she stood with breaths rushing in and out of her lungs and her heart thumping in her throat. He was nothing like what her father had promised.

His hand held hers. Actually, now that he was unconscious again, it was the other way around. Her fingers were white from the grip she had on this man she'd grown far too attached to over the past several weeks. Why was she holding his hand? She hadn't wanted him to see his leg, not for the first time he was awake. Why did she care? He was her patient. Kat never got involved with patients. Then again, she'd never been with one after surgery. She had her father to thank for this. Kat pried her hand from her patient and straightened. She'd finished her end of the bargain. Her patient was out of the woods. Therefore, he was no longer her patient.

It was time to reclaim her independence.

Kat turned her back on Pete and ran for the door. She needed sleep and proper clothing, but she needed her freedom more, and this was her chance to grab it. This was what she'd been waiting on for too many weeks. Joy and elation didn't bubble inside. A fissure formed across her chest. If she didn't seize it at this very moment, it would crack and grow large enough to swallow her whole. If she thought too long about Pete's fate, if she allowed herself to get sucked into those kind eyes, she would lose herself, the parts she'd worked so hard to attain. When she reached the door, her fists went to work before her mind could calculate the repercussions. The thumps echoed like a gong in her ears, and she knew the noise could very well wake Pete. Her insides twisted at the thought of leaving him behind.

Instinct told her this man was not who her father thought he was. He might not be an innocent. Far from it, judging by the way he'd gulped her in. Being a lady's man didn't qualify someone for... What? What did her father have planned for him? Kat glanced one last time at the man on the table, praying—for the first time—that his gaze didn't meet hers. She swallowed at the memory of his hazy eyes focusing on her, scanning and cataloging all her features. This man was a connoisseur of women. His reaction to her said he wasn't at all picky. Apart from their obvious difference in skin tone, she likely had drool dried on her lips and pillow creases on her cheeks. On her best days, she was a disheveled, asexual robot whose priority was to keep people alive.

Well, she'd done her part, and it was past damn time they released her from this hellhole. If she hadn't been fired yet, she had an internship in Berlin to return to and a life. Sure, it wasn't much of one, but it was hers all the same.

The door beeped and swung wide. Before she could stop herself, Kat threw herself through the opening and ran face first into Aron's chest. He grabbed a hank of her hair and yanked her backward. She stared into the eyes of pure evil. Aron was dangerous, not Pete. Menace blasted from his gaze and tight mouth.

"I thought you learned your lesson last time."

"I'm not trying to escape."

"Then what the fuck are you doing?"

Good question. Kat had no idea what she was doing. This man would not release her whether Pete woke or not. She'd been held captive, for Christ's sake. When he did release her, she'd run straight to the police and have him thrown in jail for the rest of time. She scrambled.

"I need to speak with my father."

"Is the prisoner awake?"

Kat had never been a good liar. Her face spoke volumes before her words ever could. The question hit her like Aron's hand had the other day. She used the shock to her advantage. "It's a good thing you're large and know how to fight and use a gun. Otherwise, you'd be useless. He just flatlined, moron."

"He's dead?" Aron's bellow could wake the dead. It shook her eardrums while he shook her shoulders.

"I brought him back, but something is wrong. I need to speak with my father immediately."

The jerk ignored her request and pointed into the room. He held his tongue. Everyone in the house held their tongues. When her father had pulled her from her sabbatical and demanded she save this man's life, he'd used as few words as possible. She'd barraged him with questions, but he hadn't fielded a single one before leaving her with a house full of security. They had security when she was younger but never this much. Never this brutal.

Aron shoved her into the room and slammed the door without a word. Tears welled in her eyes. Kat stared long and hard at the large black man she knew only as Pete. If her father would not answer her questions, then she'd get them from him, the man with the kind eyes and dangerous body.

Chapter Nine

Hunter lay awake for several minutes before he gathered enough bravery to open his eyes. The throbbing was only a dull roar compared to what it had been before he'd passed out. He feared any movement would incite the vicious beast inside him to awake. He listened, alive and alert and wholly aware of the unfamiliar surroundings. Silence filled the room save for his breaths and those of another. They were soft, silken, and far away. Centimeter by centimeter, Hunter opened his eyes one at a time.

Light filtered in through a floor-to-ceiling window. In front of it, Kat lay curled on her side in a small chair facing away from him. Cascading curls dropped over her shoulder and spilled down her back. She had ditched the cotton and lace pajamas. In their place were boxy, baggy scrubs. Still, the angle in which she sat accentuated the dip at her waist and the swell of her ass. The special operations soldier inside him begged for intel, yet his gaze refused to move from the exquisite sight. Seeing nothing but blackness for so long left his eyes—and other parts—starved for beauty and compassion.

Her ribs rose and fell at a leisurely pace. For a while, he thought she slept. She didn't fidget with her hair or the hem of her shirt. She didn't rock with angst. Everything about her was still and calm until her triumphant fist pumped into the air.

"Ha! I win, Pete. That'll be five more bucks. That brings us back to even." She turned toward him, and the wide smile fell from her face. "Pete?"

Well, this was some crazy daytime TV episode he could do without. Who the hell did this chick think he was? Pete? It was possible he'd been hit on the head so hard he imagined an entire life full of blazing guns, whiskey, and babes, but not likely. His mind raced with intel and tactics that the normal person had no right to possess. He had friends—no, brothers—who depended on him. He couldn't have made them up. So this lady was several beers short of a case.

"Oh." Her fingers covered her mouth. "I know your name isn't Pete. I'd just taken to calling you that." She shrugged. "You know, habits." Her gaze bumped around the ceiling for a second before returning to him. "Good morning."

"What day is it?"

"August first," she answered.

"Well, fuck me." Hunter scrubbed a hand over his face. Smooth skin met his touch. She'd shaved him. The thought of her close to him with a blade should have scared him since he didn't know her from Eve. Instead, it woke his inner naughty boy, which never slept for long.

"What's wrong?" Kat stood and stepped tentatively in his direction.

"I spent my birthday unconscious. Not my first, but at least I enjoyed the lead-up of the others."

"Others?" Her blue eyes went wide.

"I have a wild streak. What can I say?" If she had half an idea about how wild, she'd blush. He'd like to see her cheeks pink and skin slicked with sweat.

"How old are you?"

"I thought you weren't supposed to ask that question."

A smirk gave her away. "No, you're not supposed to ask women how old they are."

"So how old are you?" Hunter gave her a devilish grin. Even though he probably looked like shit, he couldn't help himself.

"You first." She gestured in the general direction of the hospital bed in which he lay.

"Thirty-one."

"You're a baby."

"Nah. They get to suckle at the breast all day, every day for a year; it'd be nice."

Kat's lips pressed together, and her head shook. She pulled the stethoscope from the drawer of the nightstand next to his bed. "I need to check you out."

"If you insist. It's lady's choice while I'm flat on my back."

"Have you ever been sued for sexual harassment?" Kat smacked the cold flat surface of the stethoscope against his chest with more effort than necessary.

"No, babe. I like the willing."

"And what am I?"

"You're intrigued and don't want to be."

She said nothing to his answer. Her gaze averted to the ceiling once more, and he let her escape for the moment. The uptick in his heart rate from imagining her touch intensified the throbbing in his foot. Kat moved around the bed and grabbed various instruments, shoving them into his mouth and flashing them in his eyes. Finally, she pressed her fingers to his neck and assessed her watch.

"Well, nurse, am I going to survive?"

"Ego intact, I'm afraid." She moved to give him her back but stopped. "It's doctor, by the way."

"Hey, I'm sorry." He reached out and grabbed her wrist before she could get away. "Seriously, I didn't mean to offend you. You apparently have no trouble doing that to me, though. You're jumping to conclusions. You don't even know me."

Her gaze snapped to his hold on her wrist and then back to his. He released his hold. "No, I don't know you. Why don't you fill in the blanks for me?"

Her tone held several layers of curiosity but no hint of flirtation. Red alerts squawked and flew in every direction. She wasn't interested in him. She wanted information about him. He'd dealt with enough women to know the difference. His gaze roamed the room. Base Branch had numerous boutique doctors and setups around the world. He'd been in enough of them to know. But this one was different. The walls had never been this ornate, and the doctors this hot and inquisitive about him, more so than his injuries.

It was about damn time Hunter quit flirting and started thinking about his current situation. He should analyze, calculate, and interrogate. The things he did best.

Hunter sat forward with intent. Again, a bad move. The sleeping demon inside his leg roared to life with a battle cry so ferocious it threatened to level the opposition. Him. Every muscle in Hunter's left leg convulsed in the worst series of cramps known to man...and woman. Childbirth had nothing on this shit. A guttural moan seeped from between his lips, and without command, his leg curled toward his chest. Hunter reached for the source of the pain.

Kat's hands shot out. "No. Keep your legs straight."

Too late. It was past time for him to find out what the fuck was going on with his body. In all the commotion, the sheet fell away. The surprise awaiting Hunter rocked him more than his twenty-first birthday party had. That surprise involved four strippers, a crate of whiskey, dance music, and his two best friends. It had taken him a week to recover. This would take longer, and it guaranteed to rank zero on the fun scale.

A gauze-covered stub occupied the space where the lower portion of his leg used to reside.

The elite, trained, and battle honed soldier he'd become over the past thirteen years stayed calm. An emotional reaction wouldn't help anything. So...he didn't have a leg. It could be worse. He could be dead. He could be paralyzed. He could have no legs and no arms. In all the years he'd spent traveling the world, battle had been the most ruthless, relentless, and unforgiving thing he'd ever experienced. Many of his comrades never made it home to their families. Many more made it home with insurmountable physical disabilities. Others suffered the mental turmoils of war.

Until now, Hunter had been spared any major hurdles. He loved fighting for those unable to fight for themselves. Silver stars and gold bars had always been the result of his efforts but not the driving force behind them. He was due for a good challenge.

"Pete?" Her voice held a genuine level of compassion that unraveled the neatly sewn argument against freaking out.

What was a lost leg? Nothing, if you had a really great personality.

Right?

One-hundred percent wrong.

In an instant, his universe shrank to a tiny, self-centered pinpoint. At the sharp and devastating tip was his nub. Without a leg, without a foot, everything changed. Screw walking. How was he supposed to fuck without two legs? How was he supposed to work? If he couldn't climb down a ravine and up a mountain in a ghillie suit and hide among the rock and vegetation, how could he protect his brothers? And if he couldn't protect his brothers, what good was he at all?

None.

Chapter Ten

"My name isn't Pete. Goddammit."

Kat hadn't known this man for all that long—while he was conscious anyway—yet his reaction seemed completely incongruous to the man she'd met early that morning. How exactly was a man supposed to act when he found out his leg had been amputated above the knee? Sweat cascaded in tiny rivulets across his cheek and down his stout chin. His kind, amber orbs zipped around the room at lightning speed. The whites of his teeth ground together so hard she feared the enamel might crack.

"Here, let me help." Kat reached for the morphine drip she'd secured to his IV line nearly a month ago.

"No!" His strong arm released the bandage around his thigh and shot out. The impact of his five fingers and palm against her sternum threw her back a step. Breaths stalled inside her lungs. Heat and anger flew to her cheeks and chest. "You're not going to make this go away." He pointed at her and shook his head. Tears threatened to run over his lids, but his grit seemed to keep them at bay. "Not unless this is some fucked-up dream."

"It's not a dream." He hadn't hurt her, but her hand flew to her chest over her heart. He seemed oblivious to everything going on around him; the captivity, all the questions, even her.

"Nightmare?" His tone begged.

"Reality." She hated bearing the bad news. It was the worst part of her job.

His teeth clamped audibly. A roar, unequal to any she'd heard before, drowned out the chomp of his teeth. He stared at his leg, knowing it had been smashed by something heavy enough to kill him instantaneously had it landed almost anywhere else on his body. The half-moon of his nostrils flared with aggressive breaths. His imposing chest heaved. Then his gaze lifted.

"Where is Oliver?" He poured all his anger toward her with a menacing glare.

"I don't know who that is." She held her ground.

"Where am I?" Pete lurched forward. She thought he would have learned better by now. Another wave of agony twisted his body in its unforgiving grip. Kat took a tentative step forward and offered her hand. Pete—no, Not Pete—took hold as though it were a life raft in a stormy sea. He rode each wave with more determination than the one before. His gaze narrowed. "Where am I?"

"It's my turn to ask the questions."

He looked at her as though he could inflict pain while he held her hand like she was breakable. "What?" His word was a bellow.

"You want information. I want information too. I give, you give. That's how this works."

His gaze roved her top to bottom and back again. "Who are you?"

"Still my turn." She shook her head. "Who is Oliver?"

"You're a stubborn woman, aren't you?"

"I have my moments."

"All the damn time would be my guess," he muttered.

"Quit stalling and answer my question."

Not Pete's breaths came more easily as the minute passed in silence. His thick lips rolled and pressed against one another. When she thought he wouldn't answer at all, his mouth opened. "He's my friend. Who are you, Kat? Why are you helping me?"

"I'm a doctor." The answer came so quickly she hoped he didn't see through it. She was helping this man for so many other reasons, but most of them were helping herself. "I specialize in endonasal endoscopic surgery."

"In layman's terms, please?"

"I helped you because, if I hadn't, you would've died." She let that sink in for a moment. "Why is finding Oliver so important to you?" He gave a smirk, and she amended the question before he could answer. "Other than the fact that he's your friend."

His triumphantly curved lips fell. "I was extracting him from a hostile situation when the building fell on me. Are we in Switzerland?"

"A building?" Kat could not keep her mouth from dropping wide. At worst, she'd thought he'd been struck by a car. A building, though. How the hell had a building fallen on this man? Better yet, how had he survived?

He leaned forward very slowly, using her hand as leverage and to pull her closer. "You didn't just happen upon me, did you?"

"It's my turn."

"You wasted it asking a stupid question." He smirked and waited.

"No, I didn't. What kind of situation was your friend in?"

"A psychotic terrorist held Oliver and his girlfriend hostage, using one to torture information from the other."

Kat withdrew her hand and stepped back. Her mouth gaped. Nothing easily turned her stomach—after all, she had seen horrific things—but the mental image of a man holding lovers captive and inflicting pain on them to gain information coiled her insides.

"So, Kat, why are you treating me like I'm the perp in an investigation? Like I'm the bad guy?"

"Aren't you a bad guy?" Her father had told her as much. His body told her the same. The man's attitude carried distinction and honor like a badge. And his ego... Well, his ego was the most boisterous of all.

He harrumphed, and tiny lines formed at the corners of his eyes. "I suppose that's a matter of opinion."

"Whose?"

"The guy who brought the building down on top of me and, quite possibly, my friends." Not Pete's lids closed for several beats. He pulled in a full breath and eased it out in a hiss. "Before I'm finished with him, he'll think I'm a very, very bad guy."

A chill marched itself up Kat's spine. She believed every word. Down one leg or not, this man could do damage and sleep well at night. The knowledge should have scared her right from the room, but in the hallway, a different type of danger waited.

Kat licked her lips and straightened her shoulders. There was only one way out of this. Through the scary woods. "What about me? Will I think you're a very bad guy?"

"Doc." His eyes softened, and his head shook slowly from left to right. "From where I'm sitting, you're the best. You're right up there with Oliver and my other brothers."

"Do you have many brothers?"

"An entire garrison full."

And suddenly, it made sense. Not everything, but the posture, while even in terrible agony, and the sense of pride and duty, commitment, and determination. "You're a military man."

"I'm complicated." A small smile turned up one side of his mouth.

Her laugh escaped without permission, but she bit it back. "Tell me something I don't know." Whether he'd admit it, he had military written all over him like tattoos. Flags and anchors. Rifles and skulls. The country he served stained his skin more than an ink gun ever could or ever had. His dark skin held a perfectly smooth complexion, apart from a few awful scars, which now explained themselves.

"I need a phone." His sudden announcement tossed her insides to the stars.

She exhaled through her mouth. "You can't have one."

"Why not?" His head tilted.

Kat looked toward the locked door. Not Pete didn't know it was locked, and she feared his reaction if he found out, but sooner, rather than later, he would have to know. Still, she sidestepped the Blue Whale laying atop her chest.

"I had to turn mine in." She held her features as neutrally as possible and turned back to him. "I don't guess they'll let you have one."

"Who are they?" His chin canted toward the ceiling, and his gaze cut through her. "Hospital staff? Why can't you have your phone on the floor?"

The inner strength she'd worked so many years to ensure shored up her resolve. She needed more information before Not Pete knew the details about their current predicament.

"Kat?" He reached for her hand and pulled her onto the bed next to his thigh. She was careful not to touch it for fear of inciting another round of phantom pains. "Look at me," he demanded. Her body obeyed without reservation. Kat looked into his stoic, golden eyes and dark face.

"I'm most certainly a bad guy, Kat."

Her eyes darted away. She didn't want to hear that. All her instincts told her she could trust this man—over Aron, at the very least. It hurt to hear him admit such a thing.

"No. Look at me." He cupped her chin in his warm hand and turned her face back to him. "To anyone hurting innocents, extorting them, or threatening my nation, I'm a very bad guy. To a woman looking for a husband, two point five children, and a happily ever after, I'm a very bad guy. To an ally, I'm the man they want at their back. To a woman looking for sheet-ripping orgasms, I'm the man who'll have her on hers, and then on mine, and then who knows how, but it'll be better than any fantasy she's ever concocted."

A gasp parted Kat's lips. His words heated everything from the inside out. The urge to scream, "Yes, God, please," pressed against her mouth. Between them, the air sizzled and popped as though they stood in the center of a bonfire.

His hand dropped from her chin. "I used to be, anyway."

Holy shit. Holy shit. No one had ever spoken to her that way. Not ever. Her skin flushed so hot a thermometer would certainly register the change.

Not Pete looked away as though embarrassed. Kat couldn't imagine anything making this strong, capable man blush. She wanted him to pull her against his lips, the ones she'd been sinfully coveting during his recovery, and one-up her fantasies.

The reason he'd been under her care in the first place smacked her across the face. It'd probably done the same to him. Harder even. A balled fist.

He'd have a long road ahead, learning to maneuver his life in a wheelchair and eventually how to walk again with a prosthetic. She'd only been through PT on a med school rotation and hated every moment of it. Her heart ached for him and his journey because it would be a hellacious one.

"Hey." Kat reached for his chin and turned him to her. "A leg doesn't define you."

He growled, but his expression read annoyed more than angry. "It sure as shit throws some roadblocks in front of the things I love to do."

"Surely, you've met roadblocks before."

"One or two." He smirked.

"And what did you do to them?" She was almost scared to know the answer.

"Mowed them over."

"Then that's what you'll do now." Kat smiled, downright pleased with herself. She'd outmaneuvered a tactical thinker.

Not Pete turned his face in her grip. His full lips grazed the pad of her thumb. She should withdraw her hand, but something held her there. Not him, not physically, but it might as well have been his hand holding her against his sexy kisses. It would've been easier to pull away from that. Instead, she dragged her hand across his face, letting her index and middle fingers caress the soft, dry surface. His lips embraced her fingers with delicate grazes.

The blood inside Kat's veins turned molten. It coursed through her body, pooling in the most inappropriate and tantalizing places. Heaven only knew what he could do given more acreage of her skin. Damn her to the pits of hell—aka, the loss of her medical license—she longed to find out.

The door handle rattled.

Kat's heart stalled inside her chest. Aron. She leaped from the bed. "Act unconscious. Don't say anything. Please, trust me."

Her heart slammed against her ribcage like an angry rhino demanding escape. Kat turned to the monitor, reset the heart rate, shoved the sensor onto his fingers, and wondered why the hell she'd told him to act comatose.

His heartbeat registered too loud after the silence and way too fast. The door beeped.

"Slow your heart rate," she begged in a whisper.

Chapter Eleven

"What the fuck?" a male voice demanded. The accent was European. Swedish, if he had to guess. Then again, the Finnish had a similar lilt.

"Excuse me?" Kat's firm voice didn't shirk from the profanity or aggression.

Hunter tried to calm his heart rate. Hell, that was what he did. Snipers commanded total control over their bodies. In the current what-the-fuck state of semi-arousal and total confusion, it proved harder than he remembered.

"I heard voices. I thought he was awake."

"Once again, your powers of observation astound the masses. As you can see, it's just me here, talking to myself. He has no option but to listen. While you never listen. You've yet to tell me who this man is."

The strength in Kat's voice—among many other things she possessed—impressed the hell out of him. Good thing the drugs still looped through his veins. Otherwise, he'd have a full-blown erection tenting the covers. It'd be hard to fake sleep with that.

"It's not your concern," the man barked.

The longer Hunter listened, the more apparent the depth of shit in which he waded became. Right about now, he couldn't touch bottom...had he two legs.

"As for my patient, he is my concern, which is why I talk to him."

"Why would you talk to a vegetable?"

"Even though he's unconscious, it helps with the healing process. An unconscious person can hear. They may not understand or be able to respond, but sometimes, they remember feelings of hope and feel a drive to recover when spoken to. It speeds their recovery."

Interesting. She lied again.

"What are you doing?" Kat's shriek nearly had Hunter jerking upright.

"Speeding his recovery." An ominous undercurrent weaved its way through the man's words.

"No," Kat demanded.

Shoes squeaked across the floor. The scuffle of clothing and body parts haunted his waking dream with images of Kat being manhandled. Hunter would blow his cover and kill this bastard if the guy so much as wrinkled her ugly scrubs.

"I don't think so," Kat bit, proving she could hold her own.

"You aren't getting sweet on the forbidden fruit?" A sickening laugh rolled through the room. "Or vegetable, are you, Katrin?"

Why would he say that? Was she doing more than her job? Who was this man to her? Why did he care what she thought about Hunter or what her relational status was to this jerk-off? He had more important things to figure out.

"Don't attempt to patronize me. I'm simply caring for my patient until he recovers so I can leave. Somehow, I don't think your message would speed anything except my irritation."

Hunter needed to get out of here and find Oliver and Base Branch, so they could come back and destroy this asshole.

"Two days, Katrin."

"Or what?" she demanded.

"Or you'll disappoint him."

The door clicked shut. He moved to open his eyes.

"Don't," she quietly warned. "He's liable to come right back or listen at the door."   "They're holding you against your will." Hunter growled at the realization.

"It's complicated."

Anger, pure and highly flammable, rolled off Hunter. The concerns about his leg and the drugs pulsing through his veins evaporated. Suddenly, he could lift the house off its foundation and throw it to the next country. He sat, gripping the bed rails so hard the thick metal threatened to snap under his hands.

Kat's throat bobbed. Her pupils dilated, and her mouth gaped. His anger slid toward arousal, which pissed him right off. This cluster was among the most ridiculous he'd ever encountered. Her gaze jumped back and forth between his bare chest and arms.

"Look at me, Kat."

"I am," she whispered.

"Keep looking at me like that, and we're going to have an entirely different problem."

She blew a long breath between her lips and swallowed. Christ, she was too pretty for her own good.

"Have they hurt you?"

Some lip gnawing ensued before she said, "No." It was a lie. Thank goodness, she wasn't very good at the craft.

"Explain now," he ordered.

"Tell me your name first."

For a moment he stared, not understanding what she was asking. He'd more than contemplated attacking this woman's mouth and she didn't even know his name. Sure, he got around, but he always handled polite formalities first. He wasn't heartless.

"I know you're not Coma Pete. So what is your name?"

"Hunter Masters."

"Ridiculously fitting." Her eyes rolled toward the intricately carved crown molding.

"What does that mean?"

"Nothing, really." She fidgeted with her mass of curls for the first time. The move ensnared him like a bull to the matador's red cape. "It's just I called you Pete because it was friendly and safe."

"Boring," he offered.

"Never mind." She shooed his chuckle away. "I heal people. It's what I've loved since I was little. When I watched the doctor set Trey's arm, I was hooked."   "Masochist."

"No." Her pixie nose wrinkled and wiggled the glasses on her nose. "It wasn't the pull and pop. It was the broken to whole. He'd done that for Trey, and I wanted that ability."

"Power," he interjected. "Who's Trey?"

"Knowledge," she corrected. "He's my little brother." She said the last with a hint of a smile that faltered too soon.

"How did you get corrupted?"

"I'm not corrupted." Her upper lip scrunched into a sneer. "I helped you, didn't I?"

He looked down at his leg.

"It was your leg or your life."

Hunter nodded, unable to speak. The rage had passed, leaving him weak and irritated. He leaned back, letting the fight drain from him.

"You need your rest. Seriously, I didn't know if you'd ever wake. And if you did, I expected at least minor brain damage. You're a fighter."

A fighter. Shit, he could hardly keep his eyelids open, much less go hand-to-hand with the jerk who'd barged into the room. He still had too many questions to allow sleep to claim him. "How'd you get here?"

"I was asked to save your life."

Kat sat next to him and pulled the covers up from his waist. "It wasn't a hard choice." She smiled sweetly.

"You're being evasive." His lids fell but bounced open again.

"You're being stubborn." She shook her head at him. "Sleep." The back of her hand pressed to his temple. "If you overdo it, you won't help either of us."

"And we need all the help we can get?"

"I think so."

Hunter fell asleep to the gentle caresses of Kat's fingers over his palm and up his forearm. It was probably the sweetest send-off to dreamland he'd ever had.

He woke in darkness with a bladder close to the point of rupture. Where the hell was he? Why did he hurt bone deep? Sleep crusted his eyes, and a film coated his tongue. The pressure in his lower abdomen warned him to get to the bathroom ASAP. His bladder was close to bursting. He rubbed his eyes and then blinked his surroundings into focus. The hospital bed railing flooded him with reality. No wonder he hurt.

The need to escape clawed inside his chest. If he could get back to headquarters, to his people, they could make everything better. Hunter couldn't see a clock but sensed it was early morning. Maybe two a.m. Silence filled the large house—gaudy mansion. There might be guards patrolling in the bright exterior light. It spilled into the space, lighting the room as much as a full moon would. Let them have their light. As long as they didn't have dogs, it wouldn't matter. He'd evaded too many security details to count. However, before he launched any escape and evade tactics, he really had to pee.

Hunter grabbed the bed rail and slowly hoisted himself upright. Kat's long slender frame curled into a ball at the foot of his bed. When he saw her arms hugging her legs to her chest in a protective position, his guts flopped. He hated that the smart, bold woman slept with such fear. He wondered what had happened in her life to make her that way, but nature wouldn't let him ponder the question for long. He eased back the sheet and pulled his leg from underneath, careful not to disturb her. When his nub dangled off the side of the bed, the throbbing returned. It stole his breath for several moments before normalizing to an annoyance more than pain. His good foot, his only foot, met the cold, hard floor. Its toes spread wide, giving him the sturdy foundation he'd need to balance. He scanned the room for something to use as a crutch, but a vast expanse of nothing stood between him and the door he guessed was a bathroom. His bladder wouldn't allow him to wait, and his pride wouldn't allow him to wake Kat.

The first hop was the worst. It was probably a lie, but he needed it to work up the courage to hop again. His blood pressure spiked and dropped with each leap. The room expanded and shrunk in the tunnel of his vision. He pulled deep lungfuls of air in and didn't govern long exhales through his lips. It felt as though he weighed a thousand pounds. While his friends always ragged him about being a thousand-pound bulldog, he'd always been agile on his feet. Then again, he'd had two of them and hadn't been bedridden for seven weeks. As he hopped, he scanned the room for a telephone, computer, CB radio, or anything he could use as an SOS machine. Nada. The great distance between him and the bathroom closed until finally, he reached the interior. He grabbed the wall for balance while he closed the door and flipped on the light.

A hideous hospital gown hung around his knees—knee. He ignored it and the fact he only had one knee and used the cabinetry as a crutch to help himself to the toilet. When he got down to business, he averted his gaze to the ceiling. Pure relief flooded his body. His dick was still attached and filled his grip as it always had. He kept the cheering to himself but peed with a smile on his face. He flushed out of habit and immediately regretted it. His body reacted in sniper mode, going silent and still for a full minute. No one burst through the door. He hopped to the sink, washed his hands, and searched for a toothbrush and paste. After finding two in the cabinet, he bet on the blue one. Normally, while brushing his teeth, he assessed the growth of his scruff, but today, the ceiling tiles held more interest. He flossed and washed and dried his face, all while teetering on one foot.

Well, he couldn't stare at the ceiling for the rest of his life or hide in the baggy gown. He had to face the demon dangling at the end of his thigh.

Growling as quietly as he could, Hunter ripped the gown from his body, tossed it onto the vanity, and hopped to the full-length mirror on the other side of the sink. If only it were a fun house mirror at Halloween. It wasn't. There were no tricks or treats tonight. Only pure, mind-altering hell. He pulled his gaze up from the gauzy stub. For the most part, Hunter Masters was still there in the reflection. Sure, his muscle definition had gone to shit, but that was nothing two weeks of training couldn't fix. Yet so much was missing.

The gauze haunted him in its horror film simplicity. Part mummy. Part ghost. Part Frankenstein's monster. Hunter held his breath and tore at the binding. Loop by tedious loop, it unwound from his hips and down his thigh. Every inch of removed gauze revealed smooth, unblemished skin, the skin he'd known his entire life. And then the skin stopped. The bandage fell to the floor in a heap, revealing a line of darkly puckered skin about six inches above where his knee used to be. As scars went, it was hideous. More so than his burn, which whitened and crinkled a strip of skin on his right hip. More so than the knife scar on his right shoulder. This scar marked the end of an era of walking, running, and fucking without conscious thought or effort. Those things no longer existed.

But he existed. Hunter tried to find comfort in that.

His hand caressed the bumpy scar just above his heart. The thirty-eight-caliber bullet had entered his chest two days before his sixteenth birthday and had threatened to make him miss it and all the other birthdays to come. He did manage to escape the ruthless streets of Chicago's West

Side before the shit got too bad. If he could make it through that, he could make it without a leg.

Then again, maybe not.

The door flew open. Hunter turned to size-up the attack and almost fell on his ass. He gripped the edge of the counter in time to save himself. Kat stood in the center of the doorway. Her hands flew to her hips, and an irritated scowl quirked her mouth. He stood hunched naked on his one leg and awkwardly turned, still precariously close to falling to the floor. She seemed completely oblivious to his nudity. Damn. His ego couldn't take much more.

"Why didn't you wake me?" Her tone sliced through the tiled space like a mother scolding her child. How he expected one would sound, anyway. His hadn't stuck around long past the cutting of the cord.

Her tone, his embarrassment, hell, everything rubbed him the wrong way in that instant. "Why'd you lie about me being unconscious to the man who came in the room?" He shouted the words like he didn't give a shit if the world heard him.

She didn't shrink from his bite, but her battle-ready shoulders sank with her exhale. "I don't know, exactly."

It whittled the point off his anger. He hopped his foot under him and straightened. They both ignored his dick flapping in the wind. Bummer. "You're a smart woman, Kat. You know something about this"—he pointed at the main door and out to the lawn—"isn't right. That's why you didn't tell them."

"Plenty of things aren't right. For starters, you removed your bandage." Her hands dropped from her hips, and she pointed accusatorially at his nub.

Hunter turned to the side, slowly shifting his half leg behind his good one. Having her openly staring at the raw, puckered skin had him exposed more than an open field firefight.

"It's necessary to prevent infection until your wound fully heals. Which it would have, but your drain line got infected. I had to remove it, clean the area, and put in a new line." Her accusing arm fell to her side with a smack. The balls of her cheeks flushed bright pink with anger, and her chest heaved. "We don't need any more backslides."

"I can replace the bandage." Shit, maybe it was a good thing he didn't have a mother. He'd lived through a lot, but this nagging business needed wings to fly the hell away.

"It's not that easy." Her head shook, and she stepped farther into the room. "It's especially not with you in bed...where you should be."

"Well, I'm not in bed."

"Exactly." She buried her face in her hands and hid there for a while. When she crawled out from cover, the anger stayed behind. Softer, sweeter eyes assessed him top to bottom. "You don't have to hide it from me, Hunter."

Fuck. Of course, she noticed. She wasn't dim.

"There's no place on your body I'm not familiar with." Her words held no guile. No advance either. Just his luck.

"The first woman to get me naked and not give a shit."

Her brows pulled a few Gs but fell more quickly than a fighter jet crash landing. The thoughts soaring through her head were unreadable, and she didn't speak to let him in on the intel.

Kat stepped to the cabinet, near the toilet, grabbed the clean towel, and draped it over the closed lid. "Sit."

He could argue, but there wasn't any point.

While he hobbled over, she left the room. Thank the Lord for small favors because he was due a couple. Then he shouldn't complain. Air still filled his lungs, and thoughts his brain. A short time after he was situated, she returned to the room with sterile packs of gauze, tape, scissors, and iodine solution.

"I'm not mad at you, you know?" She lay another towel on the floor next to his half leg, knelt, and spread the supplies on them. "I just need you to understand how fragile your body is right now."

"Fragile?" No one had ever used that word to describe him or anything related to him. It didn't taste good on his tongue.

"Your body has been through..." When she turned, her gaze landed directly on his cock. "It's..." She gave the ceiling a once-over, but her gaze zeroed right back to his goods.

Maybe he hadn't lost all his powers. A tiny sense of pride seeped back into his soul.

"Your body..." She swallowed, huffed, and turned away. Kat's fighting fingers ripped open a pack of gloves and snapped a pair into place. "Your body has been through significant trauma." The sound of ripping paper filled the room as she went down the line, exposing each package's contents. She removed the gloves, donned new ones, and then turned to face him. "Can you cup your penis, please?"

"Kinky, Doc."

Kat inhaled to lecture him, for sure.

"I'm kidding." He used his left hand to cover himself.

Her gaze remained on his crotch.

"What?" His gaze dropped to the area in question. Had he missed some altering injury? None that he could see...with his hand in the way. His balls and parts of his anatomy peeked out on either side of his hand.

"Two hands, please."

A smile sneaked on Hunter's lips. He banked it as best he could and obliged her without further comment. Her cheeks were as pink as they'd been when she'd been ready to murder him for jeopardizing his health, of all the contradictions.

She soaked an extra-large weaved cotton pad in the solution and dragged it across the end of his leg, which was no longer a foot. "Does that hurt?"

"No."

One thin brow and a narrowed gaze assessed him. "Then why the face?"

"I'm making a face?" He strived for cool and calm.

Hunter's stomach roiled. It wasn't blood or open wounds that got to him. He killed people on a bi-weekly basis sometimes. No problem there. He didn't do wound care. The healing parts of injuries weren't for him, though he'd suffered through plenty. This, though... the nub...

"That doesn't gross you out?"

Her chuckle reverberated over his sensitive thigh. "Would hardly be good at my job if it did."

"And you are, good at your job." He admired the care she took with him.

A sweet smile curved her lips. Her gaze remained on the job, but she whispered, "Thank you."

Chapter Twelve

Christ, when he was unconscious, his dick had been admirable. Semi-erect, it caused her throat to constrict and her thighs to clench. Beyond inappropriate.

Thank goodness, she'd removed his catheter after he'd passed out when he first woke. She couldn't imagine doing that with him conscious. Then, he'd been her patient. Now, she couldn't think of him that way. She helped him, sure, but no longer as his doctor.

She'd never fraternized with a patient, never crossed the line, but this man made her feel everything she'd always chastised and belittled. Had she belittled them because they weren't important to her or because she'd never expected to experience them? The answer scared her. It was too-bright lights, no makeup, real reflection.

"So, dinner and dancing...or should I cart my ass back to the bed?" Hunter's face lit with mischief.

"You'll be wining and dining the ladies in no time. Dancing may take a little longer but not much." His ability to make light of a ten-ton situation warmed a narrow path to her heart. "For now, let's get you dressed and back to bed." She pulled a new gown from the cabinet, unfolded it, and offered it over.

"I can't say I've ever found myself in this situation." He sighed, and his hulking shoulders bobbed.

"What's that?" Kat shouldn't ask. She had a feeling she knew exactly where this was headed, yet she couldn't stop interacting with him.

"You're the first woman to have me naked and want me dressed." His head hung and shook.

"You'll survive." She bit back a smile and hurried him on with a wave of both hands.

"Better?" He pulled the fabric low over his thighs.

Not in the least. It was safer, though. Not one for lies, she ignored the question and offered her hand. Hunter grabbed hold but made no attempt to move.

Kat swallowed and smiled awkwardly. "Once we get you up, I'll get on your left side and wrap my arm around your middle. You hold my shoulders, and I'll act as your crutch."

"Even half a leg down, Doc, I'm not light."

"And I'm not a—"

"You're not a pussy. I remember." His grin turned lethal.

"That's not what I said." Her hand snapped to her hip.

"You didn't say what?" A twinkle flashed in his eyes.

"Hunter Masters, stand."

He obeyed her order without placing any pressure on her hand.

"Arm around me." Kat shifted to his side and coiled her arm around his waist. The warmth of his body radiated through the thin gown. She'd had a hot stone massage once, and this was like a hot slab of granite against her from shoulder to thigh.

Thinking about the massage portion of the event hitched the breath inside her lungs.

"Let's step"—his fingers made air quotes—"with the inside first. If I put too much pressure on you, I'm hopping. You can choose to let go or hold on for the ride."

The ride... Goodness! Leg or not, he would be one amazing ride. She imagined, at least. "Four. Three. Two. Step." They moved together. Kat absorbed his weight with little effort. "Four. Three. Two. Step." The movement compounded the weight of his thick frame on her shoulders and hips. "Good. Again."

None of the steps took them far or fast, but they maintained the rhythm with her lead.

"Why do you hide your beauty?"

Kat choked on her, "Three." They managed to keep the pace even with her stutter. She wiggled in her scrubs and shoved her glasses up her nose. "What are you talking about?"

"You have stunning curves, a firm waist, and a striking face, but you hide them behind baggy clothes and drugstore reading glasses."

"I dress for my job." Her hackles rose. She shoved the glasses she didn't need up her nose.

"You dress to be taken seriously as a doctor, but you are a closet ten. A damn shame."

Kat's mouth gaped. Her ire made sure her jaw didn't stay on the floor long. "What's a shame?"

"That you don't own yourself."

Kat's cheeks stung as though he'd slapped her across the face. Those words were so close to the truth they camped between the T and the H with an F U between them. She contemplated jerking from his hold and letting him fall ass first onto the floor, but it took too much effort. Her body turned to stone, ceasing their progress.

He shifted slightly and appraised her. "If you don't own yourself, how do you expect a man to ever truly possess you?"

"I don't," she snapped.

"You're not a lesbian."

"I'm a doctor. Your doctor. That's all." Even though she'd just argued with herself otherwise. She propelled forward without warning, and his only choice was to keep up. Men like him didn't hit the floor unless they dived for cover. What would it be like to be possessed by a man like that? Her cheeks heated.

Kat had helped patients transition from one place to another before. Hell, she even straddled the odd one here and there to get the best angle to reset a broken bone. Her proximity to Hunter was nothing compared to the intimacy and vulnerability created by his words, though.

They neared the bed, and Kat thanked heaven. She needed to put distance between them, not her deepest, darkest fears. "I have to reposition you to get you on the bed."

"Whatever you need, Doc."

The invitation wasn't necessary. Her body, however, reveled in it. With every step, her clit throbbed and pulsed. She gritted her teeth and begged herself to ignore the forbidden fruit dangling in her face...after a lifetime of self-imposed semi-starvation.

She drew a deep breath and then stepped from his side to his front. Her left foot planted between his legs while her right stayed on the outside of his left thigh. Just great. Now, she'd inadvertently straddled his amputated leg.

His right arm joined his left behind her neck. The two thick limbs lay heavily and comfortably across her shoulders. The maneuver brought them chest to chest and face to face. To keep him stable, she linked both her arms behind his waist and pulled him close. It might have helped his stability, but it sent her reeling.

"If you wanted a hug, all you had to do was ask." Hunter peered down at her with a mix of curiosity and hunger.

"I think I liked you better when you were unconscious."

He leaned forward, nearly grazing his cheek along hers. His lips touched her ear. "I think you're not a very good liar."

Hunter lowered himself onto the edge of the bed but didn't release his hold. Had he, she might not have retreated anyway. His gaze sucked her in, tossed her about, and refused to release its hold.

Movement tickled her neck. His arms slid from across her upper back and shoulders. A small sigh loosened the tension in her traps...until he grabbed both sides of her glasses and pulled them from her face.

"I see you, Doc."

Kat saw Hunter with nothing between them. He'd stripped away the physical shield she hid behind. Her gaze caressed his cheekbones, skittered down his jaw, and lingered on his mouth. He set her glasses on the bed, never stealing his gaze from hers. She should move. She could move. But he looked at her with such intent, and no one had ever looked at her that way. She longed to stay even though she knew she shouldn't. His fingers returned to her face. The soft pads caressed the light bruise on the side of her eye and then skated to her jaw.

"What happened?"

"Nothing."

"I already told you." He cupped her jaw and pulled her closer. "You lie for shit." Soft, warm lips kissed the abused flesh. His fingers entangled in her mass of curls and held her in place. He backed away far enough that she saw the determination in his gaze. "Who hurt you, Kat?"

She didn't want to discuss the impossible situation that plagued her...and him. The more she knew about this man, the more confusing things became. Her father wasn't an affectionate man, but that didn't make him bad. Aron, the guard, was surely bad. Maybe Hunter's wit and charm hid a more sinister side. Still, that didn't explain why her father was tangled in this web. It certainly didn't explain why she was face to face with a former— minutes former—patient and doing this...

Kat closed the gap between them.

She tried.

Hunter gently tugged her hair, ending her progress a millimeter from his lips. She hung there suspended between desire and embarrassment. Why had she assumed he'd want to kiss her?

He used her hair as puppet strings and tilted her head to the side, exposing her neck. His lower lip skimmed along the exposed flesh back to her ear. "I could torture the information out of you." The hard edge of his teeth nipped at her lobe and scraped along her jaw.

A whimper breached Kat's throat. This man knew about torture; the sexual kind and the terrifying kind too. He could probably do either on her if he needed to. Still, she kept quiet.

"The hard way it is, then."

Kat's hands took over where her brain shorted out. They roved up his sides to his chest. Through the thin cotton, her fingers toyed with the gnarly old scar too close to his heart and then slipped up his neck.

"The hard way for whom, I don't know." His lips slid across hers. She stretched to meet them more fully, but again, he held her at bay.

Hot breaths heaved, and the pulse between Kat's legs grew deeper. The threads of control unraveled in her fingers. Her palms slicked, and she gripped the fabric of his gown as fiercely as she could, searching for something. Balance? Relief? She couldn't be sure.

Hunter sucked her lower lip into his mouth and then pulled back. His gaze thinned on hers. "You're in there, Kat. I feel you dying to get out."

She hated that Hunter saw right through to the pitiful existence she'd maintained. Yeah, she had accolades and degrees, but she didn't have friends. She didn't have a family. All she had was her job.

What was she doing with her life? She'd been with this stranger longer than anyone in her life. Kat was a loner. Her father had raised her that way, or better yet, she'd raised herself, alone.

Behind her, the main door into the room rattled.

All the desire she experienced a moment ago, a breath ago, vanished in a monsoon of fear. "No." Everything inside her froze. Everything outside too. She held a death grip on Hunter's gown and stared blankly into the eyes of this man she'd practically begged to make out with her.

"It's fine, Kat. Move." His hand slid from her hair and pushed her back a step. He rolled back onto the bed and pulled the covers up to his chest. "Deep breaths and let them out slowly." He did as he ordered her to do. In no time at all, the rapid rise and fall of his chest regulated to easy, shallow breaths.

Hers still jostled her boobs like a run on the treadmill without a sports bra.

Hunter's eyes closed a second before the door opened and Aron strolled inside. Kat didn't want to face him, but the will to live and to protect Hunter overtook the fear. She stalked to the other side of the room, heading for the couch where she'd taken most of her meals.

"About time you showed up with my breakfast. I'm starving." She layered on the dramatics, tossing herself onto the firm surface, folding her arms, and pointing her chin at him.

His hands were empty. The smile on the guard's face held more than an IV bag full of malice. A chill pooled in the center of Kat's chest.

"There's no way you talk to him that much." Aron stepped toward Hunter.

"Don't you dare touch my patient." Kat jumped from the couch and ran. She stopped only when she'd positioned herself between the two men.

"You didn't learn your lesson the first time, did you?" Aron grabbed her wrist so hard the blood flow ceased immediately. Tingles rushed up her arm and into her fingers. Before she could contest, he yanked her out of his way.

Kat flew sideways, head first toward the crash cart. An involuntary grunt escaped her lips as she smashed shoulder first into the series of metal drawers. The cart tilted and crashed like a collection of cymbals to the ground. Medicine, suction tubing, and a blood pressure cuff skittered this way and that. She rolled over the fallen defibrillator and came to a stop on her hands and knees.

Aron smirked at her and stepped toward Hunter.

Rage boiled back to life. It'd been distilled by time, captivity, and abuse. She stood with the clunky defibrillator in hand, reared back, and launched it at the sadistic man.

The machine caught his right shoulder and spun him toward her. Triumph glitter bombed her brain for a second before she realized what a mess she'd created.

"Be glad your daddy gets back today. It means I can't leave any more bruises, but it doesn't mean I can't hurt—"

Hunter launched himself from the bed. His fist swung, powered like a chugging locomotive, and connected perfectly with the side of Aron's head. The man's body went slack and melted into a puddle of asshole next to the bed.

Relief didn't visit long. Her knight in a hospital gown sailed through the air in a fast descent. He didn't even try to catch himself on his one leg. His broad back absorbed the impact.

"Are you hurt?"

They asked the question in unison with about as much gusto as someone who'd just gotten the shit kicked out of them.

"I'm fine," she lied.

"I hurt like the devil shoved his pitchfork up my ass, but I'll live if we get moving." Hunter army crawled himself to the edge of the bed and pulled up.

"Where are we going to go?"

"Somewhere we're safe."

Hunter fell before Kat realized what was happening. Aron held Hunter's foot until he hit the ground. Kat lurched forward and jumped onto the bastard's prone back.

"Kat, no," Hunter hollered, but it was too late. She straddled the enemy with vicious intent. A feeling she'd never experienced rushed through her, warm and charring. Her goal was to maim and dismember.

She should have started with a person who couldn't take a punch from Hunter and live to tell about it, much less flip her off like she was a bug. The world tilted, and she slid onto the floor and rolled to her side away from Hunter. Aron stood, grabbed his favorite wrist, and yanked her to stand. He whirled her around to face Hunter.

"You have a thing for the cripple?" Aron jerked her hair back and made her look at Hunter as he scrambled to a sitting position near the bed. "Well, I'm going to kill him and let you watch."

"No!" The scream that catapulted itself from her body shook the room and her world.

"Yes," Aron growled.

"It's okay, Kat." Hunter's voice was calm, almost resigned in the face of his impending doom.

She couldn't understand why.

"No." Her head shook, indiscriminately, even with so many strands of her hair tangled in Aron's fingers. She couldn't allow Hunter to die, not after she'd spent so long saving his life. Neither could she stop it from happening. Aron outweighed her by her body weight or more.

"Kat, look at me. It's going to be okay," Hunter's deep voice crooned.

"Yeah, Kat. Look, but it's going to be far from okay. As soon as I'm done with him, I'll deal with you. And you won't like it." Aron jerked her by the hair.

Her teeth chattered hard. A headache formed, swift and nearly debilitating.

"Nothing left but to quit running your mouth and give the cripple a go." Hunter shrugged and grinned.

Why was he antagonizing the man threatening his life and her well-being? She hoped he knew something she didn't. How to kill with his bare hands with a newly amputated leg would be a nice step in the right direction.

"Let her go." Relief flooded Kat at the familiar voice.

Chapter Thirteen

Difficult to fucking impossible. Great.

Tor Royan stood in the doorway of Hunter's makeshift hospital room. The man who'd mutilated Oliver ordered the overgrown meathead to release Kat. The man whose sadistic plans had severely injured Tyler, his other dear friend, didn't come alone. Three heavily armed guards stood in the hallway, jockeying for a look inside. The man who'd ordered the kidnapping and enslavement of so many women stared at the man who'd attacked Kat at least twice and quickly retreated from her side. Tor Royan, the man who stole his leg and life as he'd known it, lifted the barrel of a sleek silver pistol.

Murder and mayhem consumed Hunter's brain.

"Thank you." Kat coddled her left wrist in her other hand but had yet to look up. The fear he'd seen pouring from her eyes like tears had vanished in a near instant as Royan had ordered her released. Little did she know that they'd jumped from the flames into the motherfucking lava pit.

He willed her to look at him. He willed his leg to grow back and AKs to appear in his hands. Too bad the big guy was busy with people better and worse than he was.

When Kat finally looked up, a sweet smile spread her lips. She hurried to his side. If he grabbed her and dove for cover, he could save her until they'd killed him. Then what would happen to her?

"You told me it would be okay," she whispered.

His chest caved in on itself. He'd promised something he couldn't make good on.

"I should have listened to you." Kat's smile grew.

"No, you have to escape now," he growled. "He will hurt you, Kat, worse than your darkest fears."

"Aron? He won't hurt me now."

"No, the man at the door, Tor Royan." He put as much emotion into his features as he could without his face exploding from his skull.

The color drained from Kat's face. Maybe she'd heard of the man. The CIA and FBI had, not that he was near the top of the most wanted list. As numbers went, this guy was small potatoes. The expression on her face said she knew the name.

"I'll create a diversion. You run. Do whatever it takes, Kat. Kill if you have to, but get out," Hunter ordered.

"What about you?"

"Don't worry about me." He was gone the moment he disregarded his partner's words and went after Royan on his own. He'd just been gifted a few days with a beautiful, caring woman. Not a bad way to go.

"I don't understand." Fat, brimming tears collected in her bright blue eyes.

"Katrin Sara Royan, get off the ground." Tor's words ricocheted through Hunter's brain like a cancer that moved at the speed of light.

No. No. No.

There was no way his doc was related to that sadist.

His gaze searched Kat's. The truth sat right on the surface. He wished she could lie convincingly, just this once.

Maybe they were distant relatives. Cousins, three times removed? The only doctor in the family and he needed an off-the-books job done. All the files said he had one child, a son, name unknown.

Tor shoved Aron toward the other guards with his hands cuffed behind his back. The gun Tor had been holding no longer filled his hands. "Take him." The regal, psychotic man shooed Aron away like day-old trash. Hunter knew the man wouldn't live to see next week just as he wouldn't. "Katrin, I asked you to save his life, not coddle him." He turned to the one guard left. "Bowdin, lift him onto the bed."

Kat blinked away her welling tears and turned. "If he's not moved properly, his artery can rupture, and it will kill him within a minute."

It sounded like bullshit to Hunter, but maybe this was her angle. Hunter rolled with it, acting the part of a weakling, which wasn't far off the mark. Dammit.

"Nonsense," Royan insisted and scooted the guard forward with a wave.

"Father!" Kat stood between Hunter and a guard for the third time. That didn't much register. The guy could have raised his gun and fired a shot between Hunter's eyes, and it would have shocked him less. Royan was her father.

His ears rang. Red blurred his vision.

"You paid for my medical school, so trust me to prove it wasn't a waste." Kat addressed her father, the very deadly Tor Royan.

"Fine but wear gloves." Tor's nose turned up to the ceiling. "I don't want the foul man contaminating you."

Kat looked at Hunter. Sorrow filled her eyes, but her posture remained rigid and determined. He expected her to argue. Well, Tyler had a saying about assumptions, something about possums and asses, and too often it proved true. Today he could have done without the I-told-you-so. She moved toward the fallen crash cart and reached for the box of gloves.

Hunter wasn't contaminated. Sure, he'd fucked a lot of women but always with protection. What's more, he got checked routinely. More than that, he didn't want Tor to dictate her actions. His rage reached a new level. Disgust. If she'd really wanted to take care of him, she'd have gotten him a phone at the very least, and the hell out of here at the most.

He didn't want her to touch him. If either of them was contaminated, she was. The blood of her depraved father coursed through her veins. Hunter scooted, grabbed the bed's frame, and hoisted himself up onto the edge of the mattress.

"Leave the gloves, Katrin, and come with me. He needs no further assistance." Tor had yet to look Hunter in the eyes. That would come later when his daughter wasn't around to see the demon her father hid behind suits and a haughty attitude.

As before, she chose her blood. When she skirted past him to her dad, she didn't meet Hunter's gaze either. The door shut behind them, and its WTF echoed in Hunter's ears.

Chapter Fourteen

Silence fell over the room. Even her heartbeat paused to see which man she would choose.

In Kat's world, two plus two equaled four, good men served others, and bad men lived behind bars. Suddenly, nothing added up. Her father had said Hunter was bad, yet Hunter believed the same of her father.

She turned toward her father and walked like a well-beaten dog, knowing no good would come from her master's hand, yet still loyal to a fault.

Her gaze refused to meet Hunter's. She studied the tips of her ugly shoes, trying to make sense from the senseless. His disgust for her had been evident from the moment he'd realized that Tor Royan was her father. While she'd never been thrilled with the way her father expressed his affection for her, she'd accepted him long ago. If the things that Hunter had said about him were true, Hunter would never want to speak to her again, and she couldn't blame him. She also couldn't protect him without answers.

"Don't ever take that long to obey me again, Katrin." Her father turned and strode down the hallway. "Let's go."

Behind her, a new guard closed and locked the door. The beep of the barred door punched her in the gut. She hunched. Her arms wrapped around her middle as she stared at the door she'd been on the other side of for so long.

"You won't want to keep Mr. Royan waiting." The guard motioned her away from the room.

Standing at the opposite end of such a grand corridor, her father seemed a small man. She used that image to bolster herself. He was only what she allowed him to be.

Kat stiffened her spine and hurried to catch him before he disappeared around the corner. The new guard followed at a leisurely pace, which forced her feet to move faster. She didn't need another run-in with one of her father's hired guns. Her worry abated near the end of the space. The guard turned down another hallway, and she finally reached her father's side.

"Where's Aron?" The large dining hall they stepped into swallowed her question whole.

"He'll be dealt with." Her father's sleek wingtips glided over the floor, leaving only a whisper of sound in the expansive room.

"What does that mean?" Kat slapped her hands to her sides and stomped along in her ugly medical clogs. The frantic clops sounded as though she were a two-ton bull with friends ready to stampede.

On the other side of the room, a dining table equipped to seat half the country—the rich half—stood with a butler and two servers. They averted their gazes and schooled their expressions so much they looked like vacant mannequins displayed in the window treatment at the rent-a-servant store.

"It means no one puts their hands on my family without consequences." His voice maintained a low, almost melodic volume and tempo despite the ruckus she'd created.

"Consequences like...?" She leaned in to better hear an answer that didn't come. When he didn't fill in the blank, she tried a different tactic. "Firing him?"

The butler met her father at the head of the table and pulled a high-backed oak chair in perfect time for him to sit. "I apologize, sir. I didn't know you had company." He waved two fingers in the air, and the rent-a-servants sprang into action. One fetched a silver platter filled with a perfectly polished place setting while the other disappeared through a swinging door into what she suspected was the kitchen.

Kat stood back, watching the exchange in awe. The house she'd grown up in had been nice, but nothing compared to the opulence of carved, gold-leafed ceilings or the servants. It seemed that her father had become quite accustomed to luxury.

When the butler rounded the corner in her direction, she looked at him for the first time... because he stared at her like she was yesterday's garbage. Tarred and leathered skin pulled around light blue eyes. His sneer revealed teeth better suited for denture commercials than chewing food. "Allow me, miss." He pulled the chair from the side of the table and motioned her in with his annoying two-finger gesture.

She wanted to tell him to shove those two fingers up his ass. These were the people who fed her during her imprisonment and did nothing about it. "I'll stand."

"Not sitting. Not dining?" He posed it as a question, but it came across as an edict.

"Not caring at the moment," Kat spat and sidestepped the man.

The servant stopped in the middle of laying the place setting out. Her wide gaze toggled back and forth between her and the butler.

"As you wish." A nod of his gray hair and the servant gathered the finery in one scoop and retreated.

Butler didn't use the two-finger gesture, and the small win bolstered Kat's resolve. She planted both hands on the table. Their slap pinged off the crystal flute of champagne—a mite early for celebration—and the empty china. Her feet spread, bracing for the blowback of her crass actions and determination to get answers.

Her father's eyes snapped to hers for the first time since leaving her prison. "Aron is not your concern. He'll never touch you again."

With that non-answer, he dismissed her. His gentle efforts focused on pouring creamer into his steaming cup of tea. He poured as if nothing were wrong. As if, on any given day, he held a man captive against his will. As if he hadn't held her against her will.

The butler slipped into the background. He regained his two-finger wrist twitch—dammit—aiming it at the servant who exited the kitchen with a covered tray.

Had Hunter only told her that her father was a horrible man, she would never have believed him. He'd tried to protect her as he had from Aron. Hunter had begged her to escape before he knew Tor Royan was her flesh and blood. Goose bumps marched across her shoulders and up her neck.

"I need answers." Kat bent her elbows and lowered her gaze to meet her father's. She injected all the pleading she could muster into the request.

The server placed a dish of egg whites, asparagus, and cheese in front of her father. Rent-a-servant whirled back toward the kitchen, taking his swollen gaze with him.

"You know how I dislike talk while at the table." Her father glared.

"Then you should stand." Kat reflected his expression. "I've done as you've asked for almost two months." And her entire life. "Who is that man?" She pointed toward her prison. "Why did you tell me he was dangerous? What has he done? What did you do?" Her hands flailed about, searching for the words to get him to understand. "Why does he think you're...?"

Black clouds gathered in her father's dark eyes.

It froze the words in her mouth. Was that admission she saw? For certain, it was a side of himself he'd never allowed her access to.

"Leave us." He stood. His massive chair cried as the weight scraped across the shiny floor.

Everyone vacated the room, and she wished they'd take her with them.

Tor Royan, the new, scarier version, squared to her. A sickly sinister tic pulled at his mouth. "Your uncle is dead."

Kat staggered.

"He was murdered," her father hissed.

Her calves hit the front of the chair, and she sank into it. The world tattered yet again. She gripped the edge of the padded fabric for dear life.

Markus Royan, her uncle, bested her father in size by several inches and many more pounds. He'd been a rough and tumble kind of man but loving and playful too. As father figures went, Markus had been hers. He'd visited her at boarding school more often than her own father had. He would stay the entire visitor's day, not just the hour her father usually gifted her with. He'd taken her out on day trips to the city, and he'd been the first to let her try beer and cigarettes. The awful tastes and smells lingered on her memories so closely; he couldn't be dead.

"That man, the one you're so concerned about, and his people killed my brother." Her father roared the last, turned, and headed toward the hallway that held his office.

"Where are you going?" He wasn't much company, but the thought of being left alone with that information opened dark, haunted closets in her psyche.

"I've lost my appetite."

Kat stood on rubbery knees and started after him.

"I'm not in the mood for company." He continued through the large room but stopped at the threshold. His gaze didn't meet hers, but he offered a quarter turn. "I think it's time for you to bathe, change, and get your mind together. You'll meet me in the dining room for a proper lunch."

The suggestions didn't leave room for rejoinder. For once, she didn't have any, surprised or otherwise. "Yes, sir."

She walked back to the room she'd been locked inside. An echo chamber assaulted her with memories of her Uncle Markus; his laugh, his deep growling voice, his happy salutes, the clinking of glasses. Her father's haunting voice whispered between the lines. The comments all held more than a hint of judgment and dissatisfaction. Then came Hunter's gentle command and the careful concern for his friends and even her.

Kat stood in front of the shower, ready to carry out her father's bidding. Inside the small tiled room, the competing voices grew louder and louder to a maddening crescendo. A scream ripped from her throat. She slapped her hands over her face and sobbed. Her knees bent, and she slowly melted to the floor. Tears ran hot through her fingers. Gasps shook her shoulders.

Her uncle had always told her he was a bad man. Actually, he had said he was a bad fucker of mothers, but not to tell her father what he'd told her. Kat had lived a life sheltered from the world. Education and the ability to explore the things that interested her most kept her satisfied enough to ignore the lack of affection and familial love between her and her father. Kat never focused on the negative. She'd always made the best of things.

Those days were done. A stranger cared more for her emotional and physical well-being than her father. If she listened to her father, that stranger had also killed her uncle. When? For the past seven weeks, he'd been under her care. If he'd killed her uncle before, why hadn't her father said anything?

If her father wouldn't tell her anything, Hunter would...or so help her, she'd start using truth serum to get answers out of people. Med school hadn't covered the topic, but she could concoct a mix of drugs that would do the job.

Using the hem of her oversized scrubs, Kat wiped away her tears. It took several swipes, but her face was dry by the time she reached Hunter's door and jerked it open wide. The hospital bed lay on its side. Blood stained the white sheet hanging haphazardly over half of the cockeyed mattress. It was only a spattering, though, not enough to equate death.

She was accustomed to blood and even death. Violence, not so much. Unease settled in Kat's belly and unpacked its suitcase.

"Hunter?" Her voice sounded hoarse and hesitant. It rattled around the empty room like a ghost. She walked on concrete-lined feet to the bathroom. The closer she got, the higher her heart beat in her throat. It reached her tongue at the same time she broached the doorway.

The pristine little room stared back, no Hunter, but also, no more signs of a struggle. She skipped the closet then ran through to her bedroom and out the door to the hallway. Her feet carried her through the maze of corridors. One by one, she dipped into unused guest rooms, seating areas, and linen closets. Each disappointment ratcheted her desperation to find Hunter.

Kat stayed away from the kitchen, afraid to run into the butler. The guards should've been her concern, but they seemed to have disappeared. None of them stood watch in their usual locations. By the time she had reached the wing of her father's office, she sprinted toward the mansion's back entrance. She'd been escorted in that way too many days ago and had seen a proper receptionist station complete with a vase of flowers, a notepad, a cup filled with pens, and a phone.

If she couldn't get answers, then by God, the police authority could. After all, this involved murder, abduction, and imprisonment.

The inescapable sound of flesh meeting flesh split the air. A deep muffled grunt followed along with several men's laughter. Unease farther built the framework for a house in her stomach as though it planned on staying a while. Every ligament and tendon inside her body shook. Her blood turned gelatinous, clogging her veins. A scream lit the hallways on fire. The man inside the room must worship the Lord of light. Their cheers and chants multiplied.

"No! Please, I'll never touch her again! Please stop." The last plea turned into wailing.

Aron hadn't spoken much during her captivity, but she would remember his voice for the rest of her life. Would she remember his screams or his threats more?

Kat stepped toward the door, away from the phone. She didn't like the man—he was pure evil—yet the healer inside her railed against the abuse. Besides, if they beat Aron, what would they do to Hunter? Desperation and the need to find him propelled her forward.

A hand clamped her shoulder and pulled her backward. She stumbled over her father's wingtips. "What are you doing, Katrin?"

Chapter Fifteen

Leather straps pinned Hunter's wrists, waist, and ankle to a truly fucked-up St. Andrew's Cross. He'd been on one or two in his day. Not the hardcore stuff. Kink only. Kink was fun. None of the crosses he'd been strapped to had hosted pointed spikes akin to a short bed of nails, only thicker and sharper. From looking at the thing when they'd wrestled him in here some ten minutes ago, the spikes were attached to long, movable metal rods in slots underneath. This meant the moment that sick bastard Royan didn't like an answer Hunter gave, he'd ram one of them home... right into Hunter's flesh.

He grit his teeth, ignored the blood that seeped slowly from his split tongue, and strained. His coma-weakened muscles bunched, pulling more futilely than the thirty times before. The skin covering his wrists gave a little more. Sweat added to the sting of the already seeping wounds below the straps.

The all too familiar whack of a squarely delivered punch bled in through the chamber's thick metal door. It wasn't him...yet. Men laughed, maybe three of them, while the human punching bag gagged for breath. The setup struck Hunter as odd. Royan, the man who got off on torturing his enemies and competitors alike, had pawned off the

demolition of the guard who'd manhandled Kat. If
the man truly cared about his daughter, he'd be the
one doling out the ass whooping. But no. He was
saving his skill and treasure for Hunter.

"Fucking great." He worked his wrists again
but didn't try the ankle again. At this point, he only
had one, and he needed it to function at top speed.

Hunter had heard tales of Royan's chambers.
The youngest brother liked to brag about the room
before Tyler's woman—Markus' and Tors' past—put
a bullet in his head. Everywhere he looked,
different tools of the torture trade hung. He tried to
ignore the saws and pliers and jugs and knives, but
damn, he wasn't a robot. Plus, he knew each of
those tools' capabilities in the right hands.

The setting was torture tactic one. Listening
to them beat the ever-living shit out of one of "their
own" was the second.

Hell no. Scratch that.

Kat was torture tactic numero mother-f-ing
uno. She was the mind fuck to end them all. Dick
in one ear and out the other. Mind fucked.

Hunter had known his fate from the moment
he'd realized this was no Base Branch boutique
hospital. No one would go to the trouble of keeping
him alive and waiting through a goddamned coma
unless he had information they wanted. No way in
hell would he give them anything. It'd be nice if
they'd kill him fast. Knowing he can't help her in
his quarter-loss state hurt more than any physical
thing they could do to him.

Over the years, he'd been in tough spots but
never helpless. The relentless spirit inside him, the
one that rocked out twenty-four seven with its
middle fingers in the air and its foot on the
accelerator of life, Royan had it by the short and
curlies. He could only hope for one of two options,

and both were as farfetched as his need to protect
Kat from her father. One; Oliver—after not finding
his ass for the better part of a month—gained intel
that led him and their entire team of special forces
marching up Tor Royan's asshole within the hour.
Some real pie-in-the-sky bullshit. Two; Tor—after
getting what he wanted from Kat—released Kat
back into the wild where she belonged. Some real
pigs-flying dreams.

Oliver and the rest of the team hadn't found
Hunter at the site of rubble and ash. They probably
thought he was growing grass by now. If by some
miracle Oliver didn't believe he was dead because of
the whole no body, no death thing, he had no way
of knowing the location of Royan's HQ. The sicko
had mazes, bunkers, and safe houses all over
Europe. Tor Royan trusted no one, which made him
unstable. Hell, he'd sent his own brother on a
guaranteed suicide mission. There was no chance
Royan would trust Kat to keep quiet about the
things she'd seen once she returned to her life.

Hunter raged and shook against the bonds.
Fear crept behind his defenses. If Royan knew he
cared about Kat, would he use her to get the
information he sought?

Chapter Sixteen

Oliver sat on the bench in front of his garage-size locker in the Base Branch Armory. Half the contents of his go bag littered the ground while he repacked the thing for the third time in two days. Throughout the gun-and-ammo-laden room, his brothers in arms did the same, cleaning pristine weapons and counting, checking, and logging the gear they knew better than their own dicks. It was the usual pre-mission ceremony gone awry, the idiosyncratic madness that came from a holding pattern held for too damn long.

"Hey man, I need to talk to you." Boots infiltrated his view of grenades, first-aid kits, and MREs. Oliver didn't have to look up to know who spoke.

"I'm kinda busy."

"Tough shit." Tyler Grace tossed down his duffle in front of his locker, two away from Oliver's. Its impact reverberated like an explosion, sending shockwaves and mangled memories through Oliver's body and brain because of the chasm between them. The locker that would never again be used, not by Hunter anyway.

"I've read the schematics and memorized the terrain, weather patterns, escape routes, and plan of attack."

"Good for you. Get your ass over here, now."
Tyler turned heels and marched away.

Oliver tossed his favorite assault rifle onto the
duffle, something he would never normally do. He'd
been doing a lot of shit he'd never normally do, like
avoiding the fuck out of one of—no—his only
remaining best friend. He lumbered through the
stock of weapons and able-bodied men to the
mouth of the empty gun range.

"What is it?" Oliver groused.

Tyler opened his arms wide and tackled him
with a bear hug.

It hurt worse than any attack he'd braved in
his life. Visceral instinct ruled his reaction. He
shoved at Tyler's chest, a chest that until three
months ago had been in recovery. Oliver shouldn't
push him. He shouldn't do many things, like obsess
over a girl so much that he got his best friend and
partner killed.

"Get off me, Tyler."

"Man, this isn't just for you, you know. I lost
him too." Tyler's emotion-thick voice rumbled in his
ear, hurting all the more.

"Because of me." Oliver's rebuttal came as a
bellowed sob.

"Fuck you. Hunter had a mind of his own. He
made his own damn decisions. Always. No matter
what any of us said about them."

"Fuck you." The room caved in on Oliver,
pressing in his lungs. He planted two hands
between their bodies and shoved. The bulldogger
had a way of clamping you down and not letting
you go from years of wrestling cattle, damn him.

Oliver's emotions erupted in an ugly sob that
wracked his body. A scream accompanied it, and
then he couldn't shore up either gushing dam. At
some point, he quit pushing Tyler away and gripped

his shoulders for dear life. He knew if he let go, he'd be torn down by the current of bitterness and rage and never again find the surface. He wept at his loss, at their loss.

"I can't fucking do it, Tyler. I don't know what to do. I just can't..."

"You live, Oliver. You live for Hunter. It's what he wanted."

"You don't know what the fuck he wanted. You weren't there." Oliver released his friend. "He wanted to beat the shit out of me. The last thing I ever did to him was punch him."

Tyler held fast. "And how many times had he punched you before?"

"This was different."

"The fuck it was. Hunter was Hunter, and you are still you."

Director Tucker whistled to get everyone's attention as only he could. One long trill cut through the bullshit of twelve men shooting the breeze and continued through the silence until the man ran out of breath.

Both men pushed off each other, scrubbed hands over their sopping faces, and hotfooted it into the room with a cache of weapons and mass of men ready for battle and ready for blood, Tor Royan's blood. That DNA belonged solely to Oliver, and everyone knew it.

"We have confirmation?" Tyler hollered from the back of the room, out of order and out of line, but clearly not giving any fucks.

Tucker's jaw flexed, and his dagger gaze flashed the get your shit together look but held his tongue. Everyone was on edge but had been since Oliver had gotten back...without one of their own.

"Still no confirmation, but the tap on the Brödraskapet network is live and feeding new information by the minute. We have Oliver and Hunter to thank for that."

Everyone in the room turned to him and gave an approving nod. Like he deserved it. Hunter wasn't there to take his credit. Oliver deserved nothing, but he'd say a big thank-you to the guy upstairs if a chasm would open up beneath his feet and swallow him whole.

"We're getting closer," Tucker continued. "Cord Strong and his army of Branch trainees are shoveling through the miles of intel. As soon as anyone confirms anything, we roll. Until then, I don't want to see any of your ugly mugs in this place."

Rumbles and curses erupted. Oliver's skin stretched taut over his muscles and bones.

"Sir?" He couldn't keep the desperation or slicing boom out of his question.

"You heard me. You guys have been stinking this place up for the last week." Because he'd restricted missions to critical only. The call grounded most everyone to keep forces rested and ready for Tor, and boy were they. "I'm ordering everyone to the Stronghold Compound for a friendly barbecue. We could all use the camaraderie. All are to attend unless you're on skeleton staff."

The rumbles built again.

"Polluting the air in here isn't going to make us move any faster or fight any harder. You need to remember what we're fighting for because it isn't vengeance."

The fuck it wasn't.

"Tor Royan and his men have had this coming a long time before." He didn't have to say before they killed one of our guys, but the words echoed in Oliver's head.

As anxious as everyone had been to get on a mission, the mention of food and beer caused the tension in the room to shift to friendly banter, and soon, the operatives filtered out, save for Tyler and Tucker. It was at times like these that Hunter's absence hurt the worst. Hunter would never make another stupid joke about an Uh Oh Orco or slap him on the back of the head for saying something stupid.

"So I've got to go pick up some beer." Tyler shoved his bag into the locker and closed it. "See you at the party?"

"Yeah, man." Oliver nodded and held his breath, waiting for him to leave.

"You're not coming, are you?"

"Nope."

"One day, it won't hurt so much."

"On that day, I'll be dead."

"Keep it up and you will be."

That was the idea.

"It's no way to honor his memory." Tyler's parting shot caught Oliver in the jaw, the scarred, tender jaw. "Later, man." He nodded at Vail Tucker and slipped through the vault door.

Tucker propped a hip on the bank of lockers that used to house his, Hunter's, and Tyler's gear. Son of a bitch, some of Hunter's stuff still haunted the metal frame.

"Did I hear correct...you're defying an open order?"

"It's no order." Oliver wiped his eyes and shoved his hands into his pockets.

"Came out of my mouth, didn't it? Sounded like an order to me." Authority bled from the man's tone and dense frame, defying the graying hair and the faint wrinkles at the corners of his eyes. One titanic shoulder bobbed. "I even said specifically, 'This is an order,' didn't I?"

"I hear you, sir."

"But you don't get me." Tucker's head canted and a dark brow arched in a dare.

"No, you don't get it." Oliver closed the distance between them, itching for a fight to dull his senses or renew his physical pain. Shouldn't the two match? "You don't get it at all. Hunter is dead because of me."

"Yep."

Tucker's blunt and honest answer stopped Oliver cold. Mouth hanging open, he stared at the man.

"Some fucked-up shit, being responsible for the death of someone you love." Tucker ticked off the wall and balled two fists at his sides. Oliver needed those fists crashing into his sides, his face.

"Try two." He tossed the question like a grenade, only he had nowhere to hide and wouldn't if he could.

"I did."

Oliver's need to be pummeled took a backseat as, once again, the fearless leader who'd led him into and out of some of the darkest places on earth shocked the hell out of him. For the first time since the incident, probably and certainly, since the man had walked into the room, Oliver looked at him.

A deep rooted and buried sorrow rose to the surface. Oliver recognized the guilt, anger, and sadness because he'd lived with it nearly his entire life. How had the man hidden it so well?

"It sucks, worse than anyone can imagine. My baby girl was protected inside her mother's belly, and still, she felt the horrors of the world. I never got to hold her, to rock her to sleep, or even to see her pretty face. I watched my wife's face as she realized she'd been shot in the stomach and that her baby would never be born. I watched the life drain from my wife's body."

Oliver's guts twisted into hideous balloon animals. He scraped both hands over the short hair on his head and dragged them over his patchy beard.

"How'd you live through it?"

"For a long time, I didn't. The job was everything and nothing. I was a robot, living for one thing."

"Vengeance."

"Revenge drove me." Tucker gave a weak smile. "It's not as sweet as you'd expect."

He'd decide that for himself, thank you very much.

"Do yourself a favor and figure out what it took me nearly thirty years to. Life isn't worth living alone. Don't push away the people who love you."

"Yes, sir."

"You coming to the party?"

"No, sir."

"What if I said you couldn't go on a mission unless you went?"

"I'd say kill me now."

Oliver had heard about the party. Cord had been talking about it for a few days, and he knew exactly who the party honored. And that, he just couldn't do.

***

Base Branch Headquarters had never been so quiet. Tucker had fallen out hours ago. Still, Oliver sat in front of Hunter's locker staring at the placard across the top. Masters. The man had been a master of many, many things. He still couldn't accept that he was gone.

They'd been back to the scene twice, combing the site for his remains, but both trips had turned up zilch. No evidence of human remains or that Hunter had even been there. For two days, they'd searched the surrounding area and towns, talking to informants and even going door to door, looking for any hint that he might be alive.

Instead, they found nothing. Just like there was nothing here. Just like his staring would accomplish nothing.

Everything pulled him toward that party because he knew Marina would be there. He pushed himself away from it with equal force. He didn't blame her for Hunter's death. That he set squarely on his shoulders. Shouldn't he tell her as much? After all the crap she'd been through, she deserved whatever solace he could give.

Oliver didn't know if he had the strength to see her, speak to her, and then walk away. For the first time since the hospital, he knew where she'd be tonight. After weeks of avoiding her as if she carried the Zombie virus, he knew he didn't have the strength to stay away a minute more.

His boots moved fast, carrying him to his motorcycle, through the city, and to the house. During the entire drive, he prayed that he'd wasted enough time to miss the party.

When he turned into the driveway, he discovered two things. One, compound did not accurately describe the Stronghold place. Estate did justice to the sprawling driveway lined with moss-covered live oaks that led to a massive Colonial-style mansion. Two, from the lights glowing inside and out of the six-pillar form and the music pouring from the backyard, the party had just hit its stride.

To keep from drawing attention, he parked at the opening of the massive circular drive and hoofed it toward the front door. The white wood and black lion knocker looked inviting enough, yet he still veered to the side yard. A fifteen-foot brick fence lined the perimeter, but the scrawling wrought-iron gate hung open.

Oliver stopped at the threshold to get his shit together. Too late. The simple vision of Marina knocked him back a step.

Her vibrant blond hair hung in a loose braid over one shoulder. A light shimmer replaced the dark circles that had once haunted her eyes. Smooth, full, sun-kissed skin with a hint of muscle wrapped the elegant bone structure with which he'd become all too acquainted. Teal blue fabric hugged ample breasts, a narrow waist, and a curvaceous backside made for worshipping. Most striking of all was the wide grin stretching her sweet lips.

She stood between a blonde who had more than a foot and fifteen muscular pounds on her and a big guy Oliver didn't know but hated on principle. They bantered back and forth about something too hilarious for him to stomach. He rubbed a fist over his chest and breathed through the deluge of emotions.

Surprise. Awe. Anger. Jealously. Disappointment. They played musical fucking chairs with his synapses.

What the hell size ego did he have that he'd expected her to be sad? He didn't want her miserable. Judging by the smiles she passed from one person to the next, life with her sister agreed with Marina. After all, that was what she'd wanted.

Oliver stumbled into the shadows and clutched the side of the house to keep from hitting the ground. The world pressed in on him as it had in the hospital. The quacks had called it a panic attack, but Base Branch operatives didn't get panic attacks. If they did on paper, they didn't see the field, and the missions were the only things keeping him alive. He needed them like he needed his next breath, and that fucker was taking his damn time.

"Oliver?"

The sweetest voice he'd ever heard called to him. Add crazy to the books. He'd conjured her caring from thin air. If only he could get that air into his lungs. His knee hit the grass but just one. It was the small wins, really.

"Hey?" Marina's tiny hands cupped his face and pulled it to her breasts.

Best dream ever.

Breath scented with lavender and sunshine filled his lungs. Marina smoothed her hands over his shoulders and back and murmured to him. She even wore the frilly teal dress.

This wasn't a fucking dream.

His breath came again, pulling Marina's scent into his soul. It wasn't a dream, but he'd dwell on it a bit longer.

"Are you hurt?"

He shook his head and burrowed a bit deeper between her heavy breasts.

"Are you sick?"

Again, he shook his head and silently begged her to ask more questions.

"Look at me," she demanded. When he didn't move, she pressed a hand under his chin and lifted.

Mascara laced lashes squinted down at him. "Are you drunk?"

"No."

"You don't look well." Her pretty mouth pursed.

Too bad he felt as good as he had in the last four months at that very moment.

"You look amazing." He should stop himself, but he couldn't, not with her this close. His hands slipped around her waist, up her back, and he pulled her into a near crushing embrace.

Marina stiffened.

His insides crumbled.

Oliver searched for the will to let her go. He found it too easily since she didn't want his arms around her. The moment he shifted to release her, she melted against him.

He pulled her onto his knee, and she nestled her head under his chin. Her sobs came hard and fast against his neck. Each cry ripped at his insides. Back and forth, he rocked her and smoothed his hands over her supple shoulder, but he didn't say anything. He needed to say things. She needed to hear things. Only they wouldn't come out.

Under no circumstances, except her explicit directions to kiss him, should he put his lips on her skin. Clearly, loss of blood had caused brain damage. His mouth pressed to her shoulder just to the side of her thin dress strap. She tasted better than he'd remembered. He took another taste at the well of her neck and then another at the curve of her chin.

It was as far as he could go without moving her, which he wouldn't do.

Marina lifted her head. Wide blue eyes stared at his mouth. "I didn't think you were coming?"

"I wasn't." His erection pressed painfully into the crotch of his pants and the curve of her thigh. God, he could take her on the ground a blink away from the laughter and revelry of forty or more people.

"But you're here." Marina's eyes sank shut. She pressed her mouth to his and pulled his chest against hers.

He let her set the pace because if he didn't, they'd be naked and compromised within the minute. Her tongue sliced over his with intent. Each stroke worked its way into his mind, draining away his sorrow and replacing it with one-hundred-proof lust. She dragged her nipples across his torso. Her hips rocked on his lap. He'd been worried about his pace when hers raced for first prize. God, he needed to take it down a notch or take her.

"Marina?"

"Mmmm." Neither her moan nor her tongue helped.

"Did you want me to come?"

Well, the question slowed the pace for sure. Ninety-nine to zero in point two five seconds. Marina straightened and covered her lips. Her gaze zipped everywhere looking for the right answer. Finally, they rested on his.

"No."

The word stung. Oliver gagged on his lust.

"Yes," she breathed, "and no."

He nodded.

"It's..."

"Complicated," he offered.

"Yeah."

Wasn't it?

"I'm—"

The trill of his phone cut her off and rocketed his already jacked blood pressure sky-high. He dug it from his pocket and read the screen. 'Confirmation. Wheels up in one hour.'

Marina must have read it too. She stood, fingers clamped in a tight ball in front of her.

"I'm sorry. I have to—"

"Be careful." Blond baby hairs danced around her sad face.

"I'm going to get Tor, for all of us."

"I hope you find what you need, Oliver. I'm looking for it, but I know it's not Tor." She wiped the tears from her eyes, smiled, and ran back to the party.   Kat stood as her prison door beeped. It opened only enough to allow her new guard and the tray he carried with her breakfast atop it into the room. It closed behind him and locked tight.

"I demand to speak with my father."

"Your father is not accepting your requests at this time." The guard delivered the same droned answer as he had the past four days.

"You tell him he's not a fucking kiosk, and he can and will accept my request right this damn minute, or I'll drown myself in the bathtub." Her throat burned from the fevered delivery. She shook her fists and snarled.

He set the tray on the coffee table and left without another word. The moment the door closed, Kat sank onto the couch. Her cheek throbbed from stretching and working it in her frenzy. She pressed a red and cracked palm to the flesh her father had slapped after tossing her back into this holding cell after she'd called him demented. It'd been the first time he'd ever laid a hand on her in anger.

"I hope it wasn't too over the top." The last thing she needed was her dad to pay a visit. The purpose of the messages was to let him know she was yet to be cowed by his action.

She opened the tray and shoved eggs into her mouth. Kat chewed without tasting. The memories continued to flood back of the first time she'd seen her father lose his carefully constructed composure. As a young girl, she'd been lonely even through the short years she lived at home, which was a much smaller one in Italy. Her father didn't live there. During one of his longer trips, Kat had found a litter of kittens behind the house. Miracle of all miracles, her nanny had allowed her to keep one as long as she kept it in the wine shed. It was never allowed into the house.

Tears threatened to well, but she fought them back with another heap of food. That cat had been her best friend. As time went on, she broke the rules but never while her father had been home. One day, he'd come home early from a trip. She woke to find Mr. Sniffles gone from her bed. The poor cat's screams mingled with Aron's and morphed into her worst fear for Hunter.

"Come on, Kat. You've got this." Her palms shrieked, but she ignored them.

Kat stood, grabbed the knife, and turned to the window behind her—the one she'd blocked the guard's view of for the past four days. Even at this distance with the gouge she'd hollowed out around the latch, anyone who looked could see her attempt at escape. No, not attempt. She would break through this window today. Sure, she'd thought the same thing yesterday, but the screw that'd been placed in the window was longer than she'd expected.

Every scrape went against the surgeon's instinct to protect her hands. Every scrape rubbed into the raw flesh for the previous day's work. Every scrape also brought her closer to freedom.

The guard came promptly at the breakfast, lunch, and dinner hours.

While she worked on removing wood from around the screw, Kat also kept an eye on the sun. Her room didn't have a clock, but she'd gotten damn good at judging the time by the changing shadows on the ground. She needed to get out with enough time that the guard wouldn't notice her missing until she'd fled the property.

Finally, the last of the wood released the screw. Kat jerked the window from its frame. To her surprise. This must not have always been a prison. She looked back at the door. The thing was beautiful, but the sight of it made her knees shake. So much bad had come in and out of that door. What if the guard caught her escaping? Her legs might have been amputated along with Hunter's because they refused to move. Fear crawled up her spine. Its nails dug into nerve endings and gouged bone. Kat followed the rules. She did as she was told. She was a good person, and good people shouldn't have to deal with shit like this.

The gears of logic turned inside her brain. It fired off synapses and revved the production of adrenaline. The situation demanded action. There were too many variables if she stayed. Kat swallowed, sat on the windowsill, and threw herself out the window. Nausea bubbled, but the leap of faith released her fear and freed her limbs. She didn't worry about guards. They were all content for the time being torturing men, one of whom used to be their comrade. No, not comrade. That term denoted some sense of loyalty. These men were loyal to no one. To her estimation, they worked for the almighty dollar.

Fresh air sweetened her lungs. A blossom of some sort scented the air, and brilliant sunlight warmed her skin. Were it any other day, she'd take her time and enjoy the surroundings. Today, she kept so low that her thighs burned with each hurried stride she took toward the back of the house. The farther she went, the faster her heart thumped.

For the past month, Kat had seen cars whip down the driveway, coming and going from the massive house. Surely, one of those vehicles was around here somewhere...preferably unlocked with the keys inside. She gulped back the nausea that tainted her tongue and slowed her strides at the corner of the house. The quiet hum of air conditioning units drowned out what little noise she made. Birds chirped in the trees. The wind blew the hair from her face. She heard no voices, no footsteps, no hint of the torture going on inside.

Kat straightened and peered around the house. Two rows of cars lined a large concrete drive in the back, making it look like an upscale used car lot. It would be so easy, if the keys were inside one, to hop in and drive away from this place as quickly as the machine could carry her. The desire of self-preservation reared its ugly head and made her see the ugly and very human side of herself. For better or worse, Hunter had tried to save her on more than one occasion, so she would not abandon him now.

A deep breath expanded Kat's chest as she worked to steady her quaking nerves. She moved slowly and steadily toward the back entrance, the one she'd been escorted through so long ago. The white door with its silver handle stood just as it had back then. Her fingers shook as she reached for the handle, curled her fingers around it, and said a silent prayer that it opened.

The damn thing didn't budge. Her hope and determination backpedaled. She looked at the cars. Instinct told her to run. Hunter had told her to run. She took one step toward the cars but stalled. Her gaze drew back to the keypad below the handle. There were an infinite number of possibilities for the combination.

Kat thought about the man who owned the house. His blood ran through her veins. They'd lived in the same house for several years. She didn't know her father at all, but she could take a guess at the combination. She entered her father's date of birth. The light above the numbers blinked red, denying her access. She tried her and her brother's date of birth. Denied once more. Her fingers punched in several other combinations to no avail. She was about to give up when one last combination struck her.

"My light." She groaned the endearment and typed in the corresponding numbers for the words. The light on the keypad turned green, allowing her to turn the knob and enter the place she'd tried to escape from for the past month.

Unlike outside, Kat sure as shit worried about the guards. The doorway led to the corridor where her father had found her snooping on Aron's torture. An eerie quiet enveloped the space. Was it too early for torture? Tea first, torture later? She closed the door quietly. Her gaze homed in on the hallway, which led to her father's gym. She shimmied along the wall. Something sharp caught her thigh, and the sound of a thousand tiny cymbals eradicated the silence. Kat's hand shocked to her leg. Her gaze moved with it to find a low end table overflowing with keys, and every one of them announced her arrival. She grabbed a handful of them, stuffed them into the pockets of her scrubs, and ran.

Four closed doors configured the corridor. All the doors throughout the house were thick golden mahogany. Save for the two farthest from her. They looked black like death as the doors to a morgue should look. Cold. Slick. Uninviting. Kat wanted nothing to do with those doors. Aron had been behind the second one. In the quiet, she still heard the echoes of his deafening screams seeping from underneath. Her entire body revolted against those doors, yet she walked to the first.

Hunter had to be behind the door, which was probably locked. They wouldn't leave it open... unless he was no longer inside. She'd checked his adjoining room that morning. He hadn't returned.

Kat reached for the door. It creaked and gave at the hinges. She jerked away, slamming her back into the corner of the wall in an effort to escape. The door only opened a millimeter. No one bum-rushed her. No one exited at all. Were she inside a horror film, this was where the audience would scream themselves hoarse, telling her to run away. She pressed her face close to the crack. A sliver of the room revealed its horrifying darkness. The light from the hallway seeped inside, dimly illuminating the bare concrete floor and walls of an unfurnished room. There was no grandeur here.

Where the hell was Hunter?

She pushed the door open and covered her mouth. A shrill cry bombarded her shaking palm. Dead eyes stared at her. The clear blue that had terrified her days ago did so in a different way. Death had clouded over the clear blue orbs since Aron's death—murder. Dried blood covered his contorted face, telling her the deed had been done before his killing. His screams poured over her on a sickening loop. She closed her eyes and covered her ears to block out the guilt. This man would have killed her, but it didn't mean he deserved this. She stumbled from the room and opened her eyes only after pulling the door closed behind her.

Over the years, she'd seen awful things. Murder even. This was the work of a devil.

Kat's eyes shifted to the other death door. She retched. Her body stole control, tossing her stomach—not its contents, but the entire damn thing—into her throat. Her eyes watered. Hands on her knees, she stumbled forward, stopping at the door. With her stomach lodged inside her esophagus, the retching ceased. Tears rolled haphazardly down her cheeks.

She wrapped her hands around the handle and pled for it not to open. Locks, she could deal with. Hunter's mutilated corpse? Her head shook away the notion as moisture gathered on her lips. She wiped it away with the back of her arm, gritted her teeth, and yanked the lever. The door gave from its frame. Her stomach blocked the scream that ricocheted through her body.

"Different day, same answer, fuckwad." Hunter's gruff voice squeezed through the opening.

A sob, a happy one squeezed its way through the terror and out her mouth. Kat caught it in both hands and shoved through the door.

"What the hell? Kat?" Hunter fought against leather bonds like a feral beast. His naked body displayed the effort of every taut muscle. Blood crusted around wounds on his wrists and ankle. His pretty lips were split on the right side. One eye was swollen shut. "Kat, talk to me. Are you hurt?"

"No." She hiccupped the answer.

"Why are you crying? Why are you here? How?" His questions came too quickly. They crawled all over her and cut off her waterworks just as fast.

"You are." She snarled the answer and closed the door.

"I've had worse." He shrugged as much as the straps allowed.

"That doesn't make me feel better." Kat sniffled.

A wheelchair sat in the corner. She ran forward, lurched for it, and rolled it to the cross they'd lashed him to. Monsters.

"Anything broken?" Kat locked the wheels in place.

"I thought I told you to leave."

"I can't leave you."

"Of course, you can. Go." His swollen eye opened wide with emphasis. Red surrounded his pretty amber iris.

Strength Kat hadn't felt since her father had her ushered away from her life filled her lungs. She stood as close to Hunter's face as the height difference would allow. "You can waste time trying to get me to go, which won't work, or you can help me."

He hesitated for three long seconds then huffed. "What do you need me to do, Doc?"

"After I unfasten the straps, wrap your arms around my shoulders. I'm going to start with your foot." She was glad his weight was already on the ground. Had he been suspended at all, the damage would've been a lot worse.

"If you want a hug, all you have to do is ask." His words were as playful as they'd been before even though his tone was strained and his voice hoarse.

"I could use a hug about now. How about you?" Kat slipped the latches free as quickly as she could. A large swath of raw skin pinked a wide line around his ankle.

"I'm not about the touchy-feely," he hissed. "But yeah, I could use one."

She worked on one wrist and then the other. A muffled groan rumbled in his larynx. Free, his arm only lowered a handful of millimeters. His vocalization intensified.

"Save the hug for later." She wrapped her arms around his middle. Gel-like moisture covered his back, slicking her arms and making the transfer even more difficult. His near dead weight compacted her chest, which made breathing impossible. She pulled, twisted, and lined him up with the chair. "Sit."

Hunter collapsed into the wheelchair.

Kat braced her hand on the back, still hugging him close for several heartbeats while she caught her breath.

"We have to move." His voice was whisper quiet, almost hollow.

She stood. The horror movie returned. Fresh blood and old clots greased her inner arms. There was so much blood. "No."

"Forget it. Let's move." Hunter fumbled with the brakes, muttering a curse.

When he leaned over, Kat caught a glimpse of the mangled mess that was his back. Her curse blended with his. How in the hell...? Her gaze lifted to the base of the cross. A thousand thick, sharp points gave her the finger. "Holy shit. Hunter?"

"Kat?"

"What?" she hissed.

"Look at me."

Kat blinked the tears from her eyes and turned to Hunter. He'd unlocked the brakes and angled himself toward the door. "Do you want to live?"

"Yes."

"Then we need to get the fuck out of this place right now. Lock it up. Cram everything into a box in your mind, toss that shit into a corner, and let's figure out an evac plan."

She nodded as he spoke, kicked all the questions into the recesses of her forever altered mind, and yanked a handful of keys from her pocket. "The back door is at the end of the hallway. There are cars outside."

"How far to the back door?" He wheeled himself to the closed door. Fresh blood seeped from holes on his back.

"Thirty meters."

"To the cars from there?" He eased the door open a crack and peered out.

"Fifty," she whispered.

Hunter motioned her forward. "If they come, you'd better run." She didn't speak. Thoughts like that didn't have a place in her mind. He turned. "Promise me."

"Fine."

"Follow me. Watch our six."

"Our what?"

"Our backs."

Kat nodded and then followed Hunter as he rolled himself across the hall and along the wall. He hesitated at each doorway, assessing the interior and scanning the corridor. When he happened upon Aron's body, his demeanor didn't shift at all. He simply closed the door and continued.

Chapter Seventeen

Strung up on the cross, Hunter had had too much time to think. With Kat behind him and the potato-peeled eyes of Royan's guard in front, he wondered again what the sick fuck would do to his daughter for her betrayal. Kat never spoke of her family, but he'd guess she didn't have a mother. No telling what Tor had done to the poor woman.

Hunter rolled faster, searching sloppier. A horde of guards could be bunked in any one of these rooms. The silence of death reassured him. He opened the last door before the promised land. *Jackpot, motherfucker.* An arsenal lined the walls. Grenades. Guns. Knives. Bombs. Just what the doctor ordered.

"Grab that bag. If I nod at it, you grab a handful and stow it inside." Hunter rolled to a stack of C4, grabbed a hunk, and worked it into a strip. She stalled in front of the wall of weaponry. "Those. That." Her shoulders rolled back. She grabbed and loaded magazines and pistols into the sack.

Kat pulled open several drawers and cabinets. "I don't see any uniforms or clothing."

He stared hard, trying to understand why, in the midst of an arsenal and a deadly escape attempt, she looked for clothes.

"You're naked." She pointed at his cock.

"Born that way and I'll die that way unless we get gone." He nodded at a display of knives near her head. "Stick to the important stuff. Those." She huffed and reached for the eighteen-inch blades above the ten-inch blades he'd nodded at. "No, I like your moxie, but the shorter ones work better. Up on the shelf." He didn't bother calling things by name because she wouldn't know them. Just like he knew shit about medical stuff.

She worked quickly, building them a small buffer.

"Good. Now, close it, put it on your back, and grab that big gun." He molded the last of the C4 around a grenade and grabbed some para-cord.

"I thought shorter ones worked better."

"Depends on the tool in the job." Hunter secured one end of the cord to the metal grating and tied the other end to the pin. He grabbed another length of cord. "Come here." When she reached his side with the gun outstretched like it were a live bomb, he took it from her, released the safety, and handed it back. "Point and shoot. Just don't point it at me."

"I can't shoot anyone." Her soulful eyes were wide. Nearly as wide as when she'd entered the chamber where he'd been tortured. Thank goodness, the tears had dried. He'd never been a fan of chick tears, but hers cut him in a way that left scars.

"I know you're not supposed to do harm and all, but you're going to have to make a decision, Kat. Him or you?"

"You can aim better than I can anyway. I'll do what you're doing." She handed him the gun.

"Not if you don't want to kill anyone." He didn't take the gun. Neither would he make her kill someone if he could help it. He hoped like fuck he could manage in this state. His eyes were swollen. His ribs and back hurt like a mother. Oh, yeah, and he was missing a leg. He was no longer strapped to the damn cross, though. "Flip on the safety and at least carry it out."

"Okay." Kat flipped the safety like a pro. A fast learner. He could have her shooting a three-inch spread at twenty yards in a day. She slung the strap over her shoulder.

His blood covered her arms and the sides of her scrubs. He focused on the task at hand, not at how much he hated the look of blood against her smooth skin. "Hand me a pistol with a magazine from the shelf."

Kat handed over a CZ Sphinx 3000 and held out three different cartridges. Hunter put the expensive as fuck gun in his lap loaded with the correct ammo and hurried her into the hallway.

"If we have incoming, I want to know fast."

She nodded while scanning the hallway.

Luckily, or not, Hunter had experience with wheelchairs. He set the grenade in his lap and whipped the chair through the door backward, pulling the door as he wheeled without shutting it completely. Brakes flipped, he leaned forward. His back and ankle screamed. Breath hissed through his teeth. He used the extra cord, wrapped it around the grenade and interior handle several times and knotted the makeshift detonator.

"Hurry," she begged.

Hunter gently shut the door. The muscles in his arms stung from the strain after the lethal combination of captivity and inactivity. He grabbed the wheel handles, ignored the searing of his wrists, wheeled to the exit at the end of the hallway, and opened it.

"When we get ten feet from the house, you run and don't stop for anything. Do you hear me? Get out of the open as fast as you can. Find a car. If I'm not there, go."

"Let me push you." She grabbed the handle of the chair.

"Two targets make one big one. Apart we have a better chance." He turned toward her, forcing her hand away.

"You mean, apart I have a better chance." Kat's hands balled into fists.

That was exactly what he meant. "Are you going to waste time arguing, or are you going to run, no matter what?"

Her lips pressed into an angry line. Tears threatened to spill over her lids.

"I've been shot at before."

"You mean shot before?"

"My point is…I'll run through—wheel through —a spray of bullets. I'm preparing you to do the same. Don't freeze. Don't wait for me. Go." Two voices poured down the hallway that were not their own. "Now."

She did as he commanded, starting in a perfectly crouched sprint. Keys jangled in both her hands.

Hunter rolled over the threshold and closed the backdoor to Torture Manor behind him. He wheeled out nine feet and over two. The position allowed him sight of the roof line and back door but didn't set him up like a carnival target. The urge to look back at Kat and make certain she'd run like the devil himself chased her heels nipped at him. He ground his teeth. Sore gums jolted from the fresh abuse. Pain focused his mind.

He no longer heard her footsteps.

Okay, maybe not so focused.

The house remained quiet. No one patrolled the roof. Hunter gripped the pistol and raised it, using its sights to scan the grounds. Kat danced in his periphery along the line of fancy cars. His shoulder quaked. The perfect line between the front and rear notches blurred.

"Fuck." Hunter blinked, rolled his shoulders, and shifted the barrel point to the doorway, and then lifted it to the roof. Sweat collected across his chest. Gooseflesh stampeded over his skin in turn.

A *beep, beep* as loud as an atomic bomb fractured the silence. Kat must have unlocked a car's door. Fucking alarms. Hunter's organs jumped to attention.

From the back corner of the rooftop, a guard popped into view as though he'd been sitting on his ass leaned against the chimney catching a nap. The guy stretched his arms high overhead. His mouth yawned into a massive O. He wasn't one of the three who'd wrestled him to the ground, hog-tied him, and wheeled him to the torture chamber. If he were, he'd have been dead the moment his forehead cleared the brick.

Hunter drew a deep breath and let it exit his lips as slowly as his lungs could muster. His heartbeat slowed. His gaze tracked the man's ball scratch.

An engine rumbled to life. The herd of horses drew the guard's gaze. He jumped to attention, blinked wildly, and eased to the wall's edge. His jaw dropped. The man reached for his waistband. Sunlight glinted off the scope of a B&T sniper rifle.

"Amateur." Hunter centered the man's forehead and hoped like hell the guy would withdraw his weapon. Surely, he wouldn't shoot at the boss's daughter. Surely, the guard wouldn't make Hunter take his shot and alert the small contingent Royan had inside.

While the guy brought up the rifle, he also fumbled with the radio at his shoulder. One way or the other, Tor or his man in charge would know about their escape.

Hunter exhaled and split the air with a well-placed bullet. He wouldn't have a sniper eyeing Kat's exit. Not even a shitty one. The man dropped his weapon and slumped over the brick.

Shouts lifted from the hallway and carried through the door. Wheels peeled themselves against concrete. Horses reared. The back door flew open. A guard exited at a run with his weapon at his side. These guys might have been paid as professionals, but they lacked the sharp edge Hunter and his comrades whittled to a deadly point through years of training and countless battles.

Four more men filtered into the far end of the hallway. Skillful or not, one was bound to get the drop on him. That couldn't happen until after Kat escaped. He centered the first man's forehead a fraction of a second before their eyes met.

Two for two.

Live rounds peppered the doorway, shattering glass and ripping away chunks of wood. He rolled backward an inch to stay out of the line of fire. Burning rubber and the whine of a throttled engine assaulted him a second before a sleek, black car nearly reversed up his ass. Good thing he'd only rolled back one inch.

The passenger door flew open at his left side.

"Come on," Kat screamed.

Hunter flipped on the safety, tossed the gun onto the seat, planted one foot on the ground and dove for the car. He landed hard, chest first onto slick leather. A shot of adrenaline gave him the strength to pull his lower half inside the car and turn over.

"I thought I told you to go," he growled.

"The door." Kat's voice pitched high.

He gathered what will he had left and hauled the heavy door closed. A bullet fractured the glass pane less than a foot behind his head.

"Motherf—"

The car lurched backward. Hunter gripped the console to keep from being dumped from the seat.

Kat held the wheel in one petite hand and mastered the gear shift in the other. The speedometer climbed numbers like a crooked Wall Street accountant. Too much. Too fast. He didn't want to be shot. He also didn't want to be launched through the windshield and splattered across the lawn.

"Kat?"

"You told me to go. I'm going."

They shot past the back door of the mansion and onto the mouth of a driveway that was the equivalent of a two-lane highway.

"We're far enough away. You can slow—" Two men poured from the house with automatic rifles strapped to their chests. "Keep going. Keep going." Hunter lowered his window and fired two wild shots. One of the men ducked back inside. The other raised his gun and sprayed too damn close to the Porsche Spyder's front end.

The pistol wouldn't corral the man inside. He looked around the interior but came up empty. "Where's the bag, the rifle?"

"In the parking lot."

"What?" He fired off another round at the man with no effect.

"Would you have rather me gotten it or you?"

"Touché."

A blast shook the ground beneath them. It tossed the man and his AR into the air. Windows exploded from the fine building. Smoke rolled from the door.

"You did that?" Kat's brows hiked damn near her hairline.

Hunter shrugged. "You can slow and tur—"

Kat depressed the brakes and manhandled the steering wheel. Hunter's insides slammed into the left side of his skeleton. The front end of the car swung one-hundred eighty degrees. Kat shifted like a pro and shot them forward, away from the house, completing one of the prettiest J turns he'd ever witnessed.

"How the hell did you learn to drive like that, Doc?"

"My uncle has an affinity for fast cars. He won this one in a bet against an American businessman."

Hunter suspected that had been her uncle's way of saying he'd killed the American and stolen the car, but he'd keep his mouth shut.

"He had an affinity for them," she corrected. "When I was little, probably too little, he taught me a thing or two about driving."

Shit. The uncle who had nearly killed Tyler. The uncle who Cara Lee killed to save his friend. Did she know he was dead? She'd used the past tense when talking about him. Hunter's insides twisted. "Kat, I—"

Her head shook. A hundred tiny, blonde flyaways created a living halo around her face. "I don't want to discuss it. Can't. Not now."

He nodded and let the subject fall away along with the sight of the mansion. No one followed them. Thank goodness. He only had eight bullets to defend them. His discomfort mounted. He was naked, beaten, and one leg down with a woman who'd saved the life her father had tried to torture out of him. Plus, they were in the middle of no-fucking-where with no fucking backup.

"Where are you going, Doc?"

"I don't know."

"Where are we?"

"Swedish country."

"You know you can't go home?"

"I don't have a home here."

Hunter wanted to know more. Had her father raised her? How had she really not known he was a monster? He wrestled his curiosity. "There's a safe house in Oslo. It's off the grid. There's food, clothing. No one would know we were there." It housed a fair stash of weapons too, but he kept that to himself.

Her gaze landed on his lap and the gun he'd used to cover himself as much as possible. Color, vibrant and red, stained her cheeks. She pulled her chin up and trained it to the front of the car. They whipped past trees at a swift clip. He'd much rather have her eyes on the road right now.

"We're about an hour from the Norwegian border." She pointed to the right. "West of here. It's three more hours to Oslo."

"Before we head west, we need to get a new car."

"Why?" She snapped a narrowed gaze to him. "What's wrong with this one?"

He offered both bloody palms. "Actually, this car is a wet dream of mine, but they're probably tracking it."

"Tracking us?" The car slowed.

"Don't stop."

"If they know where we are..." Kat shifted into a higher gear and gunned the engine with gusto.

"They can't transport here. Right now, they're dealing with a fire raging up their asses. It should give us enough time to make the switch."

She dragged a hand down the side of her face. "Switch to what?" Her other hand left the steering wheel and shot toward the heavens. "I don't have money. I don't have friends...here."

"You didn't grow up here?" He couldn't help himself.

Her gaze slid to his. Hunter held it until she looked away. Kat pursed her lips. "No, I didn't. I grew up in Italy." She cleared her throat. "I don't know what that has to do with us being well and fucked."

It was his turn to clear his throat. She'd been so proper, hardly using a curse word in even the most curse-worthy situations. A smile spread his lips. "We're not well fucked. Not yet, anyway. I'm hardly in the condition." And boy would he ever like to show her what it was like to be well fucked.

Kat tugged the collar of her shirt, shifted on the leather, and then pulled the seat belt across her lap. "Buckle up."

"Yes, ma'am." Hunter pulled the belt across his chest and groaned. His ribs throbbed. His back burned. When he secured the metal clip into the latch, his cock had lengthened with a semi-erect hard-on, apparently not giving a shit about his current physical state. He looked around the car for a jacket or something to cover himself. Nothing. Not even napkins in the glove box. He double cupped his manhood for Kat for the second time.

Her eyes remained locked on the road. "I can stop at the next town, withdraw some money, and get you some clothes, medicine, and supplies for your cuts."

"No." Hunter swiveled his good eye on her. "No cards, no bank accounts, no calling friends or phoning work." White knuckles showed just how thoroughly she choked the steering wheel. "They'll pinpoint your location in seconds and, depending on who they've bought, could have ten cameras on you in minutes."

"What about the car? They're tracking it." She slapped the wheel.

"Let them track the car. Stop there." He pointed at a small vegetable stand at the side of the road.

"Are you hungry?" Kat's pretty blue eyes widened. "Feeling dizzy, lightheaded?" She immediately reached for him, running a hand across his forehead from one side to the other.

"I'm fine, Kat." He patted her hand and pointed again. "Pull over."

She pulled onto the dirt and grass combo twenty yards off the highway. A truck loaded with potatoes and leafy greens sat behind a row of overflowing bins with a small hanging scale at one end. One small truck and one tiny car flanked the food truck. Their patrons stood at the bins. The truck owner loaded several small flats of vegetation into the bed of her truck. A man in well-worn shoes and frayed shorts held a bunch of greens and haggled over their price. Hunter couldn't hear the conversation, but his body language told the story of hard times.

"Park to the right side of that car."

"That's not a car. That's a rusted-out go-cart."

"Car is in the word cart." He shrugged, and every injury roared with fresh pain. It would get a lot worse...really soon.

Kat turned up her nose like a true automotive connoisseur but pulled next to the late 1970s model Volvo as he'd asked. "Now what?"

"We move fast." Hunter glared at his nub. His fast had a new definition, and he hated it. He stowed the pain and disappointment in the darkest recesses of his mind and offered her a wicked smile.

"Where?"

"Into the rust bucket." He grabbed the keys from the console, opened his door and stood, leaving Kat gaping after him and his bare ass. Every muscle in his back, arms, and legs protested along with his ribs and half of his face. Blood pulsed with his every hop to the hood, and then around to the driver's door on the usual passenger side for him. The old car's ragged owner never won anything in a gamble or in life, but he hadn't let it hold him down. Where Hunter expected littered floorboards and ripped seats, he found a tidy interior and two unlocked doors.

"Hunter," Kat hissed from the slightly opened Porsche door.

"Hey!" Hunter called out to the thin man still in a price war over greens. He long tossed the fancy car's keys across thirty yards. The man turned in time to catch them from reflex more than skill.

The fella's lined face scrunched together. His gaze lowered to the fancy fob in his hand and then slowly lifted it to Hunter. The lines of confusion deepened. One corner of his upper lip quirked. When his gaze drifted lower to Hunter's junk, the man's shoulders jerked. His lids peeled wide, and he found his old shoes extremely interesting.

"Take the car." Hunter motioned to the Porsche. "Drive it to Stockholm as fast as you can. Look up a guy named Robart Manceen. Sell the car.

He'll give you a fair price. Go now or don't touch the car. It's your call to make, but make it in the next minute."

Hunter opened the old car's door. It groaned in contempt. He slid—mostly fell—into the driver's seat. The shock of impact was stolen by the realization that no keys were in the ignition, in a cup holder, or any other place he quickly looked. Of course. Just his one-legged luck. He pushed the metal ignition and used the two metal tabs on either side of where a key should be to twist. The tired engine turned over like molasses in winter three times before choking to life.

"Ha!" He yanked the gear into reverse, pulled out, and positioned the car as close to Kat as he could without scraping the paint off the high dollar automobile she scrambled from. None of the people in the small lot moved. They stared, struck dumb by a naked, one-legged man, practically stealing a car in broad daylight.

A laugh tickled Hunter's throat.

"You're stealing that poor man's car?" Kat threw herself into the passenger seat—where the driver's seat should've been—and slammed the door.

"I thought you said it wasn't a car?"

Her neck that'd been craned toward the witnesses snapped to him. "Don't be cute."

"You think I'm cute?" He depressed the gas, tossed dust into the air, and got them the hell out of sight.

"Hunter."

"It's not stealing. It's trading."

Kat scoffed and crossed her arms over her chest. She pouted like a little girl. He didn't have experience with them, but it's how he imagined they'd act anyway. "You did it naked too. You're a naked thief."

Amusement, delirium, desperation, and his sick sense of humor coalesced into the heartiest laugh he'd experienced since Oliver had been taken. It rolled through his chest, sending shockwaves of agony through his ribs, and still, he laughed on. Soon, the corners of Kat's sweet mouth turned from south to north. A melodic rumble escaped her lips. Her head shook. They were a ridiculous pair. Blood covered and on the run, but laughing and carrying on something fierce.

Too quickly, the laughter died and was replaced with hollow silence.

They were far from safe and even farther from being on a level playing field. The first tell? Both her arms wrapped around her torso in a self-consoling hug. Second? She hadn't looked him in the eyes, really excavated him with those ocean blue eyes of hers, since she found out he'd been part and parcel to the killing of her uncle.

The clunker shuddered along toward Oslo, filling the wordless cab with noise for one hundred miles or more.

"We're going to need petrol soon." Hunter gestured to the instrument panel that boasted two working gauges. Who needed a speedometer anyway?

She nodded but said nothing.

"Want to rock, paper, scissors for who pumps?"

That earned him a quarter smile. "I'll do it. I should be able to wipe the blood from my arms with the water from the window wiper pail without drawing too much attention."

He pulled into a small country gas station and parked at the pump closest to the road. "I found this during my key search." From the console, he pulled a small stash of money and held it out to her. But when she grabbed it, he didn't let go.

Her gaze finally met his.

"I'll understand if you go inside and call the police on me. They won't hurt me or keep me for long, but please don't. No one can protect you as I can." Could. He couldn't even save her from a big dumb guard. Still, he pressed on as soldiers do. "I know how they operate. I know how to keep you off the grid until you're in the clear. But if you do turn me in, promise me one thing."

She didn't speak, but neither did she look away.

"Don't go back to your old life. He'll find you. And for God's sake, don't go back to him."

Kat offered one curt nod. It forced a sweat soaked clump of hair onto her forehead. Hunter pushed it back from her face. "Thank you for saving me. You didn't have to, but I'm damn glad you did." He thought so anyway. The next legless weeks would tell.

"Thank you," she breathed.

"For what?" Almost getting her killed?

"Not making me shoot anyone."

"I'll never make you do something you don't want to do, Kat. Never."

Chapter Eighteen

The quiet drive only allowed her to see the swollen side of Hunter's face. From the hunch in his shoulders and the labor of his breathing, she could tell he was hurt. It kept her on high alert. She expected him to pass out from the pain he was surely in at least once a mile.

"Whenever we get where we're going, I need to examine your ribs."

"What's to examine, Doc? They're broken."

Kat chewed her lower lip to keep from screaming. They'd beaten him so badly they'd broken his bones. These were not a frail person's bones. These were thick, dense networks of collagen and calcium wrapped in layers of muscle. She knew exactly how much force it took to break a healthy bone. A thousand times she'd used power tools to do so in surgery. Her stomach flipped like a first day med student getting her first sniff of the toxic mix of formaldehyde.

She pressed a hand to her belly and turned her gaze to the trees zipping past. "You have to breathe deeply even though it hurts."

"Yeah, this isn't my first broken rib." He continued to inhale shallow, pitiful breaths.

"Again, that doesn't make me feel better." Kat snapped her arms together and turned on him. "You may have broken a rib or two, but probably not as many as you're boasting now. Breathe deeply. That's an order. I won't have you getting pneumonia. I've worked too hard to see you die now."

"Jesus. You're worse than my commander is." He pulled in a full breath and hissed it out between clenched teeth. "Way worse."

"Again."

"Fuck." Hunter gritted through the exercise and didn't utter another word. Well, he muttered words, but none were conversational.

Finally, three grueling hours later, gravel crunched under the creaky wheels, and they left the small highway for a winding driveway huddled with overhanging trees. The go-cart rounded the last bend, and the greenery gave way to clear sky and a deep blue lake cloaked by tall aspens. Two structures obscured the natural wonder of the place. Hunter drove past a small house and to the face of a detached building that matched the other in size. When he placed the car in park, Kat's lungs drew the first full breath in hours, days really. Just because she'd made him breathe deeply didn't mean she had to.

Hunter opened the groaning door and shifted to stand. A small cry escaped his lips before he clamped them together. Kat's tiny respite from constant worry fled. His wounds had dried to the worn-slick leather.

"I can—"

Before she heard her offer of help, Hunter peeled himself from the seat and stood—wobbled. He braced between the door and the vehicle's roof. She shouldn't look at a wounded and distressed man's cock, but his torturers left it untouched and in perfect condition. Her mouth watered, and she practically threw herself out her door to keep from pressing the thoughts dogging her one centimeter farther.

"What can I do?"

"I've got it." Hunter hopped to the wall, slid up a hidden panel, and pounded out a long series of numbers.

Two garage doors opened faster than your average garage door, not that she'd ever owned one. She'd seen the sluggish things, though, and this wasn't one of them. It zipped up, revealing a sleek gunmetal Audi and a truck big enough, accessorized enough, to crush her soul.

"On second thought..." Hunter nodded at the far wall. "Grab the keys to the Audi and pull it out. Park in front of the house."

She rushed forward before he changed his mind about letting her help. The man was stubborn and not used to help, taking on the world with his own two hands. More and more, she wanted to know what made him the indomitable man he was, but she wouldn't ask. The more she knew, the more captivated she became. Captivation meant vulnerability, and she couldn't quite trust him yet or maybe herself ever.

It took her no time to perform the task. She locked the car and rushed to the garage where he exited one hop at a time, leaving the rickety car behind the solid garage doors. Instead of asking, Kat moved to his side, slipped an arm around his waist, and hooked his left over her shoulder. After another long hobbling hike and an equally long code, they made it inside.

"I can make it to the couch." He tried to shirk her hold.

"No, you don't. Shower first." She held tight.

"All right, Doc. You've got me naked already. You wanna get wet and wild? Let's go."

If he weren't sporting broken ribs, she'd jab him good with an elbow. In the beginning, his suggestive talk had shocked her, but the more time she spent with him, the more she realized he used innuendoes to shove her away. He barricaded himself from vulnerability with sex. Hell, she should go back to school for her PhD in psychology.

"Keep it up, and I'll use non-lidocaine antiseptic on you." Not. Her skin crawled just thinking about inflicting unnecessary pain on him.

"You're a horrible liar," he wheezed and patted her shoulder. "Haven't we been over this before?"

Kat smiled, unable to stop the effects of his charm. "You might have mentioned it in passing." She rolled her eyes. "Where's the bathroom in this place?"

"Your guess is as good as mine."

She assessed the scene. They entered a small living room with a kitchen partitioned off immediately by a double-sided fireplace and on the other side by a four-top dining table. Windows revealed the wonder of a long staircase that descended three hundred meters or more to the majestic lake below. The house only gave them one option. They hobbled down a wide corridor to the first doorway. It offered a tiny bedroom with a twin bed. The second doorway across the hallway contained a large bed, and the third and final door led to a bathroom bigger than both bedrooms combined.

"Sorry, but Norwegian architecture makes no sense." Hunter gawked at the two showerheads that poked from the wall and poured—if turned on—into the middle of the tiled room. "It's one of the nicest locker rooms I've ever seen. Even has a sauna."

A small door to the right housed the toilet, and sure enough, across from the shower area with no curtain whatsoever was a door to a respectably sized sauna.

"I'm not Norwegian." Kat shuffled them forward to the showers and turned on the closest one to the proper temperature. "Here. I'm going to find a first-aid kit."

"So wet but not wild?"

Kat looked at his stubble covered face and the smile it boasted despite the agony hiding in his eyes. Maybe his gruff humor had less to do with her and more to do with him. Many people used hilarity as a coping mechanism. She would...were she funny at all.

"I'll be back," Kat breathed.

"I'm an asshole. Sorry." He grabbed the wall and hopped under the spray.

"No, you're not. You're just coping the best you know how. We both are."

She turned away before he could respond and scoured the house. Who was she kidding? She wasn't coping. After her father had thrown her into the room the second time, she shut off all emotional reservoirs. This was autopilot. This was live through to see the next day. This was insanity. The bedroom closets were the reasons the bedrooms were so small. The massive closets boasted MREs, first-aid kits, and enough ammunition to start a war but no guns.

Kat pulled out what she needed and left the rest, hoping beyond hope they didn't have to eat the pre-packaged calorie-heavy cardboard. She walked back into the bathroom and halted in the doorway. Hunter wasn't masturbating or doing anything overtly sexual, yet her tongue swelled in her mouth. Other things swelled too, all because this man simply ran a soapy hand over his dark skin. Suds collected and ran in streams down the sculpted curves of his abs and glutes.

"What'd you find?"

Her mouth fell open. She hadn't made a sound. His swollen eye was to her just as it had been in the car. Guess he wasn't as blind in that eye as she expected.

"Any chow? The butler didn't make it to my quarters the past few days."

"Oh, my God." Kat covered her mouth to stem the gasp.

"Don't worry. They gave me plenty of water."

With Hunter, she couldn't tell if he meant they kept him hydrated or if they'd held his head underwater for long minutes at a time. Goose bumps crawled over her chest and arms. She rushed forward. "There are plenty of medical supplies, but no food. I'll go get some things as soon as I assess you and treat your wounds."

"No food? There should be a shit ton of MREs in this place?"

"I don't consider that food." She set the kit on the counter, opened it, and laid antiseptic and an array of bandages next to the bag.

"You just have to pick the right ones and prep them correctly. While you are a connoisseur of high-end automobiles, I happen to be a renown MRE chef." He pivoted toward her, tilted his head back, and let the water wash away the bubbles from his head and chest. "Give me two minutes, and I'll have your mouth watering."

Too freaking late.

"I'll try one." Kat licked her lips. "But I'm getting real food, and you're having a properly cooked meal this evening."

"I can't argue with that." Hunter lifted his hand to her face.

Until his thumb dragged across her cheek and over her chin, she hadn't realized how close she'd been standing. He lifted his hand to the water and washed away the blood.

"I didn't know I had..." Kat let the words trail away when his finger returned, cupping her face in his big hand.

He pulled her forward. Her ugly medical ward shoes squeaked against the wet tile. It sounded very far away, like in another universe. Where she was, nothing existed except his hand on her skin and his lips that drew ever closer. His approach was painstakingly measured. Every millimeter he ate between them gave her ample opportunity to escape. Her feet refused to move. Not even a single warning bell rang in her brain, though she knew they'd come later.

Right now, she drank him in. The earnestness in his gaze, the triumph over agony, the determination to possess her mouth. He made no qualms about his open desire for his lips to meet hers. His amber gaze shifted only from her mouth to her eyes and back. Her lips parted, granting the permission he sought but didn't request.

Kat's pulse thundered over the water rushing from the showerhead. Desire melted her restraint and all common sense. Need pounded against her sternum, rousing her nipples. His hands didn't roam her body or grope, but his expression titillated all the same. Better even. He roused her mind and, in turn, her body.

His mouth, even split and swollen, slid slowly and sensually over hers. They filled the gap between her lips and sucked deeply against her upper one. Her eyes slipped closed. He used his hand to tilt her head to the perfect angle. His tongue glided across her sensitive flesh, teasing and taunting.

Kat's hands lifted to his neck, the only place she hadn't seen any bruising or wounds. Water splashed onto her hands. She held tight, needing a solid foundation in the tumult of arousal and sensory stimulation.

Hunter's chin moved the position of their mouths. His tongue delved inside hers, laying claim to every nerve ending in which it came into contact with. When she ate something delicious, she made this sound, an almost audible yum. It drove her father crazy, and she'd nixed the behavior until it slipped through her and Hunter's lips. She jerked in reaction. He stopped kissing her but held her in place until her eyes opened. Lip to lip, he pressed one last kiss to her mouth.

"Yum indeed." He straightened, washed the back of her hand, and kissed it.

"You should stop." Kat pulled back a step, taking her hand as she moved. "You can't keep kissing me."

"I assure you I could kiss you for an obscenely long time. Now, how about you tell me why I shouldn't."

"Because." She shrugged, tossed up her hands, and then dragged them down her face. "Everything that's happened..."

"None of which was your fault."

Did he really believe that, or was he just wooing her? Intellectually, she knew none of this sat on her shoulders, yet she bore the weight of her father's—hell, her family's—crimes, though she didn't know what they were. Not all of them. The ones she knew he'd at least condoned roiled. They smashed her collarbones and made breathing impossible. Every time she closed her eyes, she saw Aron's white peeled eyes staring back. Every time she looked at Hunter, she saw the brutal beating he'd endured.

"Take a shower." He kissed her hand one last time. "It'll help. I'll fix lunch and air dry. We can eat, and then you can play doctor on me." His brows waggled.

It eased a little of the load off her tired back. "I don't play doctor."

"Every woman has a fantasy. I'll figure yours out before long. Then I'll make it a reality."

Her fantasy. Sexually, she was as vanilla as they came and didn't have a kinky dream to be played out in a dimly lit room. Her real-life fantasy, the one she hardly ever let herself dream about, snuck in the back door of her brain. More than any title, money, or prize, Kat wanted someone to love her. To love her truly and completely despite her social awkwardness and frumpiness. She wanted someone to trust, who would trust her with their deepest secrets and greatest hopes. Never, not one day in her life, did she expect it to become a reality. Her mother had left her. Her father treated her like a possession, not a person. If you couldn't trust the people who created you, you could trust absolutely no one.

Besides, Hunter wasn't the type for forever. It didn't take an MD or PhD to figure out that one.

***

Lunch—a freaking MRE—was delicious. Hunter hadn't lied. The man made a masterpiece out of food and chemicals processed from years ago. Her clothing and market runs went off without a hitch, despite her nerves running away with her at every stranger who passed. Hunter got a much-needed nap while she cooked a delicious meal for them. It tasted amazing. She suspected it had more to do with the freedom aspect than her culinary skills. For too long, she'd eaten what had been provided. Sure, no dishes or chores were nice, but not as nice as freedom.

Warmth seeped back into her psyche. The food helped. The stunning lake view helped. Being safe helped most of all. Kat eased against the back of the dining chair.

Hunter set his plate to the side, bore both elbows onto the table, and looked her square in the eyes. "Time to talk, Kat."

Everything fuzzy, warm, and happy crashed and burned. No survivors.

"Where's the phone?"

Kat chewed on the inside of her cheek and contemplated her options. Lie and be known as a fraud. Tell the truth and face his wrath. Nerve endings knotted together. Her pulse ox dove through the floorboards. The moment she'd found the phone, she'd wanted nothing more than to call the authorities and her co-workers and dash back to her life. She wasn't ready to turn her father in, and she refused to put her co-workers in harm's way. So, she'd hidden it immediately.

He waited patiently, breathing deeply as she'd demanded.

"I don't see one." She shrugged.

Hunter sighed. "Not a lie." His thick lips rubbed together. He licked them, causing her already wobbly insides to flip. "I don't see one either. That's why I asked you where it is."

"I—"

He held up his hand. "Before you don't lie again, I'll save us both some trouble and give you four questions. You choose one to answer honestly.

A smart doctor like you should know the difference between a non-lie and honesty."

The prodding shoved the butterflies from her stomach and stoked a sweltering fire to life. "Who says I'll answer any of them?"

"Me."

"Really?" She stood and knocked her chair over backward. A first. Never had she allowed herself to show so much emotion. Now she couldn't rein it in. "How are you going to do that? Are you going to hurt me to get the information?"

Hunter stood slowly, reaching his full height —towering over her—with considerable effort. "No, Kat. I don't get off on hurting people. I'm not like your father."

The tears started without her permission. She hated them. She hated him. She hated everything. Her oblivion for so many years when it came to her father. Her meekness. Every damn thing she'd clung to through the years had been stripped from her over the past two months.

Kat grabbed her plate with the intention of placing it in the sink and storming out. The moment the porcelain met her grip, she reared back and slung the damn thing with every ounce of strength she could muster. She wasn't a gym rat, but she cracked bones—used to—multiple times a day. The explosion of impact shook the room. Damaged be damned.

She turned and tore from the room, leaving him with what he'd asked for. Brutal honesty. "I hid the phone, and you can't have it. I need time to work through some stuff."

Chapter Nineteen

"What the hell are you doing?" Kat stood in the doorway with the knob in her hand and a ferocious glare on her pretty face.

Fucking great. Ignoring her got harder and harder with each passing day. Another day and here it was, harder still.

Spending late afternoons sitting on the back porch gave her skin a healthy glow. Early morning runs helped settle the restlessness that had presented in the form of rabid pacing in the early days at the house...after her outburst, at least. Her weekly trips to the local market helped too. Shopping had some weird chemical effect on a woman's brain. Vail's assistant, Rhonda, had said once that shopping soothed their primal urges. She'd said something about nest prepping. He didn't understand it, but he liked the trade-off in her demeanor. Minus the nest business.

Kat had her releases. Why couldn't he have his?

"Pull-ups." He managed to keep a straight face and finished his first set of fifty for the day. Over the past week, he'd worked up from sets of five. Holy Mother in heaven, those first few days had hurt like the devil himself had rammed his horns into his sides. And weak. Shit. He hadn't felt so useless since elementary school.

"I see that." She shoved the door wide and stepped into his bedroom, aka the secret gym. "You're supposed to be on limited activity for six weeks, not three."

"How about two?"

"You've been working out for a week already?" The pink in her cheeks deepened to a rosy red. "Hunter Masters, do you want to puncture a lung and die, or worse, have to be driven to a hospital and found by my father's men?"

After all this time, she refused to discuss her father, his involvement in murder and other criminal activity, and skewed his responsibility with phrasing like father's men. They weren't the ones who drew pleasure from beating him with cane poles and dipping his head into a trough until he blacked out only to revive him and do it again. He felt his anger rise and wanted her to leave so he could work another part of his wrecked body. Maybe it would drain some of the frustration knotting his insides.

"No." He straightened his leg, found the floor, and released his hold on the closet's wood frame. "I want to get ready for the day I knock on your father's door and repay him and his men for their hospitality."

Her jaw screwed tight. Both her shoulders rolled in the sweaty tank she wore. He had to pull his gaze up from her legs and focus on her anger-thinned mouth. "You can't do that."

"The hell I can't." He hopped forward and rested a hand on the tall dresser.

Kat's blonde brows drew together, and her blues shifted to his nub and back to his face in question. She might as well have kicked him in the nuts. He knew he'd never be able to return to his job as a sniper and covert operative for the Base

Branch. No matter his will to and no matter how far prosthetic technology had come in the last decade, he'd never be one-hundred percent. If he wasn't reliable, he'd place his brothers' lives in jeopardy, and he'd rather slowly waste away than gamble with their lives. It was the real reason he hadn't pressed the phone issue. He hadn't cared about giving her time to think. He hadn't worried about Royan finding them. One call to his commander, Vail Tucker, and fire would rain from the sky onto that sadistic fuck. One call to his commander and a HELO would pick them up, surrounding them with the good guys within the day.

"I'm sorry," she whispered.

"Never be sorry. If someone bites you, bite them back...harder. It's survival."

"Is it?"

It was the only kind he'd known. "You're back early. You weren't supposed to see that."

"But I did." She stepped around him and closed the closet door. Like he couldn't just open it again.

"It could have been worse."

"I don't see how." She returned to stand toe to toe with him. "One jarring motion could cause the bone to slip and pierce your lung. I mean, you could've been doing sit-ups. That's worse. Have you been doing sit-ups?"

With Kat this close and the fresh scent of her sweat in his nostrils, his anger faded away. Mischief replaced it. He'd been doing leg lifts. They weren't sit-ups, but he ignored her question. "You could have caught me jerking off."

Her throat worked on a silent swallow, and then her demeanor shifted. A twinkle lit her eyes, and she held her ground for the third time this week. "I'd rather you did that right now than pull-ups."

"Right now?" After the first week cooped up in this house with her and his slightly healed wounds, he'd stroked himself to climax nearly every day. Thoughts of Kat kept him amped, but he hadn't touched her since their kiss. He adjusted the waistband of his athletic shorts to screw with her.

She grabbed his left hand and threw it over her shoulder. The skin to skin contact with her arm on his bare chest fed his spirits. After the first few days, she'd been distant. She'd always demanded he put a shirt on before she touched him. The speed with which she changed the bandages on his back warped until she could have him stripped, cleaned, bandaged, and clothed in less than three minutes. His back was huge and wounds many. "Maybe later." Her palm smacked his ass with a crack.

"Kinky, Doc. I knew you had it in you."

Kat giggled and shook her head. "I want to show you something."

"Yes!" He launched a fist into the air. "Wait. Are we still talking about masturbation?"

She smacked his other cheek. "Come on."

"I'm trying, Doc. I'm trying."

Her laugh filled the hallway and then the living area as they went.

"What's so important you'd skip your run and catch me red-handed? I need to know if I should expect interruptions like that more often. I might have to change my workout schedule."

"I'm serious about the working out," she warned while carting him to the back door and out onto the porch.

"Me too. Have been since junior high."

"It shows," she muttered. At least he thought that was what she said. Before he asked for clarification, Kat dipped from his side. She stretched her arms wide and spun in a slow circle, gesturing to the surroundings he'd avoided for as long as he could manage.

Royal blue water, fresh air, and a small sandy beach beckoned. Sun poured onto his face. Five segments of stairs separated by small landings taunted.

"Close your eyes." Kat flailed her hands in front of him. A bright smile lit all the way to her blue gaze. It eased the pain in his chest and reinvigorated his tired muscles. He didn't want to lose sight of it. "Now."

Hunter tightened his core and focused his efforts on balancing his new body. Slowly, when he was sure he wouldn't end up on his ass, he closed his eyes. Kat's footfalls scrambled down the steps, stalled at the first landing, and then thundered back in his direction.

When she stopped in front of him, her rapid breaths grazed his pecs. Saliva pooled in his mouth with the need to touch her. The desire had always been there, but it grew into something new. Need matched the feeling. Like if he didn't, his fingertips would go on strike. Like if he didn't feel her skin, his limbs would shrivel into raisin arms.

"Here." Her hand grabbed the back of his left wrist. The soft pads of her fingers trailed the scar around it and then into the well of his palm.

The contact made him dizzy with lust. No, not lust. He could always sate his lust with a quick fuck. This he imagined would take all night and into the morning. He wanted to take his time, to feel her skin, learn her curves and swells, and coax her to orgasm again and again.

Her palm met his too briefly, and then a cold, hard something took its place. His brain calculated the item to be wood of some sort.

"Okay. Open them." The excitement in her voice translated into a small smile that hiked his lips.

He wanted to look at her exquisite smile, but the item she'd placed in his hand took precedence. It forced his jaw open and his eyes wide.

"It's only temporary, and I think I measured pretty closely, considering I had no tape measure."

Hunter stared at the crutch cut from a branch that'd grown at the perfect angle to accommodate a shoulder and hand hold. Two sides of the top limb had been sheared, as well as the hand hold, and the bottom of the homemade device.

"If it's not, I can cut it down to size. I erred on the tall side to be safe."

Holy shit. This woman was more than amazing. She'd whittled him a fucking crutch. Most women would go out of their way to give him a blow job but couldn't be concerned enough about him— as a human—to ask if he wanted a drink when they grabbed one for themselves. The gesture nearly buckled his good leg.

"If it hurts you, I can look for another branch." She shifted from one foot to the other and shoved her hands into the pockets of shorts that hugged her slender curves. "It took a week to find that one. But if it doesn't work, I'll start looking after lunch."

Hunter swallowed.

"If you're not ready for—"

"Doc?"

"Yeah?" She pulled her hands from her pockets and crossed her arms over her chest. They boosted the swell of her cotton covered breasts, shorting his brain for a second.

"Short of you turning up in the chamber and setting me free, it's the best surprise anyone has ever given me."

A smile bloomed on her face. Her arms slipped from their knot, and one hand covered her grin.

"Thanks, Doc." He wedged the crutch under his arm.

"Call me Kat, please."

When he arched a brow in question, her gaze hit the boards beneath their feet. "What is it?"

Her pink cheeks darkened a shade or five. She dug her hand into her pockets again; only this time she used the back ones. Palms to buttocks style thrust her breasts toward his face. If he was a rosary saying man, he'd drop to his knee here and now to keep from ravaging her. Too bad for them both, he had no idea what the string of beads meant other than, "Please Lord, get me out of this shitstorm."

"We've kissed, Hunter, so I can't be your doctor."

"I thought you said I couldn't kiss you anymore."

"I did."

"But now you're saying you're not my doctor because we kissed."

"I am."

"Which leads me to believe that if you're not my doctor, I can kiss you."

Kat flapped her hands as she tended to do when she got frustrated. "Walk to the edge of the porch, please."

"What?"

"I don't know what to do with you. Literally.
Figuratively. I just don't know." She screamed at
the sky and shook her fists. "You want me to trust
you, kiss you, and I don't know who to trust. The
people you're supposed to be able to rely on most in
life turned out to be some of the most horrible on
Earth. Now I can't trust myself, much less you."

"Fair enough."

"Seriously?" She stood statue still and not
even breathing from what he could tell.
Her whisper spoke of mistrust. Wasn't that what all
this boiled down to?

"It's been my life experience you can't trust
anyone."

"It has?"

"Parents are human. Humans are pieces of
shit. The degree varies from person to person, but
just because they're your blood doesn't mean they'll
treat you worth a damn."

A pile of time passed in silence. Kat shook
her head.

"My father..." Then she stopped. She huffed a
breath and motioned him forward. "If you've been
working out, you can do the stairs. One flight at
least."

"Stubborn woman. Talk to me."

"Stubborn man. Walk to me." She stuck her
tongue out at him.

"Very professional."

"I don't have to be. You're not my patient."

"Remember you said that."

She spun around, giving him her back, and
drew two deep breaths before turning back. "Walk.
One step at a time."

There was a way for them to both get what
they wanted. He simply had to strike the balance.

"One step for one answer," he bartered. "I'm walking. You're talking."

"No."

"Fine. One step for one kiss." He could live with that.

"No. I don't want to discuss any of it."

"You need to." If she didn't vent some of these demons, they'd consume her from the inside out. Personal experience was a fucker.

"No, I don't. I'm fine." Damn fine...to look at. Her fissures grew deeper by the day.

"Then thanks for the crutch, Doc, but I have sit-ups to do." He tapped his surprise and pivoted toward the house.

"You really know how to get under my skin, don't you?"

"It's part of my job." Right now, he didn't have a job. He'd never have the job he had before his world came tumbling down. "Was," he corrected.

"I have a different proposition for you." Kat braced her hands on her hips as though she'd conquered a species. "You ask one question. I answer. You take a step, I ask a question, and then you answer."

"Hardly seems fair. I'm answering and stepping. Shouldn't there be a kiss added in somewhere?"

"Take it or leave it." She smirked.

He had her right where he wanted her, thinking she was in control. "I've always liked an uneven match."

Kat stepped down backward. If Hunter tried it, he'd fall on his rump. Hell, he didn't know if he could do it facing forward, but no time like the present to find out. "What's your favorite childhood memory?"

Her lips pursed while she searched her database for the answer. She absentmindedly dipped her shoulders side to side. "It's interesting really. My best memories intertwine with the worst."

Hunter nodded. He knew exactly what the hell she was talking about.

"The anticipation of my father's visits powered me through the long weeks of tutoring while the reality never grazed the fantasy."

"Which was?"

"That he'd really see me."

"That's why you pour so much care into your patients?"

"Maybe." She shrugged. "Maybe I do it to atone for the sins of my family."

"Did you know, before?" He knew he was pushing it, but if he could keep her talking, he'd get information, and he might not fall on his face in front of her.

"I should have." Kat stepped to the side. "Now put your right hand on the railing and give me a step. I'm here if you need me."

Hunter tested the tensile strength of the thick crutch. In no culture was he considered light fare. It held most of his weight without creaking or shattering as his grip tightened on the smoothed branch. He shifted all his weight onto the twig, prayed it'd hold, and stepped down with his right leg. His only leg. The press of his foot to the ground, the actual art of stepping, instead of hopping, stole his breath. He wheeled the crutch around and stood stunned to have moved his big ass without direct reliance on another person.

"That was wonderful," she practically cheered.

"Considering I used to walk everywhere without a single round of applause, it's not that great of a feat."

Her gaze narrowed.

"Fine." He adjusted the waistband of his shorts. "It was pretty damn nice."

She rewarded him with a big flash of her pearly whites. Then her expression turned serious. "What's your favorite memory from childhood?"

He should've expected the question, but it sideswiped him just as waking up without a leg had. Time to dig deep. Leaving that hellhole had been amazing, but he'd been nearly a man...in his mind anyway. Then it came in a flash. "Playing hide and seek in an abandoned house next to one I lived in."

"Who'd you play with?"

It was her second question. He thought about not answering, but turnabout was fair play. "There were anywhere from five to twelve kids in the home at any given time. I wasn't picky, though I especially liked playing with the older kids. They'd get so pissed when they couldn't find me."

"I bet they did. You have a way of working people up."

"Are you worked up, Kat?"

He took the next step with more confidence and no prompting from Doc.

Little nipples pressed against the front of her fitted T-shirt, giving him the answer he wanted. "You don't have to answer that."

"Why not?"

He stepped down again, closing in on her. With the damn stick, he felt more on a level playing field than he had since waking from his coma. "Because your body answered for you."

Kat placed a hand over her throat.

"Nope, that's not the spot." He stepped again, and she scrambled back.

"Wait. You're messing up the process."

"I thought I was moving it along." Hunter stepped again. This time his ribs tweaked, stealing his momentary reprieve from bodily pain. He breathed through it, though, without revealing anything but his determination to Kat.

"Wait." She thrust out both hands. "What happened to your father?"

Well, that stopped him cold, but it didn't take him long to recover. "I never knew him. Don't expect my mother did either."

Her gaze dropped to his chest. It glazed over as if she were far away for a moment.

"Are you close to your brother?"

She blinked and focused on him. A look of bewilderment crinkled her nose and mouth as though it were an odd question. "No. We didn't grow up in the same house." Her shoulders bobbed. "I lived in Italy. He lived in Sweden. He's technically my half-brother. I didn't know about him until I was eight. My father brought him to the house where I lived during one of his visits. That was the same trip that Trey broke his arm."

"One of his visits? Your dad didn't live with you?" Hunter doubted the kid broke his arm. The sick fucker father of his probably broke it for him.

"That's three questions." She put a hand on the railing and cocked her leg out. The stance melted his mind. "Do we need to go over the rules of this game again?"

"You broke them first." He stepped down two, forcing her back.

Kat's palm flattened against his chest. "Take your time."

"I can do that, Doc." His gaze dropped to her hand. The contrast of their skin spiked his temperature. "All day. All night. As slow as you want it."

"How many women have you been with?"

"Uhhh." Hunter choked on his tongue. No one had ever asked him that. It was the don't ask question of relationships long and short, and she stomped all over the tradition.

"Ballpark." She folded her arms, stealing the magic of her touch, and then offered a devilish smirk.

"How many have you been with?"

"Three."

Christ. He'd been with three women before he'd entered high school. Not the wisest move. But he'd had a free supply of condoms from the health department, a libido unmatched to most, and women—not girls—willing.

"Serious relationships?"

"No, not really. It was more a mixture of hormones, curiosity, and rebellion."

"Kat, the rebel." He liked the images that thought conjured.

"So?" she prodded.

"Isn't it my turn to step or ask or something?"

"Now you're worried about the rules of the game."

It was clear no rules existed where Kat was concerned. He'd already spent more time with her than any other woman in his life. Hell, he hadn't even slept with her. No, take that back. He'd slept with her. Another rule shattered. He just hadn't been inside her.

"Kat, look."

"Looking." She hiked her brows and grinned.

"Christ," he groaned. "More than ten and less than…seventy." Had he not worked on a mission in remote parts of the world so often, that number would've been higher.

Kat opened her mouth to speak, but he couldn't handle her judgment. When the fuck had he ever cared about that? "Before you give me the hazardous to your health speech, you should know I always used protection and got checked before every mission. Routine. Can't jeopardize my life or my brothers."

"Not through STDs, but bullets and bombs are fine? I don't get you military types."

His ribs and head throbbed. He hadn't walked or thought this much in a while. Military he could explain a shit ton easier than his sex life. That thing was riddled with some deep-seated shit. The military. His honor and duty. Now that got his chest tingling and his blood pumping more than most women. It was his life's purpose.

"It starts as a way out for a lot. For a few, it's a lofty but untenable notion of patriotism. For me, it was both. Those notions endure through basic and your first posts unless you're a pussy of the highest degree. Then, if you're good enough, specialty training starts. They push you, pound you, piss on you until they've stripped away every preconceived notion and everything you thought you were."

"Goodness."

"Then they put you back together." His chest warmed. Shit. He loved it. "An alliance stronger than birth replaces your marrow. Loyalty to your country is your skeleton. Determination barricades your mind. Relentlessness strengthens your muscles more than any exercise. Your lungs run on adrenaline. Your heart beats for the mission. Duty to those less capable forms an impenetrable skin."

As he talked, Kat's eyes softened. Her lips parted. The breaths filling her lungs came in rapid succession.

"Bullets and bombs play a role in your tactics. They don't penetrate the warrior you've become."

Emotion squeezed his throat. He'd become the warrior, fought the fight, defended the weak, and now he was one of them. The warmth faded and an arctic gust blew between his ribs and threatened to freeze his heart.

Fuck. He'd get past it. His warrior parts remained even if in pieces. But...motherfuck.

Kat stepped forward to the level on which he stood. The movement yanked him from his pity party because she now stood close. Her brilliant eyes zeroed in on his. Long lashes interrupted an otherwise honed study.

He'd kissed a lot of women, and none of them had taken a percentage of the care that Kat took with him. There was no question she intended to kiss him. Again, sheer volume and experience. She had the parted lip salivation, rapid breaths, and a throbbing arterial pulse he'd come to know and get off on, but Kat had something more. Caution and tension measured her assault. And Lordy was it an assault.

Her fingertips tickled the scar over his heart. Gently, they drifted up, molding to the ridge of his redeveloped pec. Honeyed sweet breaths danced over his collarbone along with her fingers and then onto his neck.

Hunter's pulse rushed in his ears as though this were his first day of special operations training. He swallowed hard and told himself not to move.

She needed to do this. He wanted her to do it. Anything and everything he'd take from her and return tenfold if he could.

One of her palms cupped his left cheek, and she pulled his face down to hers. Dammit all, but she didn't kiss him. She rubbed a trail over his nearly healed brow, down his cheek, and across his jaw with her other hand. Her forehead pressed to his in the most intimate gesture he'd ever experienced.

She pulled him down farther still and molded her lips where her forehead had been. Her mouth dragged down to the tip of his nose, over to his eyes, and then his cheeks. Finally, her delicate mouth grazed his hard mouth so gently it hurt. Though fully clothed, he stood before her naked for the first time. Panic welled. What might she see? What might he reveal? It was too much. Where was the sexual tension he'd stoked in her since he'd gained consciousness? It had been there only moments ago. He'd seen it with his own eyes. These kisses spoke of compassion, not passion, and he hadn't the slightest idea what to do with them.

Kat placed one last kiss on his mouth and straightened. Befuddled and exposed, Hunter did what he did best. He tossed up his hands and went for a playful demeanor that'd gotten him through everything else. "Woah! Woah! We didn't agree on the step and kiss portion of this game. Now you're trying to change the rules midstream."

Her knowing gaze darkened. She licked her upper lip and pulled it into her mouth with a small groan of satisfaction as though she were tasting him.

His jovial notion boiled down to pure desire.

She stepped into the spot where his left foot would have been and pressed her body against his.

Her lower belly trapped his burgeoning erection between their bodies. Kat wrapped her arms around his neck and pulled him down to meet her mouth.

Hunter wasn't happy his leg was gone but, damn, talk about an unexpected perk. Kat's body fit perfectly to his, filling in the space and leaving nothing between them. Her mouth ravaged his. Sucked and nipped at the places on his mouth not slit by abuse. She sucked his tongue into her mouth and tangled hers around it. Soft moans filtered into his throat. He gobbled them up and readied for more, but she pulled away.

Kat grabbed the railing and panted.

"I guess it'll work." Breaths filled and fled his lungs at an accelerated pace. He wouldn't say he panted, though that was exactly what the hell he did. She said he worked her up, but damn if it wasn't the other way around.

He turned his back to the railing, rested the crutch next to him and reached for Kat. His fingers hooked inside the waistband of her jeans. When he pulled, she came willingly. The need to pick her up and wrap her legs around his hips used his broken ribs as toothpicks...because, if he followed through, that was what they'd become. He settled for sliding his left arm around her back and pulling her close.

Their mouths met in a heated tangle of lips, tongue, and teeth. Hunter's left hand slid up her back and threaded into her hair. His right hand smoothed up her abdomen. Smooth skin drove him wild. Firm muscles fought back against the bite of his fingertips as he pinched her tiny waist in his grip and shifted the V of her legs over his throbbing, shorts-covered cock.

"Yes." She sighed.

Hunter filled his right hand with the underside of her sweet ass and rocked her against him.

Kat's arms tightened around his shoulders. His ribs screamed, but the haze of lust buffered him from acute pain. Her hips undulated in small circles up and down and around his length. He forgot the world and all their problems with it.

"Kat." He hissed her name and nibbled a trail down her neck to the little hint of her exposed collarbone. His teeth sank in—not too hard, but enough that she cried to the sky and rubbed her body against his with total abandon. "That's it, Doc. Let me hear how much you like it. I want to know what gets you wet."

He dragged his right hand down the seam of her pants to where their bodies met and back again. Her breath hitched. A long, muffled moan followed. His fingers ran the trail harder this time. She bit his neck just below his ear.

"Hunter."

His name was a plea and a warning. Fuck, he could beat his chest, but he decided to save it for later. He detangled his fingers from her hair and slipped his hand under the hem of her shirt. The smooth cotton of a thin bra met his fingers. The distended peak of her right nipple offered the leverage he needed.

"Oh, Hunter. Oh."

"I've got you, Kat." He pinched the firm skin lightly between his fingers and rolled. His right hand continued the assault on her steamy seam while he tugged and gently twisted her nipple.

Kat held tight and rocked her clit against his shaft.

He nipped her earlobe. "Sweetest thing. I know you want to come. You know I want to hear it."

"Yes." She nodded against his neck and moaned.

When he expected her to blow, she grabbed his face. Their eyes locked in what was his most intense exchange on or off the battlefield. She pressed her lips to his, rode him to the brink, and cried her release into his mouth. Her body shook in his hold. He held tight, fearing she might vibrate right out of his grip.

After more than a minute, she slipped from his hold and hid her face behind her hands. "I can't believe—"

"Believe it and get used to it." He pulled her hands from her face. "Until you decide to give me a phone, I intend to make you come as much as possible."

"You must not ever want to leave." She gulped.

At this moment, he didn't want to go anywhere. The world wasn't the same one he'd known before the accident, but the one he was getting to know intrigued the hell out of him. "Must not."

She held her fingers to her lips. A smile peeked out of either side. "I don't know whose question it is."

"Me neither."

Their chests rose and fell for a full minute without a word. They stared. Was she as befuddled as he was? Cross his heart and hope to die, he'd never used that word before. Befuddled. Yet it perfectly described the feelings colliding inside him.

"Are you hungry?" Kat adjusted her shirt.

"Famished." Hunter let his gaze drag from one side of her to the other and then from bottom to top. "And I just had a taste of something exquisite."

She cleared her throat, straightened, and motioned to the house. "I think we've gone far enough today."

When he looked around, he realized he'd walked a flight and a half of stairs. He was farther from the house than he'd been since their arrival. His gaze returned to the most beguiling woman he'd ever encountered. More than any meal, he wanted to devour her, but she wasn't his usual fare. She left him vulnerable, and vulnerability in his current state—hell, ever—wasn't a great idea.

"You're right." Hunter picked up the crutch she'd made him and wedged it under his arm. "Do you want me to cook tonight? I have an itch for steak."

"They have MRE steaks?"

"Bet your fine ass they do." He winked.

They headed inside, and he got to work in the small kitchen. Kat pulled up a chair at the table. She held a thick book and leafed through the pages for a minute before clearing her throat.

"Hypernova...a type of star explosion with an energy substantially higher than that of standard supernovae and is one of the most catastrophic events in the universe." Kat shrugged. "So see, all this stuff we're dealing with, it's small potatoes."

"When compared to a hypernova, yes." Hunter ripped open two beef steak packets.

"Hypocaust...a hollow space under the floor of an ancient Roman building, into which hot air was sent for heating a room or bath."

"Okay, wait. Is that a dictionary?" He set aside the MREs, propped his hip on the counter, and studied her.

"So?" Kat stole her gaze and flipped the thin pages.

"So you're just reading the dictionary?"

"What else is there to do?" She huffed.

He stepped toward her.

"That doesn't make me feel like I'm jumping out of an airplane without a parachute?" she quickly added.

Pride puffed his chest. He stopped at the table and scooped up the book. It was a Norwegian-English dictionary. The little genius had just managed to pick two words pronounced the same way in both languages. "You read the dictionary a lot?"

"I didn't have friends. I had tons of time. So, I read."

"The dictionary?" he asked again.

"I like learning the meanings of words." Kat tossed up her hands and bobbed her shoulders.

"Did you ever learn the meaning of ønske?"

She looked at him as though he'd lost his mind. "No," she breathed.

"I have." He set the book down on the page for ønske. The word meant desire in English. He returned to his meal prep with a huge smile on his face.

Chapter Twenty

Kat felt like a teenager. Scratch that. She felt how she expected a normal teenager felt when in the throes of their first all-out obsession with a boy. Had she any idea that over the clothes make-out sessions were so mind altering, she'd have done it as a teenager—screw her hang-ups and in-a-bubble raising. She closed the car door, locked it with a twirl—a freaking twirl—and headed for the house.

What did you get the man who'd given you more orgasms in three weeks than you'd had in your life? Something equally life changing. Kat clutched the box to her chest, pushed through the front door, and hoped she hadn't miscalculated the gift or the actual measurements.

The house was quiet. Instantly, she longed for the healthy bass beats from the radio she'd given Hunter a hard time about only two weeks ago. The lights were off. Stunning sunlight poured in through the windows. She tiptoed down the hallway but found all the rooms empty. Her heart dropped to mid chest, very near her stomach.

"Hunter?"

Hollowness echoed through the space that up until this morning had been rife with conversation, laughs, the tumult of her orgasms, and irritation of him not letting her return the favors. She hurried to the back porch, lugging the large box along. He wasn't on the porch or the stairs he'd worked himself on each day. A twinge of panic settled in her heart, pressing it deeper still.

Had her father found their hideout and taken him away? Had he left on his own? She didn't know which would hurt worse. Lord, she was sick in the head. Of course, if he were abducted, that would be worse. If they took him... Her mind wandered down a dark path but stalled. If they'd taken him, there's no way Hunter would have left without a fight equating to broken furniture and body parts left behind. Not his.

The house looked neat but lived in with his coffee cup, the largest one she'd grown to think of as his, still on the railing. He'd won it in a fair rock, paper, scissors war. Where would he have gone? Why wouldn't he tell her? Just when she was about to lose all control, her gaze caught movement in the lake. Even at this distance, she could tell it was Hunter. His arms slowly, gracefully churned the water, propelling him from one side of the bank to the other. Instantly, the pressure holding down her heart lifted.

"Oh Kat, what are you doing?"

She was getting gooey over a guy, one who had no intention of getting... anything with no matter how many times he insinuated it. The man hadn't made a move. He'd gone so far as to outmaneuver her advances with excuses about protecting her. He had in so many different ways. It was about time he saw her as something other than his mission. She hurried to the back and leaned the box against Hunter's bed.

"Just planning to have the best night of my life."

Kat hurried out the house and down the long series of stairs. She eased to the end of the pier, hoping not to distract him from the laps he swam in front of the wood outcropping.

A pile of clothes laid to the side. She sat near them, removed her shoes, set them to the side and hung her feet over the edge. The chilly water stole her breath for a second. Watching such a thick man move through the water so effortlessly diverted her attention from the temperature. He moved his face out of the water only enough to suck a quick gulp of air, and then he was under again, pulling and pulling until long past the time Kat's lungs would have demanded air.

Hunter reached the other side of the lake, straightened with his back to her, drew one deep breath, and then dove beneath the surface. He left hardly a ripple in the water, and soon those settled, leaving not a whisper of the man who amazed her more and more every day. Their daily steps and questions always challenged her boundaries. She put up with it because, though uncomfortable, it helped to discuss things. Plus, they usually ended the session with an orgasm. Hers. Today would be different.

Kat's gaze scanned the surface. Bubbles—heck, even a ripple—would soothe her anxiety, but an eerie quiet settled over the water as though the birds even held their breath in anticipation of his return to the surface.

Silently, with barely a ruffling of the surface, Hunter's head broke through the darkness an inch from her left foot. A smile beamed, showcasing his white teeth and beautifully healed lips.

"Kat." He winked with his left, no longer swollen shut, eye and leaned forward. His lips warmed her cold big toe before easing back and between her legs.

He warmed her through and through with the slightest gestures. Only they weren't slight at all. Last week, he'd taught her how to break an attacker's hold and return a shocking blow to the face. The eyes and the nose made small, but effective, targets.

"Aren't you cold?" she whispered, afraid to break the still.

"No. I'm..." His shoulders bunched as he swept his hands through the water, keeping himself afloat. He pressed his wet lips together. The whites of his eyes revealed a track of thought he didn't share.

"You're what?" Gorgeous. Kind. Protective. Off-limits.

"Ah, it's dumb."

"I'm a huge fan of dumb. Dumb keeps me in business." She gave him a smile.

"In the water, I'm..." Hunter huffed. "I'm... normal again. I don't have to hop or crutch around. I just swim...like I have since I was a kid."

"That's not dumb." Her chest ached for him. "It's wonderful."

Hunter tried to hide his smile, but the joy was etched all over his face.

"You don't want to get out, do you?" She laughed, beyond thrilled with his excitement.

"Nope." With one crank of his arms, Hunter propelled himself back, revealing his rebounding chest, etched abdomen, and the V pointing at the spot that almost peeked from beneath the surface.

Her mouth watered. She'd tried to get him naked or catch him masturbating for three weeks now. The man was a master of getting up and dressed before she stirred. He was the master of many things, and she wanted to get deeper firsthand experience. She stood, yanked the cotton shirt over her head, dropped it next to his pile, and unfastened her jeans.

"Kat. What are you doing?" His voice rumbled off the water like a warning roll of thunder.

"Taking a swim." She shoved her pants to the decking and stepped out of them.

"I'm naked."

"I know." Kat unfastened the soft underwire bra, slipped it from her arms and hooked a finger in her panties.

"I don't think you should do that. We haven't crossed that line...yet." He spoke as though he didn't want her to go any further, but his intense gaze told an entirely different story.

"Has anyone ever told you that you're a bad liar?" She pulled all the strength, confidence, and determination she'd gained over the past several weeks and slipped her panties down her legs.

In the beginning, Hunter had been sans clothing in front of her more times than she could count. Even with all her orgasms, this was the first time she'd been naked in front of a man in years.

"Never." He cleared his throat. His head shook. "Christ, Kat. Are you trying to kill me?"

"That's the opposite of what I'm trying to do." She walked to the edge and assessed the depth. Three feet from the dock and Hunter treaded water.

"What are you trying to do?"

"Swim." Kat dove to his left. Cold wasn't the right word to describe the pin prickle down her spine and the icicles in her veins. The water enveloped and shocked every inch of her skin while also invigorating her. She flipped and whirled under the water as she never had. Freedom. It made everything sweeter. Especially the anticipation.

Her head broke the surface. Sunlight poured down, competing with the water. Hunter split the water in a direct line for the ladder up the side of the dock. Kat put her legs and arms to work, and they answered the call rather easily after all her running and body-weight exercises at the house. She cut him off several feet away, placing herself between him and the dock.

"What are *you* trying to do?"

"Escape and evade." Hunter's gaze narrowed to her breasts peeking through the clear blue water.

"A big man like you shouldn't be scared of me." She gave him her best I'm innocent eyes.

"I'm not scared of what you'll do to me, Kat." He churned the water between them.

The large motion moved currents across her belly and pelvis. "You're scared of what you'll do to me?" Kat scoffed. "You wouldn't hurt me." He continued toward her, and she continued back. The wood brushed her shoulders. She reached for the rungs above her head and blocked his path.

A small growl brewed in his throat. His hand grabbed the ladder on either side of her breasts. Hunter pressed his body to hers. The contrast between cold and hot shorted out her brain. Her nipples pressed against his. The full length of his cock brushed the inside of her thigh. Kat swallowed and resisted the urge to roll her hips. Just barely.

Hunter's face lowered so close, but his eyes remained fixed on hers. "I'd never intend to hurt you, Kat, but when I'm inside you, I won't get out. Not until I mark you." His head shook. "There'll be no pulling out. And I don't think either of us is ready to be responsible for another human life."

That was his holdup the whole time? Why hadn't he said so? She'd have gotten them the box —at least, the little one inside the big one—weeks ago. "That's all you're worried about?"

"I refuse to play around with a kid's life because I want to bone the fuck out of someone, Kat."

"And you shouldn't. That's not what I meant. I think it's wonderful that you take it so seriously. So many people don't." She leaned forward, connecting their mouths.

The contact of their mouths set off a spark that ignited a frenzy. Hunter pressed closer and pulled higher. His thick length wedged against the V of her thighs. He shoved higher still, strumming her clit with the ridges of his penis. It stunned a moan from her lips, which tried their damnedest to eat his mouth whole. Her finger tightened on the ladder's rungs to keep from putting too much pressure on him, which seemed ridiculous. He was a bulldog of a man. One leg or two, he could hold her high and do mad things to her body. He had only days ago. That somehow didn't compare to the current onslaught he poured over her.

Hunter released his hold with his right hand, squeezed her waist, and drove her down across his cock several times. He ripped his mouth from hers. His lips devoured a line across her jaw to her collarbone and across her chest.

Stunning scenery surrounded them, but Kat closed her eyes. She focused on the touch of his lips, the scrape of his tongue, the bite of his teeth, and the strum of his hard flesh against hers. Each nuance of this experience etched itself into her memory. This could sustain her for years to come.

The grip on her hip eased, sliding up her abdomen. He cupped her left breast high. His mouth drew near her aching nipple. Kat opened her eyes and watched Hunter marvel at her body a moment before his tongue flicked out. He lashed her tightly beaded flesh over and over.

Kat clamped her thighs together, trapping his dick between them. Her hips writhed, rocking her clit harder along his dick. Over the clothes had been amazing, but this short circuited her every nerve ending. She arched and panted. Hunter took the invitation and locked his mouth around her sensitive nub, suckling her deep. Each tug on her nipple felt as though it were attached to her clit. Sensations battered her from every angle.

She broke. Her climax screamed from her lips. Hunter tore his mouth from her breast and watched while she cried her orgasm into the wild like an animal. His amber eyes flared with intent. Her hips eased their attack on his cock, and her breaths slowed. Still, a hunger ate at her.

"Kat, please tell me you got condoms on your mysterious mission."

Her mouth refused to form words, so she nodded.

"Where?" A level of desperation crept into his voice that she hadn't even heard when he'd been strapped to a table in a torture chamber.

"Your room." She smiled.

Hunter smacked her butt lightly with his free hand. "Up you go. Double time."

A yelp left her lips. She scrambled up the ladder, grabbed the crutch she'd made him, and held it for him at the top. Hunter ascended the rungs faster than she had with two legs and took the crutch.

"You first." His gaze consumed her body head to toe. "I want to watch that ass sway when you walk." Kat giggled and turned toward the house. Hunter's mouth descended on her shoulder. His teeth and lips sank in. A growl rumbled into her ear. "God, Kat, you're fucking exquisite. Now move boots."

"Yes, sir." She headed toward the house, taking the steps slowly. She didn't want to rush—

"You move any slower, and I'll think you don't want me inside you."

She laughed and ran up the steps. Hunter kept pace with her to the door. She pulled it wide. "I should have used my naked body as your incentive to walk steps that first day."

"You can use your naked body as an incentive for anything." His fingers gripped her ass cheek.

"I want you inside me, Hunter." Kat leaned into his touch. His chest met her back.

"Nowhere else I want to be, Doc." His lips nibbled on the crest of her ear.

Her feet shuffled forward with the first taste of apprehension. She was sure about having Hunter inside her, but the gift setup gave her pause. What if he didn't like it? What if it killed the mood? While behind her, Hunter closed and locked the door. She hurried ahead, ready to remove the condoms and hide the big box, but just as before, he caught her in a blink.

Sunlight poured into the room. It illuminated the perfectly made bed with its gray comforter and white accent pillows. It also created a spotlight over the long box. She moved to it, picked it up, and hugged it as she had earlier. For the first time since she'd stripped, a wave of self-consciousness washed over her as she turned to Hunter.

"Well." Hunter grinned and gestured to his fully erect, massive cock. "I appreciate your faith in my goods, but I have to break it to you. I'm not that big."

She'd beg to differ. "It's not just condoms."

"Whew!" He made a show of wiping sweat from his brow. "I'd hate to disappoint you."

"I'd seen and experienced enough to know you couldn't disappoint me."

Hunter eased forward and gently planted his lips on hers. The gesture was so tender it stalled the air in her lungs. It hugged her heart tight. He sat on the bed and waited quietly, patiently as though he knew exactly what was inside the box. His openness tickled a smile to her lips. She couldn't say anything that would make this any easier or better, so she handed the box over, moved the crutch to the wall, and sat next to him.

He ripped the box open down the long middle seam. The sleek black prosthetic with its silver accents and metal foot stared back at them.

Silence filled the room, but it wasn't an empty quiet. Hunter filled it with a thousand thoughts. None of which she could hear. She didn't need to. His reaction would tell her all she needed to know.

After a minute or more, Hunter grabbed the prosthetic and let the box fall away.

Kat rejoiced without a word.

Hunter held it upright and rotated it three-hundred-sixty degrees, examining each aspect of the exterior. "Damn, that's a high-tech piece of machinery."

"The highest," she nearly squealed. "It has a micro-processor in the knee and a hydraulic ankle."

He turned to her. His head shook. "How did you...?"

"When you were far enough post-op but still unconscious, I took a mold and sent it to a friend. Aron thought it was a box of samples for testing. He hated the blood and fluids, so he sent it without looking."

"Can't say I blame him...for that."

"I waited until I was certain it would be complete before contacting my friend last week. To be safe, I had him mail it to the post office in Moss. Not here."

"Christ, Kat. I know this thing wasn't cheap."

"Free." She smiled and shrugged. "He owed me a favor."

"I'm afraid to ask what you did for him."

She shoved his shoulder. "I saved his daughter's life."

Hunter hooked his hand around the back of her neck and pulled her close. He looked into her eyes for so long she thought he might not kiss her. A smile stretched his mouth as wide as she'd ever seen it, and she couldn't help but mirror it. His lips slowly descended over hers. The contact almost tickled with tenderness. He kissed her sweetly as if it had meaning.

Kat gasped into his mouth. What she'd wanted for so long was about to happen, and it terrified her. She'd been ready and willing to have sex with him and walk away when they left this place...when they were able to go back to their lives. When he kissed her like that, though, it gave the act more depth.

The moment the concern crowded her mind, the tempo of Hunter's kiss changed from slow and sensitive to devilish and determined. His tongue delved inside her mouth. Pressure gathered at her nape as his fingers tangled in her mass of hair and pulled her head back to better access her lips.

He broke free. "Kat?"

"You're missing the best part." She pointed at the prosthesis. "Look inside."

Hunter tipped the metal leg toward him. The box of magnum condoms dumped out onto his lap, wedging between his massive cock and newly chiseled abdomen. A black lace nightie she'd bought to entice him followed, covering his intimate parts.

"Sweet Jesus. You're fucking perfect."

"Hardly." Kat took the prosthetic from him, leaned it against the dresser, and then stood in front of him with the fronts of her thighs brushing the bed. She plucked the nightie off his lap and tossed it to the side. Next, she picked up the box of condoms and tore one from the package before ditching it on the floor. "But I'm open to instruction." She ripped open the foil and knelt.

"Fuck." He dragged out the word into a moan.

Her fingers lightly grazed the silky skin of his wide head and then danced over his length. On the ascent, she wrapped her fingers around him. At the base, her freaking fingertips didn't meet one another. Fuck was right. He would stretch her to the limits. She swallowed her concern and stroked him several times. The weight and feel of him in her hands overrode any worry. He wouldn't hurt her.

Kat pulled the condom from the wrapper and rolled it on, stretching the latex over his skin. Hunter pulled her to her feet. He placed kisses over her chest while his hands spread her legs apart. His gaze remained fixed on hers while his fingers delved between her slick folds. Water droplets collected on their skin from the lake. The cold she'd felt long ago evaporated from the heat their bodies created.

Hunter took his time, stroking and massaging her clit to a dangerous peak. His touch traveled farther between her legs and then slowly slipped inside. He started with two fingers, gently easing them in and out of her damp pussy. Her head fell back. His forearm banded around her back, holding her upright while his lips homed in on her right breast.

Soon, the easy pace gathered steam. Kat's hips undulated. Her head shook back and forth. "You can't make me come again."

"Watch me."

"Not like this." She levered her head upright and found his half-lidded gaze. "I want your cock inside my body. I've waited long enough."

"Oh, yeah?" His brow arched. "How long have you wanted it, Doc?"

"Since I could've lost my medical license for it." Kat crushed her mouth to his to keep him from saying anything that would stall the process of getting him inside her. She hiked one knee onto the bed next to his thigh, but his leg barred her other. "Please."

"You're not ready yet." Hunter massaged her opening with three fingers.

"Yes, I am."

"Have you ever been with a big man, Kat?"

"Average," she growled and fought against the orgasm gaining traction on her.

"No one has ever called me average."

She pressed her mouth to his again, shifted her weight, and stole her leg from his. Her sense of triumph lived as long as it took her to lift and brace her knee on the other side of the bed and lever herself over his cock. When her opening met his head with an abrupt stop, she gasped.

"It's about time you start trusting me." He spoke the words against her lips.

Kat wanted it so bad she bore down on his crown and rocked her hips. The orgasm threatening to attack turned tail and ran. His massive head breached her body, and pain ripped through her. Silver spots danced in her vision.

"Breathe, Kat."

She couldn't. It stung. Surely, if she moved one way or another, he'd split her in two.

"Look at me." His voice was quiet and calm but demanding.

Her eyes focused on him. He pulled her hand up from its death grip on his shoulder and lowered her middle finger into his mouth. His gaze anchored her while his tongue toyed with the pad of her finger. He sucked it down to the base and worked it to the tip where he left just a hint of saliva on the tip.

"Rub your nipple."

Kat's mouth fell open.

"I thought you took instruction well?" A twinkle of challenge lit his gaze.

She'd never done anything like this. Not while anyone watched, at least. Her hand shook, but she moved it to her breast. The moisture was cold on her skin. She held it there without moving.

"Like you mean it." He put his middle finger to his mouth and licked it. "Like this." His hand dropped low, and the pad of his finger slid along her swollen clit down to the point and then back. He used straight strokes, then circled her flesh, and then depressed the nub and whirled it around in a circle.

His gaze narrowed to her nipple, demanding she participate. The quiet order made touching herself easier by freeing her from the concern of perception. She eased into the touch as he had on her clit, starting slow. Their fingers worked in tandem, stoking the kindles of her desire to a roaring fire once more.

Kat's inner muscles relaxed. Her hips rocked to the beat of their caresses. Little by little, she worked herself on his dick and took more of him inside. Her breaths turned to heady moans. Her light touches morphed into the all-out groping of both breasts.

"That's it, Kat. Fuck. Let me inside that sweet pussy."

"Yes." She'd never had anyone speak so crassly to her, and it shot a wave of lust straight to her core. She loved it. "I want more."

Hunter gripped her ass with both hands, stopping her cold. She wiggled to gain control and more of his length, but his hold was absolute. "Tell me, Doc, do you want more of my dick or more of my dirty mouth?"

"Yes." She nodded. "Both."

"My pretty angel likes it kinky." He sucked the nipple of the breast she cupped. "I knew you had it in you."

The small claim of ownership should have scared her or, better yet, not registered at all. Oh, it registered all right. Right between her lifted breasts and her labia. Before she could stew, Hunter pulled her hips down and thrust up. Her ass cheeks met the tops of his thighs.

"Oh, Hunter." He filled her so completely— lust, emotion, and raw desire choked her.

"Breathe, Kat."

"I am." She abandoned her breasts and wrapped her arms around his shoulders.

He leaned his lips against her ear. "You wanted me inside you. Now I can feel the pulse in your womb. It's hammering against my dick." His fingers kneaded her ass. His mouth snagged hers in a quick kiss. "You feel like fucking heaven." The words were mumbled against her shoulder as if not meant for her.

No. Kat just projected. Guys probably said that to women all the time. Hunter had probably said that to— Not a helpful train of thought. She lopped it off. Still, the roots took hold. They were rotten and tainted the soil.

"Hey, come back here."

"What?" Her gaze focused on Hunter. He studied her for a second.

"You're worrying, and this isn't the time to worry."

"Ah!" She growled. "I hate that you can read me so well."

His mouth wore on hers for a moment. "I love it." He offered her a sinister grin and then flipped them over. His thick arm hooked around her back, and he crawled them up the bed with one hand and one leg.

Kat sank into the covers and let Hunter press his chest to hers and study her. His gaze mined deep, and then his hips thrust. They retracted and lunged again. Her legs fell open, receiving every part of him. He gave it all, battering her most sensitive flesh with a ram built for total domination.

She forgot everything and felt. Her body gave over to his demands. Each thrust abraded her slick clit. Each thrust rubbed her sensitive nipples against his chest. Each thrust ratcheted her higher and higher until...

Free-fall.

Her fingernails bit into his shoulders. She came under his watchful gaze, moaning and speaking words that didn't form a cohesive thought.

"You're beautiful, Kat." He pounded into her. "Watching you come just does it for me." His head shook. "Every time you came with your clothes on without touching me, I almost lost it."

"Lose it now," she begged. More than anything, she wanted to see him lose control over her.

As if he lived for her order, Hunter's jaw tensed. Every muscle in his shoulders and chest strained. His abs contracted, and he lifted himself off her slightly. "Kat." He shivered in her hold and then collapsed atop her. Their breaths and heartbeats mingled for many minutes. "I have a present for you too."

"Oh, I got it. All of it."

Chapter Twenty One

"Ha!" Kat cleared the chamber, flipped on the safety, and slid the Smith & Wesson M&P Shield into the clip at the small of her back. She whirled toward him with wide eyes and a fat grin. "Ten out of ten." Her palms clapped together and then flew high above her head. "That's one-hundred percent." She pointed at him. "In case you didn't know."

Hunter couldn't contain the pride swirling in his chest or the erection in his pants. He cleared the uneven terrain in three strides, locked his arms around Kat's waist, and hoisted her into the air. This time, she didn't chide him about the added weight on his prosthetic. Instead, she wrapped her legs around his waist. Her palms clutched his face while her lips smashed into his. Instantaneously, he renounced the decision he'd made during the night. When she slept next to him, it was easy to see they couldn't ignore the outside world much longer. After all, Tor was probably up to some no-good revenge shit. If Hunter lay dormant and one of his brothers—hell, anyone else—got hurt, he wouldn't be able to face himself in the mirror. The sun beat down on their faces with the lake at their backs. The open sky smiled upon them. Kat held him like she never wanted to let him go. It was easy to forget the horrors of the world and simply be with her and that fucking radiant smile she flashed him morning, noon, and night.

"In case you didn't know," he said, nibbling her collarbone, "if you'd started practicing five weeks ago when I gave you the thing, you'd have shaved two seconds off your time by now."

"Do I need to put something in your mouth to shut you up?" She giggled and plowed her fingers over his short hair.

"Yes," he groaned. "Tuscan chicken and stuffed artichokes, please."

"That's not what I meant." Her face arched to the sky, and she laughed. It shook her belly against his. He seized the opportunity to hike her higher in his arms and bury himself in the valley of her breasts. He drank in her scent buffered only by thin cotton. Then he filled his mouth with as much of her breast as possible with no hands. "Now you're getting it."

"Not yet, but I will," he warned with a mouthful.

"Food first," she insisted, "I'm hungry too."

"You're the one who insisted on maiming five-hundred cans." His words muffled against her chest.

"I don't hate guns anymore. It's actually fun and... I don't know..." She wiggled from his hold. "Empowering."

Hunter set her on her feet and kissed her forehead. "You hated your fear of guns and lack of gun knowledge." He offered her his hand, and they turned back to the path that brought them through the woods and to the house. She slipped her palm next to his, and they started the walk. "Just like this thing." He waggled the tennis shoe covering his prosthesis on a stride. It landed easily on the ground and allowed him to continue without thought. "I hated it until I learned how to use it. Now, I can beat you back to the house."

"Always a show-off." She pulled herself close and pressed a kiss to his shoulder.

When she looked at him with those vulnerable blue eyes, he lost himself in them; so much so, he contemplated not asking the question. It could send her running. Then again, it might show his willingness to compromise. As a rule, he didn't compromise, but he would do it for Kat. After all, she'd been through enough already.

His heart thundered in his chest, and it had nothing to do with running, walking, and standing with his prosthesis for a record number of hours. He braced and tossed, "If I promise not to kill your father, will you testify against him?"

He'd like the man dead, without a doubt, but it would hurt Kat. If she testified, if his team flushed out the evidence, they could put Tor Royan away forever and get some intel in return. The thought of Tor getting ass-raped in prison would put a smile on his face for years to come, but he'd keep that to himself.

"Those are the options. Death or betrayal?" After all their hours talking, days fucking each other senseless, and the realization he thought she'd come to about her father, she balked like the man were a Nobel Peace Prize winner.

"They're better options than he deserves. Better than he's given others."

Tears welled in her eyes. She held them at bay with a sniff and jut of her chin. "He's my father."

The same man who'd held her against her will. Hunter wouldn't throw that in her face because she knew it.

"I'm going to change and go for a run." Her hand slipped from his.

Hunter let her walk ahead of him. He wouldn't chase her. The demons inside her did that too much already. She reached the first split in the path, only ten feet from him. He wouldn't chase her, but it was about time he challenged her.

"Aren't you tired of running?"

She stopped midstride and turned on him.

"Aren't you tired of fighting?" Her hands spread wide. "I don't understand why you're so eager to get back to a life that left you pounding on death's door."

"I'm not eager, Kat, but we've been here for two months. I've been MIA for five goddamned months. No matter how much we want to, no matter how easy it would be to stay here with you, we can't hide here forever."

Three long strides brought her closer. "I'm not hiding," she snarled.

"You're not? I sure as fuck am."

"You are?" The tightness around her mouth eased and her brows arched.

He nodded. "Do you think a sexy little thing like you could keep me from going if I wanted to?" His shoulders bobbed. "I mean, you could shoot me now, but if I wanted to leave, I would've used the phone you hid under your mattress the first week we were here."

Her gaze hit the dirt.

Hunter stepped forward and lifted her chin. "The truth is, at first, I stayed because I couldn't face my old life and the changes that are sure to come. Then I stayed for you. I wanted you comfortable with me, to trust me, and come in with me when I decided it was time."

"All this was to tame me like a fucking animal?" Kat jerked her face from his hold. Tears welled in her pretty eyes. She reared back only looking at him from the corner of her eyes. "And now you say it's time to go. So I'd better hop to and turn my father in?"

"One week in, yes. That was my plan. Then...I stayed for me." He eased his hand toward hers as though she were an injured creature, and she was. The strangest feeling gathered in his chest; a mangled mix of heartburn and drowning fear. When she let him hook two of her fingers with his without running away, the tiniest bit of it abated.

"What do you mean stayed for you?"

"The past two months have been some of the most challenging of my life, but they've been—without a doubt, or even a close second place—the best of my life." Her sharp features softened. Hunter huddled the rest of her hand into his. "Out of anyone in this world, you've cared for me more, and—"

She threw herself at his chest, nearly knocking them both to the ground. Hunter braced his prosthetic leg, steadied his foot, and hugged Kat to him. Even though she made no sound, hot tears soaked through his shirt.

"And I care for you more than I knew it was possible to care for someone I don't call my brother."

Her arms squeezed him to the point of oxygen deprivation. He kissed the top of her head and exhaled his worries and fear. There was no fucking way to know what would come next, but if she came with him, he would make things as good for her as he could. No worries of retribution from her father. No looking over her shoulder.

"I'm scared." Kat sobbed.

"Me too."

"You are?" She sniffled and wiped at her face before looking at him with a narrowed gaze.

"Of plenty, but I'm not scared of going in. Not if you go with me."

Kat pressed her lips to his. Her eyes were sad, but that perennial determination shone through. She turned toward the house and pulled him along. "It's still under my bed."

He kissed her hand. "You mean the bed you used to sleep in?"

"Yeah." She nodded, and a hint of a smile met her lips. "What's the plan?"

"I'll call my commander, say hello from beyond the grave, and he'll tell me what's what. There might be a legitimate level of cursing."

"Oh, I haven't heard any of that lately." Her lips pursed and eyes rolled.

"Hey, you're getting just as bad."

"Only when I come," she protested. Like that wasn't all the damn time.

Their conversation quieted, and their steps never rushed on the long walk. When they got inside, they walked to the bedroom and sat on the tiny mattress. She offered him the phone she'd left connected to a charger. Before he turned it on, he turned to her and planted a simple kiss on her lips. As much as he was ready for the next step, he didn't want to leave their hideaway.

The phone shined to life. Hunter input the number he knew by heart and turned on the speakerphone. He wanted Kat with him one-hundred percent. Because after they learned that she was a Royan, he would only have so much control over their fates.

After a mechanical beep, he said, "Oscar. Romeo. Papa. Hotel. Alpha. November. One. Nine. Eight. Six."

Kat scooted closer to him, forcing that funny as fuck feeling into his chest again.

After a series of beeps, an operator answered. "Voice confirmation complete. Missing in Action Agent Masters, how may I direct your call?"

"Commander Tucker, please."

Several moments of silence filled the line.

"About motherfucking time, goddammit." Tucker's gruff voice filled the small room. "What's your status, soldier?" Under the bristled outer layer, a hunk of concern lay solid and unyielding.

Hunter muted the line for a second. "Don't worry. It's just a dude's way of saying you scared the shit out of me and I'm glad you're not dead." Kat offered him a faint smile. He unmuted the line. "A little worse for the wear, but all in all, I'll survive."

"Then why the fuck has it taken you this long to make contact? Your friend is about to jump off the deep end."

"It's complicated, sir." For so long, he'd put himself into a box, not allowing thoughts of Oliver and Tyler. Knowing Ollie wasn't doing well sliced deep.

"Where are you? I'll send a HELO and get you the hell home and de-briefed."

"I'm in the safe house on the outskirts of Oslo, sir, and I'm not alone."

"Please tell me you have Royan."

Beside him, Kat jerked. Hunter laid his hand atop hers and pulled it to his cheek. "I have a friendly. She saved my life in every way, sir. In every way."

"Put her on the line, Masters," Tucker ordered.

"She already is, sir."

"You trust her that much?"

"And then some," Hunter said.

"Miss?" Tucker addressed Kat.

She leaned forward and drew a deep breath. "Yes?"

"I cannot ever thank you enough for saving Masters' life. We are forever in your debt and will do whatever we can to assist you."

"I..." Kat looked at him as though at a loss. "You're welcome."

"I'll need you to come in with Agent Masters. We'll ask you a thousand questions but get you back to your life as quickly as possible."

Kat nodded. The tears gathered in her eyes again.

"Sir, when can we expect you?"

"Since you're in Commander McCord's district, and I already stepped all over his shiny shoes with Oliver's extraction gone fucking awry—sorry, miss—I'm going to let him bring you in. Besides, it's closer, and he can get you debriefed sooner."

It wasn't home. Then again, if Tucker came and got him himself, he wouldn't let anyone know Hunter was alive until they had all their questions answered and he exceeded the holding period mandatory for agents who have a huge chunk of time unaccounted for. He got it. They had to make certain he hadn't gone rogue and switched teams. Surely, bringing a Royan in with him wouldn't bode well for a short transition, but it was better than hiding.

"Yes, sir."

"Hang tight, Masters. The cavalry will be there before you know it."

"Sir?"

"What's up, Hunter?" For the first time, his superior was asking as a friend, not his boss.

"I know you can't tell Oliver yet, but make sure he doesn't do anything too stupid on my account."

"I'll try my best."

"Thank you, sir."

"Damn good to hear your voice."

"Yours too, sir."

The line went dead. He threw his arm around Kat and held her tightly to his side. So many things were swirling through his head. He'd lived the military, covert ops life for years. Kat hadn't.

"When they arrive, they'll blindfold us with black bags. They'll separate us. They won't speak until we get to HQ. Then they won't stop. It'll be question after question. You'll talk until your throat is sore, and your brain is mush. Then they'll ask you more questions. They'll do the same to me."

Kat buried her head under his chin and nodded.

"Answer all their questions as honestly and completely as you can. Know that they will not hurt you." They wouldn't. Not even knowing she was a Royan. But, so help them if they did. Gimp leg or not, he'd bring the world down around their ears. Gooseflesh crawled up his spine and down his arms. That was the first treasonous thought he'd ever harbored. It made his stomach knot, but he didn't know for which side of the fence it coiled.

Damn, but this woman affected him a shit ton more than he ever anticipated.

They cleaned and packed up the house, leaving everything as close to how they'd found it as possible. Too soon, Hunter heard the far-off whop of helicopter blades. He found Kat on the back porch, staring out at the lake. Without a word, he wrapped his arms around her, pulled her back to his chest, and held on as tightly as he held anyone, ever.

Hunter had never wanted a happily ever after. He didn't believe in it. But if he could imagine a life with anyone, if would be with Kat. She was strong, brave, vulnerable, and caring. She was everything he never knew he could want. She was everything he couldn't have.

"You know what you said about the hardest and best time of your life?"

"Yes."

"I know exactly how you feel."

He turned her to face him and kissed her with everything he possessed. She kissed him back just as fiercely. A few seconds before the HELO crested the trees, Hunter pulled back. Kat blinked away the moisture in her eyes, released his hand, and turned toward the future...without him.

The helicopter breached the horizon. Late afternoon light shined off the beautiful black bird. Two men stood in each of the open cargo doors, hanging from the belly of the beast. Bracket mounts for machine guns decorated each side of the fighter, but the guns were hidden in compartments inside while in friendly territory. A mixture of excitement and misery whirled in his stomach. The sight reminded him of everything he loved about life as a soldier. A life he'd never have again.

Kat stepped closer to his side. Whether for him or her own comfort, he didn't know, but he welcomed it all the same. As the bird descended in the large patch of grass to the left of the lake, Hunter hiked a ruck with his meager belongings onto his shoulder. Kat did the same. They walked toward the HELO a united front.

A guy who'd give Tyler a run for his money in the size department hopped from the door in fatigues, a T-shirt, big ass boots, a side arm, and long blade. His prep boy blond hair ruffled in the wind the blades created. He exited the vortex, stopped in front of them, and offered his hand to

Kat first. "Miss?" A British lilt stronger than tea and crumpets wrapped itself around the word.

She looked at Hunter for confirmation before offering her hand for a brief shake. Hunter's chest puffed tenfold, but he managed to keep it still under this man's scrutiny.

"Juliet. Uniform. Sierra. Tango. India. Charlie. Echo. One. Nine. Four. Five." The agent Hunter knew from hearsay and a bit of legend as Law Pierce demanded a salute. He'd worked undercover longer than any other agent in Base Branch and for one of the most gnarly fuckers on Earth.

Hunter gave his salute willingly. "It's a pleasure to meet you, Commander Pierce. I'm Missing in Action Agent Hunter Masters. Oscar. Romeo. Papa. Hotel. Alpha. November. One. Nine. Eight. Six."

Pierce returned his salute. "Call me Law. I'm happy to call you found agent Hunter Masters. I was with your US team, searching the rubble for three days."

"Thank you." Hunter nodded but didn't look at Kat. If he did, he might lose his shit.

"I'm just sorry we couldn't find you sooner." Law's gaze dropped to his prosthetic leg.

Up until that moment, he'd actually forgotten about the damn thing for a blissful moment. "Well"—Hunter shrugged—"I'll take it over a tomb any day."

"Oorah!" Law clamped him on the shoulder. "Hoorah, warrior." He hiked a thumb toward the bird. "Let's get you back. The big boys are dying to know what the fuc—heck happened to you."

Kat harrumphed, he'd surmised, about Law's almost fuck and recovery.

"And you, miss, I hear we owe you a great debt of gratitude."

She shrugged. "Just doing my job."

Hunter chuckled.

"Hush," she chided.

"This way." Law pointed them ahead and followed behind.

Inside, he directed them to sit next to one another on the tail side of the HELO and buckle. The other guy who'd been in the other doorway pulled two black bags from a compartment behind his seat. Law lifted his hand palm up, and the guy stopped. His brown gaze flew from the bags to him and Kat and then back.

"Just because I'm down a leg doesn't mean I can't handle protocol." Hunter's clipped tone told a little too much about his discomfort with the situation.

"I don't doubt it, but I was being a gentleman." Law pointed at Kat. "It's a two-hour trip. I figure we can hold off for a while."

Kat's hand found its way into his. Even though he hadn't intended to give away their relationship so early on, it was the anchor he needed to pull his shit together.

Law motioned to the pilot, and they soared in seconds. The pressure on his fingers increased, and Hunter glanced at Kat. Her wide eyes transfixed out the open doors at the treetops that whizzed past.

"Do you want the bag?" Law offered with a chuckle.

She declined with a stilted shake of her head.

Hunter rubbed the same pattern on the top of her hand he had every night before they fell asleep. Soon, her rapid breaths slowed and her frantic gaze eased. When they hit the coast and zipped low across the water, her mouth gaped, and a smile curved her mouth. The scene was nowhere near as beautiful as she was.

With what Hunter expected was England in sight, Law gave the approval to bag them. Kat patted his hand in reassurance. Still, the instinct to maim and murder the young soldier who covered her beauty in a black sack roared to life.

"At ease, Agent," Law ordered. "I'll handle her with the same care as I do my wife."

Kat's chuckles seeped through the bag.

Both men looked at her, and then back at each other.

"I hope not." Kat laughed. "She probably wouldn't appreciate that."

The cabin filled with laughter.

"Not at all," Law agreed, emphasizing each word.

Hunter accepted his bag without incident. Before long, they landed on a rooftop between two or three skyscrapers. The whirling blades and working engine bounced off the surfaces and ricocheted about, leaving no question. He'd done enough rooftop entries to know. They shut the bird down and escorted them inside. Down a long corridor, a right, and into an elevator they went quietly; him, Kat, Law, and then the other soldier. The car descended for what seemed like an eternity and opened into a small room. He could tell because the reverberation of their footsteps didn't travel far.

"Hold out your arms," Law ordered.

Kat's arm brushed his, and he fought the urge to grab her. The separation was coming, and the dread of it tore at his guts. No one patted him down. A door opened at the opposite end of the room, and Hunter guessed they had a new body scanning system like they'd gotten in DC.

Through the door, Law put a hand on his shoulder to still him. "Ma'am, come with me, please. Hunter..."

"You're coming with me." The voice was new, deeper, and came from maybe three inches higher than Law's had. It possessed a seasoned authority. Any other time, Hunter would've made a crack about coming with a dude. Now he listened to any sign of a struggle or stress on Kat's end. He heard none as her quiet sneaker steps faded from his hearing.

"Yes, sir."

The man didn't offer Hunter an arm or grab his. He simply took off down the hallway with deliberate footsteps in the opposite direction Kat had gone. Hunter followed   to a different elevator. They dropped another level or two and then exited left. British boss input his code.

"After you." His voice gave Hunter the orientation through a narrow doorway he needed, and he entered a small space. The door closed with a metallic thunk. A metal on concrete scrape filled the area. "Have a seat."

Hunter did his best blind man feel for the chair and sat under a bright light. It seeped through the bag, heating his skin. He knew exactly where he was. Over the years, he'd been in plenty of interrogation rooms. Usually, he was on the other side of the table. After the man pulled the bag from Hunter's head, the bright lights stole his vision altogether for a second.

A massive man with a neatly trimmed Wolverine-like beard and 'do stared intently for a long time without a word. Hunter stared back, refusing to fill the void with chatter. The guy wore jeans and a threadbare T-shirt as though he'd been interrupted mid vacation. Or maybe he wore comfortable clothes for doling out a beatdown. Time would tell. The wedding hunk of metal on the guy's left ring finger would hurt like a bitch.

Finally, the man extended his hand. "I'm Baine McCord."

"Hunter Masters." He shook the hand of the commander of the European headquarters for the Base Branch.

McCord walked to the other side of the table, dragged the chair back, and sat. "Where the hell have you been, Masters, and what happened to your leg?"

For more hours than Hunter could track, he told the story of following Tor Royan through a maze of tunnels until deciding to come in and most things between. The part about Kat being a Royan garnered no reaction. The things Hunter left out or glossed over, McCord attacked point blank. What he refused to answer—the personal stuff between him and Kat—the commander doubled back on from every angle.

They blew through thousands of tactical questions. Hunter drew out the path they'd taken to the safe house and mapped a course to Tor Royan's home base. It gave him purpose and a sense of duty he probably wouldn't find after this was all said and done.

McCord called a water break, handed his notes and Hunter's map to someone on the other side of the door, and then closed it.

"Is Kat still in questioning?" Hunter was used to long Q&A sessions, but Kat wasn't. By her own admission, she rarely dealt with people on a long-term basis. She'd be fatigued, for sure, and possibly close to her breaking point.

"Do you love her?" The commander might as well have kicked the chair out from under his ass and pinned him to the floor with a boot to his throat.

Hunter stared at him be-fucking-wildered by the question.

"It's obvious you care about her." McCord crossed his arms over his chest. "What I need to know is if given a choice between your duty and your woman, who would you choose?"

"She's not my woman." Hunter's head shook in direct defiance of his words. "She's her own woman." Was he trying to convince himself? No. His duty came above everything. "I put duty before my own life."

"What about hers?" McCord asked.

Hunter stood so quickly he forgot about his prosthetic leg. He wobbled but used the table for balance. The only hope he had against a man of McCord's stature was getting him on the ground.

A smile—the first hint of humanity—crept onto the commander's lips. He held both palms up. "Settle down. No one's going to hurt Katrin." McCord tried to rub the full-out grin away but failed.

Hunter wanted to knock it off his face.

"I have my answer." He chuckled. "Even if you don't realize yours yet."

What the fuck was that supposed to mean?

"Since you're up and I'm tired of talking, let's take a walk." McCord opened the door, and they returned to the elevator. He depressed the button for the underground parking garage.

"Where's Kat?"

"Safe."

"Specifically," Hunter demanded.

"Look..." The commander swung his wide frame around. Hunter braced himself for a fight or the bullet to come. Maybe the guy didn't buy his recounting of events. "I read your file. I don't know what it's like to grow up with no one who cares about you. My mom saved me from that fate, but my father took her away from me. So I know how it is to grow up trusting only yourself." McCord shrugged. "It's a defense mechanism. It works like a charm, too, until you find someone worthy of your trust. Their presence shows you just how alone you are."

The doors opened, and the commander walked out as though he hadn't said a word during the ride. Hunter had no choice but to follow along confused and irritated. The fucker still hadn't told him where Kat was or how she was. A sleek car idled at the end of the sidewalk.

Where were they taking him? Would he ever see Kat again?

Hunter's heart beat out of his chest. He didn't know where the fuck or what the fuck, but he was ready to tear the place apart to find her. His body tensed to spring.

The honeyed sound of Kat's laughter filtered through his mania. His head snapped right toward the waiting car. She sat in the back seat, covering her mouth and giggling as though she hadn't a care in the world. He nearly plowed over McCord in his rush to get to her. When she saw him, her hand fell away from her mouth, revealing the brilliant smile she had just for him.

He sat beside her without instruction. Her hand clamped around his. Wherever she was going so was he. He couldn't look into any of the deeper meaning bullshit. But he knew that without a doubt.

Law sat behind the wheel. He'd changed from his fatigues into more casual attire. Kat too looked fresh and content. McCord crammed himself into the front seat, and they pulled away from the curb.

"Where are we going?" Hunter needed to know.

"To a place scarier than you've imagined." McCord laughed.

"That's for sure." Law snorted.

Chapter Twenty Two

Kat sat with Hunter to her left at the end of a six-top breakfast table in the center of a massive kitchen. Mostly empty dishes with remnants of delicious roast, potatoes, and carrots cluttered the space between her and Law. He crouched on the ground on the other side of the table with his jaw hanging near his knees. Magdalena, Law's wife, stood clutching his hands over her swollen belly.

"I can feel…" Law squealed with a level of excitement Kat had never seen in a grown man. Especially one who commanded a room the way this one did. "Bloody brilliant."

Around Kat and Hunter, the room erupted in whoops and hollers.

"Is that an arm?" Law gazed up at his wife, wonderment contorting his features.

"Hell if I know." Magdalena giggled and shrugged. Her blonde hair fell over her shoulders.

"I want to feel." Sloan McCord, Baine's stunning wife, scrambled up from her perch on her husband's lap. She weaved around Law but waited patiently behind him for her turn.

"I want to feel!" Alma, the oldest of Baine and Sloan's adopted daughters, jumped to her feet. Next to Kat, the two little girls, Alma and Alisa, wrestled their way into the small gap between their two chairs.

"No, me first." Alisa, the youngest, thrust a pointy elbow into Alma's ribs in an effort to get ahead.

"Neither of you feel anything until you eat your supper." Baine's deep timbre stopped them cold. They sat in two little heaps of dejection. Their large pitiful eyes filled with moisture almost on cue.

"None of that." Sloan pressed her hand to Magdalena's belly. Her face was a mixture of awe and parental determination. "If you hadn't interrogated Kat and Hunter, you'd have been finished eating twenty minutes ago."

Alisa's big brown eyes slid to Kat in raw accusation. Kat slid to the back of her chair, giving the girl a clear shot of Hunter.

"That's cool. Give me up to the enemy." His strong arm hooked around her neck and pulled her in front of him like a shield.

Alma climbed onto her chair, spun around backward, and rocked it onto two feet rodeo style. Alisa continued her stare down.

"She has baby dolls," Kat whispered, "and she's not afraid to use them."

"It's her most devious torture tactic." Baine nodded.

"Well, here's mine." Sloan straightened from Magdalena's belly, flicked her long ponytail off her shoulder, and zeroed her amber eyes in on the girls. The woman had the most striking features Kat had ever seen. Her skin was a perfect mix of light and dark.

If she and Hunter had a baby, it would have the same stunning complexion.

The moment the thought flew through Kat's mind, she screamed it out the door. What the hell? All this togetherness, the family atmosphere where no blood was shared, did crazy things to her brain.

It made her think impossible things were possibilities.

"Sit and eat, or no book before bedtime." Sloan's edict met with two gasps. The girls sat in the chairs and grabbed their respective utensils.

"Man, that's low." Law scooped two handfuls of dishes and headed to the sink, shaking his head. Before he got out of reach, Magdalena smacked his butt.

"I know, right," Baine agreed.

"It's the only thing that works." Sloan tossed her hands into the air.

"Have you tried electroshock?" Law asked over his shoulder.

"It wouldn't faze them." A prideful grin stretched Baine's mouth.

"Who would have thought such deadly operatives would be reduced to such deviant behavior?" Hunter chuckled. "No bedtime story."

"Seriously." Magdalena grabbed two plates and headed in her husband's direction.

"So you all live here?" Kat asked. The old colonial mansion was certainly large enough to accommodate them all. Heck, on her way to the bathroom, she'd seen a dining table large enough to seat the entire surgical staff at her old hospital.

"Yes." Baine nodded. "I grew up here with my mother and grandfather. When my mother died, he left the place to me before he passed." He pulled Sloan atop his lap and patted her leg. "It's the perfect place for our unconventional family."

Hunter's gaze bobbed back and forth between the two couples, thinking probably close to the same thing as Kat. She didn't have the daring Hunter had to ask without actually asking.

"No." Sloan hugged her husband in a blatant act of possession.

Law chuckled at the sink. "Yeah, nope."

"Well." Kat stood and grabbed her and Hunter's plates. She needed something to break the awkwardness, though she was the only one who seemed to experience it.

"No, you don't." Magdalena tsked. "It's Law's turn to clean up dinner. We all have our nights, and last time it was his turn, we caught him bribing the girls with ice cream to clean the kitchen."

"I still don't see what's wrong with that." Law shrugged.

"He'll take those." Magdalena stole the dishes from Kat, brought them to Law, and then returned to Kat's side. "I'm sure you two are tired. I'll show you to your rooms...or room?" The pregnant woman's brows waggled.

"Room," Hunter declared without consulting Kat. She should have been embarrassed. After all, she was the daughter of a man their organization sought to capture at best or kill at worst. A shiver crawled down her spine, but the warmth of his claim on her—as small and insignificant as it was—chased away the sorrow.

He stood. Every eye in the room went to Hunter's prosthetic leg except hers.

"Wow." Alisa gasped. Her chubby little index finger pointed at the anomaly.

Alma's eyes grew to the size of the Goodyear Blimp.

Baine and Sloan's gazes locked in an expression of sheer terror that looked unparalleled to any they'd seen in the field.

The girls had been upstairs getting their baths before such a late meal. When they'd come into the kitchen, Hunter had already been sitting at the table, and their minds had been on food and inquiry.

"He has a robot leg," Alma squealed.

Magdalena covered her mouth.

Law winced.

Kat held her breath.

Hunter eyed both of the girls for a split second. His hips shook slowly at first, and then gained speed and waggle. He picked up one foot, and then the other, jerking the rhythm of the robot that worked its way up his body. It was so spot-on Kat felt a twinge of jealousy that—even down a leg—he could dance ten times better than she could.

"It's so cool," Alma screamed.

"Awesome," Alisa cheered.

Their tiny hips wiggled, and their butts shimmied. The room erupted in whoops and hollers. Law attempted to shake it.

"Save it for the bedroom, big boy." Magdalena planted her hands on his hips, holding him still.

Baine looked at Sloan, and his hands shot high. "Don't worry. I haven't met my quota for all that." He shook the cup holding a finger of brandy in his hand.

After the girls closely inspected the robot leg, Law ushered them off to bed.

Baine stood and offered Hunter his hand. "Sorry for the ice routine earlier. I had to figure you out."

"Did you?" Kat asked. "I've been trying to do that for months now and can't say I'm any closer than when I started."

"People aren't nearly as complicated as we give them credit for." Bain winked at her.

Hunter shook Baine's hand. "Thank you for putting us up tonight."

"We're not putting you up; we're protecting you, both of you, until the situation is resolved."

"Resolved?" Kat needed to know what he meant.

"Until Tor Royan and his organization are no longer a threat. Now that we know where to look, thanks to your intel"—his finger bobbed between them—"we know he's actively seeking you."

"He's my father. I didn't withhold that in my interview," Kat explained.

Baine nodded. "His intentions aren't that of a father."

Hunter's fingers wrapped around hers. He pulled her closer and addressed Baine. "I'd like in on the operation."

"I know you would." Baine might have known that, but Kat didn't. Her heart plummeted. If she had to choose between her father and her...Hunter, she knew exactly who she'd choose. She just didn't want to.

"Don't tell me it's my leg," Hunter growled.

"I won't because it's not the issue." Baine scraped a hand over his beard.

"What is?" Hunter demanded.

Baine's dark gaze dropped to their joined hands. "You're too close to this."

Kat expected him to toss her hand away and denounce the charge. Her lungs seized in preparation for the blow.

Hunter's breath hissed through his nostrils.

"We don't kill for vengeance, and we don't show mercy when it's not warranted because we care about someone close to them," Baine offered.

"It's a narrow line we live on." Sloan stepped closer and hooked her arm around Baine's, looked up at him, and then returned her gaze to them. "We live on it, so we can live with ourselves. Were this any other operation, you'd know that. Because it's different, you're too close to see it."

Hunter squeezed Kat's hand. "True enough."

"You two sleep well, and we'll see you in the morning." Sloan waved them off.

"Follow me." Magdalena motioned them toward the back door.

Whether for ease of travel or the fact he could release her hand without making a scene, Hunter let go of her hand. Her entire limb grew cold in an instant. Icy shards crept toward Kat's heart and corrupted her mind.

Magdalena led the way across a gravel drive and into a quaint coachhouse. Where the mansion boasted beveled glass, gold leafing, and spectacularly high ceilings, the cottage possessed a comfort only a tiny fireplace, hugging low ceilings, and a mixture of textures could possess.

"This is lovely," Kat breathed.

"Thank you." Magdalena walked through, turning on lamps as she went to add to the light of the one left burning in the living room. "I grew up here. Baine was my adopted brother of sorts. My father lived and worked here for Mr. McCord for fifty-five years."

"I'm sorry." Kat couldn't imagine losing her father, and he wasn't half the father Magdalena's was. The pictures that filled the mantels proved that much.

"Please. He's not dead." Magdalena snickered. "Far from it. He's living with his girlfriend a few hours from here."

"Oh." She gasped.

"Our bags?" Hunter asked about the ruck and backpack by the door.

"Yes, bring them up." Magdalena led them up the stairs. More family photos cluttered the wall and short hallway that led to a master suite. "He had taken care of us for long enough. It was time for us to do it on our own." Her petite hand patted her belly. "Well, not on our own exactly. We'd finally found our paths, which allowed him to follow his."

"That's..." Surprising and sudden emotion clogged Kat's throat. She swallowed it down. "That's awesome."

What would it have been like to have a family, a father who cared for her? Anyone, for that matter. Apart from her career, she was utterly alone in the world. Her entire body frosted over, making her an actual desolate tundra.

Chapter Twenty Three

Hunter watched Kat's brilliant smile fade incrementally from the kitchen to the house. The deeper they moved through the cozy space, the more dull it became until it wasn't there at all. Her arms hugged her middle as though she were freezing in the tepid setting.

"Thank you, Magdalena." Hunter dropped their bags by a dresser, stepped forward, and offered his hand.

The feisty woman nodded. Her gaze slid to Kat who sat on the edge of the bed and shriveled in on herself like a plant left without water or sunlight. "I'll lock up after myself."

"Thanks." He walked her to the bedroom door and then waved her to the top of the stairs where she paused.

"Take care of her."

"I intend to." Hunter watched her descend the steps and then closed and locked the bedroom door.

Kat sat staring into nothingness as though she were the only person on the face of the Earth. She looked so alone. Before the military had molded him, Hunter had known that feeling. Hell, he might know it again after they kicked him out. Whether that happened or not, he never wanted her to experience that hollowness.

"Kat, what's wrong?"

Hot tears slipped down her cheeks. Her arms wrapped farther around herself and held tight. Silent emotion shook her chest.

His insides twisted. He longed to cup her face, thumb away her tears, and kiss her nose, and then her eyes, and then her forehead, and then—

"I'm jealous." Kat hiccupped. "I'm mad," she growled. "I'm... As much as I thought I was a successful, together person, I'm just fucked up." Fresh tears accompanied her admission.

"Why are you jealous and mad and fucked up?"

"I envy Magdalena and her father. I'm pissed mine is a psychopath. For so long, I've just pushed on and made do, and I'm tired of it. I want something normal. I want someone to care about me the way people are supposed to care about each other." Her hand shot out in the direction of the main house. "Look at them. They care about each other. It's not some surface level bullshit. It's real. It's the 'I'll give my life for yours' kind of love I never thought I needed."

Hunter held himself back, unsure about what would fly out of his mouth if he opened it right now.

"Growing up, I had nannies and tutors. If given the chance, they'd have sold me for a vacation to the French Riviera and found another job when they got back." She sniffled. "My eyes have been opened, and I hate what I see. I'm tired of being complacent and ignorant of the void in my life. I have a career but no life."

Kat's words were a well-hidden sniper. They took him out at the knee cap. The good one. "It's amazing, really."

"What?"

"How similar we are. We're both fucked up by a lack of people who gave a shit in our early years.

We overcompensated with careers. We're presently unable to duck and cover from the bullshit flying around. Your dad. My lack of a leg."

Kat looked him square in the eyes. "I was meant to save your life."

"Even after the information overload that came with it?"

"Yes." She wiped the tip of her nose with the back of her hand. "You showed me there are things worth living for."

"Damn straight, there are."

Hunter walked to her. The need to comfort her, to hold her close, and to make love to her drove him to his knee in front of her. He grabbed her hands. He cupped them in his and raised them to his mouth. Each knuckle and every space between received a tender kiss until he'd covered the back of her hand. When he finished, he turned them over and started at her fingertips.

"What are you doing?" she breathed.

Indeed, what the fuck was he doing? In all the times he'd ever had sex, Hunter had experienced many urges. Spanking. Anal play. Ménage. You name it; he'd tried it at least once. Never had one of the urges been to make love. Yet here he was at Kat's feet.

"I'm making love to you."

Kat's tears dropped onto his forearm and rolled down his dark skin. Something about it baptized him into a whole new world. A world where he could belong to Kat and Kat could belong to him. That teardrop marked him.

He kissed up her wrist and to the fold of her elbow. His hand crumpled the front of her shirt and pulled her forward. Their foreheads met. Every shard of her Baltic blue eyes pierced his heart. He pulled her closer still and dragged their cheeks together. His nose buried in her hair and the crook of her neck. Her scent filled his nostrils. It warmed his chest and spiked his desire. He brushed the shell of her ear with his lower lip.

There were so many things he wanted to say and even more he shouldn't. Instead of words, he dragged her lobe into his mouth and sucked. His hand found her cheek and smeared her tears down her neck. Her head fell back in surrender. He loved his way down to the little dips in her collarbone.

Hunter stood and peeled the shirt over her head. Soft blonde curls fell from the cotton, cascading over her shoulders. Kat sat there staring at him in awe as if he was something special. He'd been a hero in battles, but he'd never wanted to be a woman's hero until that moment. His fingers brushed over her lips to her chin and skipped to the skin covering her heart. It beat under his touch. It echoed in his fucking soul, driving him to the brink of the unknown.

His fingertips indulged in the silk of her skin as they slid across her chest. He hooked the straps of her bra and dragged them over her shoulders. They fell at the sides of her arms.

Kat leaned forward and loosened the hold of his prosthetic leg.

His breath hitched. "You give the care you seek, Kat. You give it to me."

She pressed her face into the hand he offered. Her eyes closed. There were so many things she wasn't saying, too, and it shot a thrill through him.

Hunter lifted her by the waist and eased her back on the bed. He dragged his hands down her belly to her pants, unfastened them, and dragged them down her legs. He undressed completely, his leg being an accessory he didn't need to love Kat.

He crawled up her body. His mouth praised every inch of her calves, thighs, belly, breasts. The parts they neglected, his hands roved. They teased and tormented.

Kat's tears dried. Her lips parted. From left to right, hcr head lolled. Her blonde strands heaped around her head, morphing into knotted mountains on either side. The swish of her restless legs attracted him like a mating call.

"Hunter?"

"I'm here." He left her breasts and crushed his mouth to hers. He dragged kisses all over her face, making her his as much as he could.

"This is..." Her eyes closed.

He drew back enough to study her expression. Tears threatened to breach her lashes. Hunter braced himself over her and waited.

They opened. Her lower lip curled into her mouth. Still, he waited.

"It's different than it has been," she admitted.

"Damn right, Kat." He stroked her cheek. "I'm a fumbling first-timer. I've never made love before. I never wanted to until you."

Her smile gave him all the encouragement he needed. His knee shoved her left leg high. Her right leg stayed straight, in the way of his hip sinking into the V of hers. Every other time, she'd accommodated him. A challenge lit her eyes. He hated to touch her with his nub. What the hell was sexy about a missing limb and shriveled skin?

"I want you to make love to me with every part of you."

Well, fuck.

He shoved her right leg high with the part of his thigh that remained. The fever of her skin warmed the sensitive skin that had only ever felt silicone, plastic and cold, besides his own mandatory touch. Her leg moved, allowing his hips to sink. His fully erect shaft pressed between her swollen lips. With her body calling to his, he forgot about his insecurities.

Kat wrapped her arms around him, lifted her hips, and pulled him close. The invitation was clear. He'd never been inside a woman without protection. Temptation had never outweighed the risks. Somehow, Kat transformed the risks into psychotic rewards and a deep-seated desire to give part of himself to her. She nodded without him asking the question, but he needed to hear her answer.

"That won't work, Doc. I need to know you're asking me to come inside you without protection."

"I do." She gasped. "I am asking you to."

"Knowing the possible consequences?"

"Yes." She writhed against his cock, nearly shifting his focus.

He gritted his teeth and fought the urge to pierce her womb with a deep breath. "Knowing that if you end up pregnant, you're never getting rid of me."

"I'm not ovulating." She sounded so sure of something women got wrong on a daily basis. He held perfectly still and waited for the answer to his question. "Yes, Hunter."

"Knowing we shouldn't do this because who knows what tomorrow's going to bring."

"Do you want to make love to me?" she panted.

"More than almost anything."

"What's the thing you want more?" Her body undulated under him.

Hunter leaned forward and melded their lips together. "I want to care for you more than I want to feel your sweet pussy wrapped around my cock."

Kat's throat worked, and moisture filled her eyes. She nodded and hugged him. Hunter positioned himself at her entrance. He pushed slowly and steadily into her body and straight into heaven. Holy shit, his entire frame shook with pleasure. Kat hiked her knees high, grabbed his back with her heels, and breathed through the invasion. He might as well have been a virgin. The threat of pre-fire stalked him like this was his first time. His face burrowed into Kat's neck, and he breathed. It didn't help. Her smell drove him mad. Every movement sent waves of ecstasy through him. He felt everything. Physical. Emotional.

"I've never been so close to anyone," he wheezed.

"Me either."

Hunter dragged his face up to hers. He pulled out to the tip and planted himself deep. Kat's lips parted. If he were a wise man, he'd focus on the risk of this entanglement, but the slick, tightness of her body and the intent of her gaze refused to allow any deviation. She filled his mind. He filled her body and withdrew almost immediately. His hips thrust deep. Her murmurs filtered into his ears, seducing him and reducing him to a fireball of desperation. He bottomed out flush with her pulsing lips, dying for release.

"I feel everything," she gasped.

Too much.

He'd stuffed many tips and tricks into his bag of how not to come before a woman over the years. Hell, in the past month, he'd used nearly every one of them with Kat to masterful perfection. This time, for once in his life, there would be no showmanship in the bedroom.

"Tonight, there's just you and me." Hunter grunted, pulled out, and drove home. "Forget the world and let yourself be mine."

Her hands grazed his face while her hips arched into his thrusts. "Only if, tonight, you're mine."

He rested his forehead on hers. "Completely." The force of his jacking hips pounded them deep into the mattress. Waves of emotion and unfed hunger collided inside him like massive thunderheads.

His shaft slicked with Kat's unabashed invitation. His balls grew heavy. Beneath him, Kat rolled her hips, matching his every thrust. He gripped the sheets as though they were a lifeline while he pierced her womb again and again. His forearms threatened to burst from the tension building inside him.

Lightning flashed behind his eyes. Pressure raced up his shaft.

"Kat." Her name left his lips like a curse and a plea.

She answered with wild breaths. Her heels dug into his ass.

Hunter spilled himself inside her.

Kat moaned. Her hips worked him for every drop. She keened. Her head tilted toward the sky, and her mouth found his in a tangle of sweet surrender. He caught her cries between his lips and swallowed them down. They'd feed him forever.

Chapter Twenty Four

The day after they arrived in London, Kat had requested an appointment at a women's clinic to get on birth control. As much as she liked the idea of creating an actual human life with Hunter that'd grow with the perfect mixture of each of them, she knew they needed to commit to a life together before a pregnancy ever happened. Through the years, she'd seen too many children brought into the world in volatile situations. She and Hunter weren't volatile, yet they weren't stable either.

Because they'd been in hiding, the Base Branch doctor came to the house bright and early the second day. When he'd left, Kat not only had the tools she needed to stave off pregnancy, but she also had a job at Dr. Dylan Cole's clinic run by his wife, Willow.

Concerned her father's men would find her, Baine nixed the idea. Hunter came to her defense, offering himself as her personal security detail.

Butterflies.

Daily tasks anchored them for the wild abandon in the bedroom. They lived each day as their last, never knowing when they'd be given the green light to return to their respective lives.

Kat cuddled Hunter's sleeping back. They didn't discuss the future. Even thinking about it was off-limits. More than she liked to admit, this holding pattern worked for her. Hunter had been the one hell-bent on facing the world. Here, with people who respected him and also guarding her, Hunter seemed almost at peace. He slept more soundly than he had since being in a coma. She hugged him close.

Working and loving Hunter fulfilled her more than anything ever had. The thought of losing the man she loved… Kat's mouth fell open with a gasp. What delineated the line between like and love? Her mind fumbled through uncharted territory while her arms clung to Hunter. Not wanting to live a day without him likely leaned hard toward the love column. She'd liked her colleagues at Johns Hopkins, but they hadn't stopped her from taking a sabbatical. To be with Hunter, Kat would—

The pounding of footsteps rushing up the stairs filled the small house.

Kat's stomach lodged itself in her esophagus. Every other time Magdalena, Law, Baine, Sloan, or even the girls came to visit, they'd knocked on the door and waited for a response. Whoever rushed toward them wasn't waiting for anything. Neither would Kat. She lunged for her pistol, snatched it off the bedside table, and aimed for the door. The barrel swaggered from one side of the frame to the other.

At that moment, Kat knew she loved Hunter because she was willing to give her life to save his. If she could only steady for the shot.

Hunter jerked from the covers. His eyes swelled on her gun for a split second before he dove for the side arm on his nightstand.

"Remember what I taught you."

She inhaled deeply and released the breath in a long steady exhale.

"You don't have to shoot. I've got it." He sat with his pistol raised.

Despite everything, a hint of a smile curved her lips. She'd come a long way from a helpless surgeon. He knew she didn't want to take a life even if she could and would for him.

The bedroom door swung wide.

A man with closely cropped blond hair, thick arms, and a honed gaze burst into the bedroom.

Kat's finger caressed the trigger with deadly intent.

The man wielded no weapons. Fresh scars accentuated his strong jaw. In a fraction of a second the intense blue gaze he hosted shattered. His stout shoulders hunched with a depleting exhale.

"It's okay," Hunter commanded as though he were willing the words to be truth. His hand rested gently atop her gun and lowered the barrel.

"Hunter?" The stranger's strong voice shook.

"Oliver?" Just like that, all the puzzle pieces fit into place. The scars. The build. The sorrow. The determination. This was the man Hunter had asked for and spoken of since first waking. This was the life Hunter had before her, coming to claim him. This was the end of their holding pattern.

Giving her life for his would have been easy. Giving Hunter back the life he wanted...now, that would prove her love and leave her with a broken heart.

Hunter dropped his weapon onto the table.

"Brother." Oliver rushed forward with his arms wide. Behind him, a thin, young woman stood just inside the doorway. Tears filled her eyes, and a smile stretched her lips.

Hunter threw his arms open, not caring at all about his bare chest. Nothing new there.

Emotions played bumper cars with Kat's ribs. Surprise. Joy. Sorrow. Anticipation. Fear. They crashed into one another, ricocheted off and struck her thrumming heart two and three at a time.

The men barreled into one another like rugby locks. Strong arms quivered. Their chests heaved. Curses flew in growled sobs. They embraced like long-lost...family. Kat clutched the sheet to her nightie-covered chest and pressed her knuckles against her aching heart.

Her movement drew the woman's gaze from the men. She wore black leather pants, a breezy pink top, and pumps to match. The sweet smile she wore outshined the outfit and her beautiful pixie face.

"Sorry to barge in." Her whispers held more than a hint of Swedish-accented English. "I'm Marina." She pointed at the man in bed with her and Hunter. "That's Oliver. He's been looking for Hunter for quite a while." Her narrow shoulders bobbed. "Once Tucker told him where you were, there was no slowing him down."

Oliver levered back, grabbed Hunter's shoulders, and shook him. "Fuck." He stood with a groan. His feet shuffled back several feet, and his hands flew to his chest.

"Hands where we can see them, or we'll shoot them off." Sloan's cool voice filtered into the room and dropped the temperature by thirty degrees. Kat, Marina, and Oliver froze.

Sloan stood in the doorway, her body shielded by Marina. Kat clearly saw the gun as sleek as the woman who aimed it at Oliver's back. Baine stood in the doorway to the bathroom with a dark expression painted on his face, and his pistol pointed at Marina's chest.

"No!" Hunter leaped from the bed, placing himself between Sloan and Oliver. His arms shot

high with both palms out. "Friendlies. Don't shoot."
The covers slipped from his naked body.

Before the words were out of his mouth, their
weapons lowered.

Hunter stood at the center of the room with
his stunning body on display. Oliver's gaze locked
on Hunter's amputated leg hanging free. Silence
and a tension wrenched higher than that of a
battlefield sucked the oxygen from the room.
Hunter cupped his manhood in two hands and
twisted to hide his nub from Oliver.

Kat's lungs flamed. Her cheeks burned. If he
said anything to hurt Hunter, he wouldn't have to
worry about Sloan, the deadly operative. She'd
annihilate the man and anyone else who hurt the
man she loved.

"At least I know the rumors are true." Marina
shoved her hands into her back pockets. "Black
men are hung like horses." One clear crystal eye
winked at Kat.

"Mar." Oliver's upper lip curled, and his
mouth dropped open.

Across the room, Sloan snickered.

"Not a word from you, Mrs. McCord," Baine
warned.

"What?" Sloan chuckled and pointed at her
chest. "I didn't say a word." Her brow arched high.
"But if I had, it'd have been a big one." Her large
grin and the glint in her eyes challenged Baine.

"I'll give you a big one," he warned.

Kat broke into a fit of giggles. Hunter turned
his amber gaze on her and offered a smile that
warmed her to her toes.

"Everyone to breakfast in the main house,"
Baine ordered. "Except for you two." He pointed at
her and Hunter. "You'll need clothes first."

"Don't know if I can eat, but I can always drink coffee." Oliver nodded.

"That sounds great." Marina offered Oliver her hand. Oliver looked from her to Hunter, as though making sure he was real.

"I'm not going anywhere, man." Hunter grabbed a pillow from the bed and held it in front of his waist.

"It's damn good to see you, brother." Oliver straightened, grabbed Marina's hand, and followed the others out the door.

They listened in silence as the four descended the stairs and exited the cottage. When the door closed behind them, the silence remained. Hunter didn't say much as he hopped over to the drawer, grabbed clean clothes, and laid them on the bed with no help from her. Not long ago, he'd required her assistance for even the simplest tasks. Now, he was completely independent. The evil cocktail of pride and sorrow mixed itself inside her belly.

Hunter moved through the progression of dressing with his head down. He was a million miles from the bedroom.

Kat swallowed the tears threatening to topple her and walked to the bathroom. With every step, she begged him to call to her, to give her a sign that she still mattered. The cold tile floor gave her more comfort than the absence of his attention. She closed the door, leaned against it, and let the sadness fall silently onto her feet.

The connection they'd had only moments ago seemed so fragile an ardent wind could carry it away.

"Kat?"

"Yes?" She sucked back the tears, wiped her face with the towel on the back of the door, and reached for the knob.

"I'm going to head down. You don't have to rush."

"Okay." Kat sat on the edge of the tub and listened to Hunter's retreat from her life. Her fists clamped into tiny balls of rage. Her mouth opened in a silent scream. Her heart fractured into a thousand pieces.

Chapter Twenty Five

Hunter took the cottage stairs two at a time and prayed the prosthesis would keep up with him. Adrenaline dumped near fatal amounts of Holy Fuck into his veins. Sweat slicked his brow. His muscles pumped full with the intoxicated blood. He reached the landing on two feet instead of his face, exhaled and grabbed the doorknob. His hand slipped off the metal, and the momentum carried him chin first into the thick oak.

"Fuck." His grunt filled the empty room. He sidestepped and mentally checked himself.

Oliver had just arrived. He and Baine were likely not through all the introductions yet. Too bad the girls were at school and couldn't run interference. When they were around, it took twice as long to accomplish the simplest of tasks.

He wiped his palm on his jeans. This time his grip held and the door opened. It closed too loudly behind him, but he couldn't stop himself from running across the gravel. Frosted wind swept under his T-shirt. He didn't slow to curse it.

The back door opened and Law stepped out with the leather log carrier. His forearm lifted in a quick defensive move that it took Hunter a second to realize was aimed at him. The large man reeled the arm back in and sized him up. "Blast it, Masters. I could've laid you out."

"You wish." Hunter eased his pace but jockeyed for a way around the operative who'd made him feel more at home than Hunter had ever felt at his apartment.

"Look." Law dropped the wood carrier to the side of the walkway and closed the door, halting Hunter's progress. "I can see you're excited to get inside and talk to your friends..."

That should have been the reason Hunter wanted inside so badly, but it wasn't close. He needed inside the house, in the conversation to make sure no one said anything to Oliver about Kat being a Royan. If that was the first thing Ollie found out about her, it would color his every opinion. More than anything, he wanted his friend to like the doctor who'd brought him back from the dead and stolen his heart right out of his chest in the process.

Law's eyes drifted off farther than the trees for a second too long before coming back around. "The transition into an old life—especially when things have changed—is harder than you'd think."

"I know I'm not going back to the field." Hunter kicked the dirt.

"I'm not talking about your physical changes." Law dragged his teeth over his bottom lip. "Judging by how fast you were clipping it to the house, your leg won't hold you up much at all. It's the stuff they can't see. Hell, it's the stuff you can't see that'll trip you up."

"Talking from experience?"

"It's like us and civilians." His new friend nodded once. "They think they know what we've been through because they saw a documentary on PTSD or they watched *Saving Private Ryan*. Fellow operatives will think they know what you've been through because they've experienced battle. They

won't get it any more than the civilian does a
soldier's life."

Law must have seen the skepticism in
Hunter's gaze. More than anyone, Oliver got him.
"Transition is hard for even the best
friendships. Just take it slow. Don't expect too
much from yourself or others."

"They'll always disappoint you?"

"No." Law grabbed the leather carrier. "You'll
do that all on your own."

His new friend clapped him on the back and
headed for the wood pile. Hunter stood suspended
in the honesty of the man's imparted wisdom. He'd
created a life for himself devoid of any real
vulnerability. If you didn't give people the
opportunity to disappoint you, they couldn't. In
doing so, he'd set himself up for lifelong defeat.

Through the door's window, he saw the only
person he'd ever let into his life pacing back and
forth in the living room. Oliver was his best friend.
They knew enough about the other's demons to let
them sleep while they'd run at life full tilt. Marina
moved into the frame of Hunter's vision and
extended her hand to his best friend. Oliver
grabbed it like the last ammo rounds in a knee-
deep battle. His steps ceased. He pulled Mar into
his arms, and a deep breath settled his shoulders.

Maybe he and Oliver had been running away
from life. As much time and trouble as they dusted
up around the world, none of it ever brought the
look of contentment to his face as much as
Marina's touch did.

Oliver didn't know the depth of Hunter's
scars. The only one he'd ever let glimpse those
mangled parts of his soul was Kat. He hadn't made
the conscious choice to let her in, but something
about her quieted his inner turmoil, lowered his

defenses, and allowed him to connect on a level so deep he hadn't known it existed until her.

Hunter opened the back door and stepped inside.

"Morning, hung—I mean handsome." Sloan laughed and set the last two plates onto the table.

"I heard that." Baine uncovered the phone's receiver and continued his hushed conversation inside a large pantry.

"I meant for you to." Sloan giggled. She turned to the refrigerator and pulled out a pitcher of orange juice. "Breakfast will be ready in ten."

"Ish," Baine added.

Sloan stuck out her tongue at her husband. "I'm not as good at timing as you are. Remember, until a year ago, my go-to meal was cereal."

"Year and a half," he corrected.

"Not quite," she shot back.

"It feels like forever." Baine grabbed his head and groaned.

Oliver and Marina eased to the threshold between the kitchen and living room. Sloan winged a thin biscuit at her husband's head. He snagged it out of the air and bit off a large bite.

Law opened the door behind Hunter and stepped inside with a full load of wood. "Ooh, I'll have one." He opened his mouth wide.

Hunter walked through the kitchen and toward his friend. He didn't know if Sloan chucked Law a biscuit or if he'd grabbed one for himself, but when Law walked around Hunter and to the hearth, he held half of one and chewed on the other. Hunter stopped in front of Oliver and stared at the man whose life he would have happily given his for. Gone was the man's signature wavy blond locks and the full beard he'd rocked since Hunter had known him.

"I don't know which is worse; me losing a leg or you losing your hair." Hunter smiled at his friend. Scars occupied what had been bloody flesh where Tor Royan had shaved off Oliver's hair.

His friend harrumphed and pulled Marina into his side. "You're just worried the ladies will die for my devilishly handsome mug."

"Ladies?" Marina smacked a hand against Oliver's stomach.

The woman who barbed his friend while openly loving him wasn't the same woman they'd rescued from the prison Tor had made for her. Muscles instead of bone etched her frame. A smirk sat pretty where a hollow frown once had been.

"I'm just starting the list of reasons I can't be his wingman anymore," Oliver explained.

"You think I ever needed a wingman?" Hunter scoffed. "That was just to help you get lai—" Marina's narrowed gaze cut him off. "Some attention every once in a while," he amended.

They laughed, but too soon the raucous sound faded. Reality stared them in the face. Marina straightened from Oliver and stepped back, breaking the small circle and leaving them face to face.

"Tucker wouldn't tell me much of anything." Oliver rolled his shoulders. "I can't fucking believe he knew you were alive for a month and didn't tell me."

"Hey, now," Baine warned, now off the phone. "Tucker has a duty to all his men, not just you, Knight." The European commander for Base Branch operations called Ollie by his last name. They didn't know one another beyond internal reports and a handshake. "Keeping intel from our own is the hardest job we have, but it serves a purpose."

"Yes, sir," Oliver agreed. "It just—" His jaw flexed.

"Fucking sucks," Baine offered.

"Yes, sir." Oliver looked Hunter in the eyes. "It fucking sucked. I still don't understand why he couldn't tell me, but what I really don't get is why you kept silent for five goddamned months." His hand scraped over his tightly cropped hair.

Kat stepped between him and Oliver. He hadn't heard her enter. "Because he was in a coma for more than a month and had a long road to recovery." Her chin jutted.

Oliver stepped back and peered around Kat. "Hunter, who's your guard dog?"

"Oliver, Marina, meet Kat." Hunter pulled Kat into his side. Shit, this was not going the way he hoped. He wanted Ollie to like his woman as much as he did. Well, maybe not that much. But he wanted them to like one another.

"Nothing against you, Kat. It's just...this situation is crazy." Oliver's gaze slid to Hunter. A deep sorrow hung around its edges. "We looked for you for a long time. There was nothing in the rubble. No body. No sign you'd been there." Ollie rubbed his chest. "I knew you were alive, which hurt more because I—" His teeth flashed white in disgust. "I couldn't help you."

"Kat saved me." Hunter rubbed his thumb over the smooth skin on the back of her hand. "Nothing against you, Ollie. It's just...Kat has more first-aid knowledge in a strand of her hair than you have in your head."

"Have you seen the size of my head?" Oliver begged.

"Both of them." Hunter nodded.

The ladies choked in unison.

"What?" He shrugged. "I was talking about his actual skull and his ego."

"Sure, you were." Marina stepped around Oliver and offered her hand. "Hi, Kat. I'm Marina." Kat sized up the young woman for a few beats before meeting her halfway for a shake. "Anyone who cares about Hunter as much as you obviously do is a friend of mine. While Oliver saved my life, Hunter saved our relationship."

He had no idea what she was talking about. All he'd done was give her the pep talk she needed to pursue Oliver. "I'm glad you two worked out."

Oliver and Marina looked at each other and then back at Hunter.

"It wasn't easy," Mar admitted. "When he lost you, he quit everything. Not even Royan's death helped him."

Kat turned from pliant to stone in his arms. "Royan's death?"

Hunter prayed they were talking about her uncle's death. The hairs on the back of his neck stood tall, offering the answer before anyone else.

Oliver nodded. "I was supposed to kill the bastard to better the world." Tears welled in his bare-knuckle brawling, motorcycle riding, all night partying friend's eyes. "I killed Tor for you, but it didn't help." He sucked back the emotion. "It didn't bring you back."

Kat clamped a hand over her mouth. It didn't deaden the scream that escaped her throat at all. It reverberated in Hunter's eardrums and liquified every cell in his body.

"What?" Oliver crouched into a defensive position. His gaze swung left and right. When he found no intruders, he turned back to them. "What's wrong?"

"Tor Royan was her father," he whispered.

She cringed. Kat's pain became his. Every tear that streaked her cheek gouged a path in his skin. She crumpled onto herself. Hunter hooked a hand under her legs and gathered her to his chest. Her face burrowed in the crook of his chin.

"Motherfu..." A hundred different emotions toyed with Oliver's features.

Hunter turned and walked them slowly through the kitchen.

Tears framed Sloan's amber eyes. She strangled a dish towel as though it were her greatest adversary.

Baine's face was a mask of indifference. When Hunter drew near, the massive man whispered, "I'll take care of them." If he didn't know the many facets of Baine McCord, he'd guess that meant to take them out back and shoot them. But over the past month, they'd grown close to the guy. He would treat his friends like family. That was what the Base Branch was...for Hunter. Family. And now, Kat had none.

Chapter Twenty Six

Around Kat, the room quieted yet a shriek rattled her skull. The soft tissue congealed into a gelatinous heap robbing her of all function. Her limbs gave up. Gravity took hold, dragging her toward the pits of hell. It was the only way she'd be close to her father ever again. Oliver, Hunter's best friend, had made it so with the casual dispense of a round from his gun.

Her assaulted mind wondered where the bullet had entered her father's body. What path had it taken through his flesh? Had it nicked any arteries, ripped a jagged wound in a major organ, or lodged in a bone? Years spent working in an ER had taught her that some bullets reached such high velocity that they exited the body in a clean line. Those usually did the least amount of damage. The ones that penetrated the skin but lacked the power to plow through the muscle, cartilage, and tendons and punch out the other side—those bounced around like pinballs. Each ricochet ripped through important tissue. Each ping off a bone left fragments so small it took hours to clear from the site.

Bile whirled in her stomach. It couldn't find the exit. So much time spent around horror stole her body's ability to eject nearly anything. Her stomach's contents were the least of her troubles. There were rolls and rolls of overexposed film containing the terrible scenes she'd experienced as a doctor; the loss, the heartache, the disappointments. Her mushy brain stored them in a dark vault in the back of her mind.

Now the frame rattled. The door bowed. Panic threatened to release every awful thing she'd ever dealt with in a flash flood of shit.

"Shhh."

The noise came from above. Heat encompassed her. The excruciating sound of screams had given way to quiet, save for the rhythmic hushing.

Moisture soaked her face. The top of her shirt clung to her chest. Hair matted to her forehead. Kat's hiccups drew her further from the discontent of her past and into the dread of her present.

Hunter's strong arms held her firmly against his thick pecs. He sat on the couch in the cottage, rocking her in his lap, but any bit of goodness and solace ended there. Her father was dead. Murdered. And there was nothing anyone would do about it because he was the bad guy. Her father had been the thing that hid under people's beds. He was the one they locked their doors for. He was the one harming the world. He was her father, and now she could never earn his love and attention.

"Kat?" Sorrow shadowed Hunter's voice. "Talk to me, please."

What was she supposed to say? Could she even form words? Her mouth tingled as though she'd been close to hyperventilating. An arrhythmic heartbeat stammered along inside her chest, giving the feeling at any moment it could fly out of her sternum or quit entirely. Her head oscillated on a steady back and forth.

"I know you can," he insisted. "Anything you want to say. Say it." His thick lips formed a line. "I can take it."

Still, her head refused to stop denying him.

"You hate me? You want me never to see Oliver again?" He shrugged. "Whatever it is. Let me have it. Don't keep these things inside. They'll only hurt you."

That wasn't true. They'd hurt him too. As sure as she knew the sun would set on this horrid day, she knew she couldn't deal with any of this. There was too much. A mountain stood high and impenetrable between Kat and the life she wanted.

"Kat?" Hunter's lips pressed to her temple. She couldn't take his tenderness a second more. If he continued to show her affection when what she needed—what she'd always wanted—was love, she'd crack in two.

She shoved from his chest and grabbed the edge of the coffee table for balance. The room rolled like an unforgiving sea. When it settled, Hunter sat on the edge of the couch ready to catch her if she fell.

Who would catch him? She wasn't capable.

Kat buried her face in her hands and screamed as loudly as she ever had. The walls of her throat shook. The raw flesh ached as though she'd done it a thousand times. She wanted to run out the door and continue forever until nothing hurt.

"Let it out." Hunter sounded calm and unaffected by the wildness that peeled layer by layer of skin from her bones.

"Why?" She shook her fist at the ground. One smacked the tabletop again and again. When her shoulder burned, she stopped, and tears pooled at her knees. "Why do I care about the death of a man who didn't give a shit about me?"

"For better or worse, kids always want the people who created them to love them. After all, they're the ones who should love you more than any other person in the world. That's the way it's supposed to be. That's what I hear anyway. It doesn't always work out that way." He pointed between them. "We know that."

"I knew my father. You never met yours." Why was she complaining to a man who'd never known his parents?

"Both our lots were shit. We made the best of them." Hunter rested his forearms on his knees; real and robotic. "I was neglected." His hands clamped into fists.

"You were abused. I'd say yours was worse."

"I wasn't abused." Her spine stiffened. The room stilled. Anger boiled inside her, turning her blood to steam and giving her the energy to stand. "I wasn't abused."

"Just because you weren't physically or sexually assaulted doesn't mean you weren't abused."

"I wasn't abused." Kat slapped her hand to her chest like an ape.

"Your father was a sick man."

"What did he do that was so bad? I want to know everything. Details this time." He hadn't murdered her or sold her. Other than leaving her alone, he'd provided her with an amazing life. She had a top-notch education. She had a career. She had a life. No, it wasn't as exciting as Hunter's, but it was her safe place away from the pain. She controlled what went on in her days, no one else.

"Knowing those things won't help you heal." Hunter shook his head and stood.

"Then what the fuck will?"

Her scream stalled his approach. His amber eyes pivoted left and right, high and low. The tightness in his jaw fell slack, and his thick shoulders hunched. "I don't know."

Kat stepped back, placing the short table between them. She bit back the tears that battered her lids and smacked at the ones rolling across her cheek.

"Kat." Hunter begged with only her name.

"I have to get back to Baltimore."

"Kat."

Her head shook. Her whole body shook. "I can't deal with this anymore."

"I thought we worked through this. Just talk to me, and we'll figure it out." He stepped forward.

"No." She threw her hands up and retreated two steps.

He stopped. They stood in silence for a long time. No one moved. No one spoke.

"Running away isn't the answer." He said it with such confidence she hoped he had an answer.

"What is?"

"I don't know." Hunter sat on the couch as though he'd taken the bullet meant for her father.

Kat walked backward around an armchair. She couldn't take the wounded expression on his face.

"I don't want you to leave."

"I can't stay." Her fingers sunk into the cushioned wings. "You can't either." She looked around the second place they'd squirreled themselves away inside, hiding from the world. "This was amazing, the best time of my life, but it's not real."

"Yes, it is."

"Look around, Hunter. This isn't our life. This is what we needed to get through."

"And now?"

"There's too much here to stay."

Hunter stood. "There's too much here to leave." His voice shook the windows. He didn't holler, but it rumbled deep like a storm in the distance.

Kat eased around the chair and walked slowly to Hunter. His cheeks warmed her palms. She closed her eyes, pulled his mouth to hers, and seared the memory of his touch and taste in her mind.

"Thank you," she whispered.

"Don't thank me."

"Thank you for showing me I'm worth fixing."

"You're not broken, Kat."

"I'm shattered, and as much as I'd love for you to put me back together again, that's not something you can do. Only I can do that. It's going to take time and many trips to the fifth floor."

"The fifth floor?" He lifted the hair from her eyes.

"The mental health and wellness department in the building where I work."

"Kat, there's—"

"I love you, Hunter. As much as I know what love is, I feel it for you."

His mouth fell open as though she'd hit him with a defibrillator. He gulped and licked his lips. "Then why are you leaving?"

"I'm an intelligent woman. Educated. I have a regular level of common sense. But I can't admit that my father abused me." Her tears came back, flowing full force. "It should be an easy thing to see, but I can't. If I can't do that, I can't love you the

way you deserve to be loved because I don't know
how to love myself."

"Are you telling me I need therapy, Doc?" He
cupped her chin and lifted it until their gazes
clashed. "Because I love you and I'm letting you go."

***

Five Weeks & Eight Intense Therapy Sessions Later

Kat shoved through the operation room door
convinced of two things. One, her patient would
live. Sunshine and rainbows. Two, Hunter would
never return her calls, and she'd lost the best thing
that'd ever happened to her. Dark clouds and fry-
you-to-a-crisp lightning.

"Hey, Royan. Good to have you back."

One. Two. Three. Four. Five. Kat breathed
deeply while she counted. Miracle of miracles, the
crushing weight of hearing her father's name didn't
flatten her into a pancake or even a sobbing mess.
Three weeks back at work and the adverse reaction
to her surname had faded to a manageable level.
Thank you, Susan. The therapist might be
expensive as all hell at two visits a week, but she
was also totally worth it. Working helped her cope
with the weight of the sewage she waded through.

Adjusted, Kat turned to find Mike Webber
shoving his way through the doors of OR two. She
pulled the mask from her face and offered an
appropriate smile that she hoped didn't allude to
the number of steps she'd taken to get it there.

"Hey, Mike. I'm glad to be back."

"Was that your first surgery?" The tall, tan
man swished his floppy hair toward the operating
rooms she'd just exited. His brown locks were just
long enough to be considered edgy while not
crossing the line of professionalism. She'd seen him

around but had only worked with him a couple of times before her sabbatical.

"Third."

"What?" He offered her a smile that showcased white teeth and a wide mouth. "And I haven't been on your team yet."

The anesthesiologist did decent work, but he wasn't her favorite on staff by a long shot. He talked a lot during procedures, mostly about things she didn't care about. Like his weekend activities, which sounded similar to Hunter's...pre-coma.

"Rogers has been with me since I started back on rotation. He hasn't lost me a patient yet." Kat walked steadily toward the stairs that would lead to her office.

"Don't tell me you have a thing for older men." Mike reached above her head and opened the double doors that led into the main corridor. "After you."

She walked even though she was certain his eyes were on her ass. A smirk crept onto her lips. "Actually, no. I apparently have a thing for younger men."

"You know, I happen to be younger." His footsteps caught up with hers.

"So is the man I'm in love with." Kat pressed the button for the elevator and waited for the car to arrive.

"You're killing me, Royan." His hand covered his heart. "You leave right after I get here and come back all doe-eyed for some European."

The elevator doors opened revealing a half full car. Mike stepped into it without hesitation.

"He's American actually, through and through." She waved Mike off as the doors closed.

"A surgeon?"

"A soldier," she corrected as the gap narrowed to nonexistence.

The first true blue smile arched her lips. It didn't matter how many calls it took or how long. She would fight for Hunter just as much as she'd fought for him to survive. Her footsteps sped down the hallway, up two flights of stairs, and into the suite she shared with four other surgeons. Their assistant wasn't behind her desk, but her messages could wait. She had another important call to make. If he didn't answer, she'd just call again tomorrow. Eventually, he had to ans—

Kat pushed through the door to find a primly dressed man and woman in her office. Their heads were close together. They were in such rapt conversation they didn't notice her enter.

She wasn't expecting a meeting. People didn't get inside without the code or her or her assistant, who was missing, letting them in.

Her palms slicked.

With shaking hands, Kat backed from the room. If she'd ignored the hospital's rules about firearms and brought her pistol, this encounter wouldn't be as terrifying. Her mouth thinned to nothing as she eased the handle back into position. She didn't breathe until she was back in the main room, and that was only to call for her assistant... quietly.

No one answered.

Kat's heart thumped. She hadn't had a panic attack in weeks. It wasn't time to have one again. Even if strangers in her secure office when no one was supposed to be in her office warranted one. She sucked in a breath and hurried to the other hallway. Her hand was up ready to knock on her colleague's office when the bathroom door opened.

Kitty stepped out, still adjusting the tight pencil skirt she wore.

"Oh," the young woman startled. "I'm sorry. Did you need inside?"

The level of freak-out reined in by half or more at the sight of the other woman. "No. Who's in my office?"

The woman's thin brows arched. Normally, Kat wasn't so brusque, but when your dead father was an international criminal with goons on his payroll, you learned a little caution was in order. A little caution and a side arm. With caution, politeness took a hike. Tough shit.

"Your two o'clock." Kitty's ultra-red lips pursed.

"I don't have a two o'clock."

"Shoot." Her pump stomped the thin carpet. "I meant to tell you before surgery. Doctor..." She thumped her fingers to her lips several times. "Let me look."

Kat followed the woman down the hallway to her desk.

"Dr. Masters from the Branch Clinic set up your two o'clock in reference to DNA." Kitty shrugged. "I didn't know you did that stuff. If you don't have time to meet with them, I can tell them to leave."

The roaring of her heartbeat in her ears muffled the woman's last sentence. "You said Dr. Masters from the Branch Clinic?" Kat wheezed.

"I did, but like I said, if you want me to boot them—"

"No. Thank you. I've got it." Kat's voice trembled.

She had zero idea what was going on, but Hunter had sent these people to her. Just the distant connection sent her hopes soaring. They could be here to serve her with a restraining order, but until they said as much, Kat would take it as a positive sign. Hunter had thought of her.

Kat rushed down the hallway and into her office. Again, the couple was so absorbed in their talk they didn't notice her entrance. She took a moment to observe their interaction. There was excitement in their wide eyes and smiles but also nervousness. The middle-aged woman squeezed the man's hand so hard her well-defined veins and hints of svelte muscles plumped on her forearms. The gentleman, who seemed slightly older than the woman, pressed a lock of the woman's graying blonde hair behind her ear.

They weren't here for fertility treatment, that much was clear. Kat couldn't think why Hunter would send these two to her office. Maybe they had a son in a coma. That field wasn't her specialty, but neither was amputation, and she'd done all right. If it was in her power, she'd help them.

The woman gasped. Her hand covered her mouth. Her husband—judging by the matching wedding bands and the way they interacted—lifted the hand he held to his chest and cupped her shoulder with the other.

Emotion wafted off the couple in pounding waves. Kat breathed deeply, preparing herself for whatever horror story these two had to share, and stepped forward.

"Hello. I'm Kat." Since she'd been back, introducing herself as Dr. Royan seemed wrong. So she'd gone with the plain old Kat for weeks. Some people actually caught on and had been calling her by her first name. Not the old guard, though. Hence, therapy.

The man stood and pulled his wife to her feet, though, of the two, she seemed the one inclined to hoist. As most older men did, this one sported the signs of a life indulgently lived. He looked too clean cut for beer. So she'd guess foods high in fat and sugar.

"Hi, Kat. I'm Patrick Austen." He extended his hand. Kat took his hand in hers and offered a shake longer than her usual. He looked like he could use it. A smile lit his eyes that turned to his wife. "This is my wife."

"Hi, Kat. I'm Trish Austen." The woman offered her hand, and again, Kat extended her shake longer than normal.

"It's nice to meet you both." Kat offered them to sit and rounded to her side of the desk and sat. Her feet ached from hours at the operating table, but she hid her grimace.

"If you need a minute to put your feet up or grab a drink, feel free." The man rubbed his knees as though experiencing sympathy pains. "Your receptionist said you were in surgery before this."

Kat studied Patrick Austen. Most people wouldn't think twice about a doctor coming out of a surgery. They'd expect it to be a walk in the park. After all, they weren't the ones on the table. "I'm sorry, but are you a surgeon?"

His massive grin answered the question. "Retired, orthopedic."

"For thirty years." Trish patted his thigh.

"I'm sorry I'm not more prepared for our meeting." She closed the file open on her desk and moved it aside. "A..."—the love of my life—"...friend of mine referred you to me, but I'm sorry to say I don't know why."

Tears welled in Trish's eyes. She blinked them away and nodded. The woman was well into her sixties, maybe even early seventies, but there was a youth and determination in her that moved Kat. Trish shifted to the edge of her seat.

"Hunter called us a week ago, and then came to our home for a meeting just this week. He is truly a stunning man."

"Hey now." Her husband poked her in the ribs.

"Oh, you hush." She shooed him away with a thin hand. "He is handsome as all get-out but even more so brave and kind-hearted."

Kat blinked back tears. He was all those things and so much more.

"What he told us was quite a surprise, but more than that, it was an answer to a prayer I've never stopped repeating." Trish drew a deep breath and seemed as though she counted to five and breathed again before continuing. "Patrick and I have been married for forty years. When you make the vows for better or worse, you never expect the worse. We've lived it for the past thirty-four years."

"I'm sorry," Kat whispered.

"Oh doll, it wasn't your fault. And as much therapy as it has taken me, I know it wasn't my fault, and it wasn't Pat's." The couple held hands again.

Kat had no idea where this was going. She wasn't a marriage counselor. As it was, she'd run away from the only man she'd ever loved.

"I'm sorry, we're not making much sense just yet." Patrick scooted to the edge of his seat.

"I'm getting to it." Trish shooed him again.

"You're doing beautifully, dear." He squeezed her hand.

"When we'd been married two years, we decided to expand our family. Things were going so well. Pat signed on with a top-rated ortho clinic, and I'd taken an advisory position with the college.

That's the University of Delaware. We were ready, but my body wasn't. It took two years and as many miscarriages, but finally, we had the most beautiful baby in the entire world." Trish beamed.

Kat smiled too.

"We love her more than we've been able to express." The woman swatted at a tear. "The next two years were the best of our lives. We rotated schedules and didn't see each other much, but that meant we didn't have to arrange daycare and could spend our time with our daughter."

Beside her, Patrick nodded.

"At the beginning of my third semester as an advisor, the college offered me the opportunity to accompany students to Europe. I'd always wanted to go. By that time, Pat had worked enough that he had the vacation to take. So the three of us embarked on our first family vacation along with six college students interested in the exchange program."

Kat's smile fell. Maybe it was her ties to Europe or the change in tone of Trish's story or the way Pat moved closer to his wife. Whatever the reason, it had Kat's stomach tied in knots.

"We had an amazing trip. The students spent most of their days in the program at the local college, and we experienced France. Our daughter liked the bread shops best. Every day, she would hug a loaf of French bread from the shop closest to the housing they gave us next to campus all the way back to the steps. Only then would she turn it loose, and that was only so she could press the button that let us inside."

Despite the smile on the woman's face, tears fell freely from her blue eyes. Her husband offered her a handkerchief. Kat's heart skipped at the old-fashioned gesture. After she took it, he rubbed a hand over his mouth. When he spoke, his voice was gruff.

"My daughter and I walked to the bakery that last day in France. Trish had duties with the students. We got the usual loaf. She hugged it so tightly, almost as tightly as I hugged her to me on the walk back to the housing. The searing pain came out of nowhere. At first, I thought I was having a heart attack. I felt a burning in my shoulder and back. Then I saw the blood. The man who wielded a knife stepped in front of me."

He looked up at the light and blinked furiously. "I wasn't a fighter, but I was prepared to take on the world to save you." Patrick wiped at his eyes.

Kat let her tears fall freely. Therapy. Don't mask your feelings. Let them flow. Apparently, today that was down her face, ruining what makeup surgery hadn't.

"I didn't know it, but there were four of them. Organized. They had a fancy car, and I was losing blood so quickly. That bastard...excuse my language—"

"Those pieces of shit," Trish supplied.

"They'd known just how to hit an artery. When they pulled my daughter from my arms, all I could do was lay on the pavement and watch the most horrifying thing I'd ever imagined happen."

Surely, when he'd said you, it'd been a slipup. She was the age their daughter would've been. She had a light complexion and light hair like they did. She just reminded them of the daughter they'd lost. No, the daughter stolen from them.

"When I got to him on the sidewalk, he was unconscious and so close to death I didn't know what happened to our daughter. The police put out a bulletin, but it was two days before Pat was well enough to speak. In a city of fancy black cars and no witnesses to the crime, there were no leads." Trish had reined in her emotions, but she still spoke with purpose and conviction. "We stayed for three months, prodding the police, walking the streets, and interviewing people. None of the pieces led anywhere."

"They forced us to leave after a one-week extension of our short-term visas." Pat shook his head. "Before we left, we hired a French investigator. He just took our money. We had given him a lot because we were desperate to find our daughter. Over the years, we've taken countless trips to France. We begged the US embassy for help. We hired American investigators. We paid off French officials."

The couple clung together as if they were the only thing keeping each other upright. They quieted.

Kat let the story sink in. She could envision everything from the little girl to the streaks of blood on the street. Her imagination even painted the face of the man who took their daughter. It was the face of Tor Royan. Then again, Kat was in intense therapy for a reason.

She wiped the tears from her eyes and licked her lips. "Did you ever find your daughter?"

"Yes," Pat and Trish answered in unison. Their eyes glossed with fresh tears and large smiles stretched their mouths.

Pat kissed the back of his wife's hand. "Hunter searched the missing person database for weeks. When he came across our story, he made contact and asked questions. We never expected... But he came back with a ninety-nine point nine nine percent DNA match to you, Kat."

Kat covered her mouth. Tears slipped over her fingers.

"I don't mean to upset you, doll." Pat grimaced.

She shook her head because words weren't yet possible. Pat pulled another handkerchief from a pocket and handed it across the table. Kat clutched the cloth like a lifeline.

"He searched Tor Royan's financials," Pat continued, "and found no record of him having a daughter until the week of your disappearance. The records also showed that Tor was in France that week, working on a deal to funnel illegal drugs through the area. Hunter was convinced you were our missing daughter."

"And you?" Kat croaked.

"We were hopeful, but after so much disappointment through the years, we were skeptical"—the woman sighed—"until you walked into the room." Trish fought off tears by using her hand as a fan but lost the battle. "I'd, we'd, know your face anywhere."

It was all too much to take in at once. She had a family. For her entire life, she'd been loved and not known it. Tor had stolen her from her father's arms and left him for dead.

Kat couldn't get her body to move. It was as if shock paralyzed her. Joy and rage formed a heady mix she didn't know what to do with.

"Please." Trish lifted her hands in prayer toward Kat. "We know this is a lot to take in all at once. The last thing we want to do is cause you more pain. Hunter didn't tell us much, but we know you weren't physically harmed and that you had at least a good education."

"He was a twisted man who never laid an ill hand on me but who abused me through neglect."

Kat smiled to put them at ease as much as she could. "It's something I didn't realize until our mutual friend pointed it out. It's something I'm working on with a therapist."

"I'm glad you're getting help." Trish nodded and wrung her hands. "It makes all the difference. We just want you to know we're here for whatever you need, as much or as little as you want. You don't owe us anything."

"Now that you're free, your life truly is yours to live as you choose." Pat nodded. "Of course, we'd love to get to know you but not at any cost to your well-being." He placed a card on the desk. "This has all our contact information; address, phone numbers, cellular phones. If you want to reach out, we're available at your disposal. Anytime."

They stood. Kat's leg wouldn't work, but she offered Pat his hankie.

"Please, keep it." He grinned.

"Thank you for listening to our story." Trish placed her hand on Kat's and held it there for a few seconds. "I know it will be hard on us all, but one day, I hope you'll share your story with us."

Kat wanted to say something. Thank you. Thank God. Thank Hunter. She just sat and watched the couple—her parents—walk out of the door and close it behind them.

Peace and longing, contentment and angst, elation and anger; each emotion cut in line in front of the other. They pushed and shoved their way to the lead. Overwhelmed wasn't the word to describe what she was. An accurate one didn't exist. Not in her vocabulary anyway. Some of Hunter's words would work, though.

She sat for hours. The sunlight streaming through her small office window finally ebbed as did her tears. Her skills as a doctor had given

Hunter another shot at life. His skills as a badass had gifted her with another shot at life; one she hadn't known she'd missed until she'd met him.

Her wet finger twined in the handkerchief her father, by blood and love, had given to show her comfort. Kat couldn't imagine the strength it took for them to walk out, but then again, she'd walked away from Hunter. Sometimes, the right thing wasn't what you wanted it to be, and other times, like today, it was exactly the thing you'd hoped and dreamed about every day of your life.

Kat slid the card she'd been staring at all afternoon toward her. Then she pulled the one from her desk drawer Hunter had given her before they parted. It was white except for a single phone number. From no family to complete love in a day—the day Hunter had opened his eyes and looked at her—the gift was almost too much to comprehend.

She picked up the receiver and dialed the home number for Trish and Patrick Austen. The line went live after the first ring.

"Hello?" Patrick answered.

"Hi, Dad."

In all the years she'd thought she'd had a father, never once had she called Tor dad. The title hadn't belonged to him.

"Kat, doll." There was a pause. "I'm so happy." He sniffled and laughed. "I'm so happy you called."

"Me too." She picked up both cards in the hand with her dad's handkerchief and crushed them all to her chest. "Me too." In the background, she heard Trish's squeal.

"I'm going to put you on speakerphone if that's okay?"

"That's perfect."

"Okay, Kat. We're here," Pat announced. His voice sounded bigger than it had before.

"I'm shocked and overwhelmed," Kat admitted. "For the first time in as long as I can remember, though, it's not by loneliness but by love. I want you in my life. I want to share my story with you, and I want us to make new stories."

"Oh, Kat." Trish sobbed. "That's what we want too. So much."

"If it's not too soon, I'd like to meet with you tomorrow. I totally understand if you have plans or think it's too much," Kat hedged.

"Doll, it's not soon enough," Pat said.

"Kat, please, come to the house any time tomorrow or tonight. I'll have food. You can stay as long as you want," Trish insisted.

"Would it be okay if I invited Hunter along?" Kat asked.

"Doll, I owe that man a couple of my nine lives." Pat chuckled. "You bring him anytime."

"I don't know that he'll come." She rubbed her thumb over the number that'd yet to connect them.

"Kat?" Trish asked.

"Yes?" Kat whispered.

"He loves you as much as we do. He'll be here. Just ask him." Her mother sounded so confident.

"I will. Thank you, Mom." The word felt new yet comfortable in her mouth.

"My absolute pleasure, Kat. We look forward to seeing you soon."

"How about tomorrow at eleven?"

"Perfect," Pat chimed.

"We'll see you then," Trish squeaked.

"We love you, Doll," Pat said.

"God, yes we do," Trish agreed.

"I don't know you just yet, but I know that I'll love you two in no time."

Their cheers and laughter filled the line for a second as Kat placed the phone back in its cradle only to pick it right back up again. She dialed the number Hunter had given her with a smile on her face. By the sixth ring, the smile faltered. When the recording told her to leave another message, Kat didn't hang up for once. She breathed deeply.

"Hunter, there aren't enough words to express how thankful I am that you came into my life. So, I'll use grand gestures. I'm willing to use my body too. Whatever it takes to get you back in my life, I will do it. If any of that sounds like something that moves you, I'd love for you to join me at my parents' house tomorrow at eleven a.m." She shifted to hang up the receiver but stalled. "Thank you, Hunter, for showing me love and helping me learn how to love. Whether I see you tomorrow or never again, I'll love you forever."

Chapter Twenty Seven

If Kat took any longer, Hunter's fingers would freeze completely and have to be removed due to frostbite. She loved him as a single above-the-knee amputee. Would she love him with no fingers? Probably not. His fingers played her body like an instrument and were starved for the sound of her, the feel of her. The past five weeks had been more torturous than her captor's chamber. He shifted his ass cheek he'd propped on the hood of his '69 Mustang Boss—right to left—and looked at his watch.

9:15 a.m.

He expected her to bound out of her condo any minute now and head to her car to start the hour and a half trek to her parents' house. No way in hell would he let her make that drive alone. Meet her there. Who was she kidding? Hunter wasn't the romantic type, but Cara, Carmen, and Rin were a heart and flowers dream team. Even Tucker had thrown in a decent idea or two. After one meeting, operation Get the Girl was a go.

Stage One: Find Kat's Mother had shocked the hell out of him. When he'd expected to find a clandestine grave on one of the Royan properties, he'd found Patrick and Trish. Stage Two: The Reveal, letting the Austens know their daughter was alive and well, had lifted him to a level of fulfillment he'd only experienced in Kat's presence.

According to Patrick and Trish, Stage Three: First Contact had gone beautifully. Which progressed him on to Stage Four: Wow and Woo. He had flowers and a dictionary. Each of the words they'd learned while hiding in the cabin was highlighted in yellow with yellow tabs as well as some words highlighted in pink with pink tabs. Those she needed to familiarize herself with.

He'd arrived early, in case she'd decided to get a head start. The girls had told him the surprise was over half the fun. He wasn't to knock on the door but wait for her—in the cold—with the ønske burning a hole in his chest. The hot and cold should've balanced each other. Instead, they created an irritation he couldn't shake until she was in his arms.

Getting out of the car hadn't helped. Maybe pacing would. He knew it wouldn't, but what the hell else did he have to do until she came outside? Hunter shoved his hands in his pockets and started up the sidewalk. When he came even with her building, he saw large hollowed out footprints in the snow from a row of hedges on the west side of the two-unit condo. Kat's unit. The footprints in themselves were curious. No one walked in the snow when perfectly clean sidewalks were available. Also, the only thing on the side of the building were windows. Windows into Kat's house.

Hunter's palms slicked. Suddenly, the frigid temperature was the least of his concern. He talked himself down for a three count. Then his gaze traveled the line to Kat's little coupe.

As casually as was possible with at least a peeping Tom in Kat's midst and at most a person her father had wronged seeking revenge, Hunter grabbed his phone, dialed Oliver, and walked perpendicular to the footsteps toward the back of the building.

His friend picked up on the second ring.

"When's the date, bro?" Oliver asked.

"I have a situation. Suspicious as all fuck footprints outside Kat's condo and car. Get some of our crime scene guys—"

Talking or, rather, the belligerent rant of an unfamiliar male voice coming from inside Kat's condo stopped everything; his heart, the world, the future.

"Hunter?"

"Shhh." He crouched low and moved close to the brick. Through the closed blinds, he could see nothing, but this close, he heard the one-sided conversation too well.

"I'm the loyal child, the one he kept close, in confidence. The one who didn't get him killed. You did that, you and that agent."

Hunter moved around to the front of the building. "Trey Royan, the fucking weasel I've been looking for, is inside yelling at Kat about getting her father killed. I've gotta go."

"Wait for backup."

"It's at least thirty minutes by HELO. She'll be dead by then."

"Remember what happened last time you bailed without backup?"

"I am, and I'd do it again. That and more. Just like you would for Mar."

"Stay safe, brother. I'll be there as fast as the bird will fly."

Hunter placed the phone on vibrate, shoved it into his pocket, and tried the door. The knob gave, and he eased it open a crack. If only he'd been here before. He had zero idea of the condo's layout. The mix of voices sounded as though they still came from the back of the building, but was there a straight shot from the back to the front? Was Trey watching it?

Fuck. Were he in full gear, he'd have a mirror, flash-bangs, and tear gas. All the things he'd need to get Kat swiftly and safely out of harm's way. Instead, he had the technological equivalent of a Swiss army knife and his side arm. He pulled the smart phone from his pocket, switched on the camera, and eased the lens into the crack.

The door led into a small living room. A key chain lay on the floor surrounded by shards of glass and plastic. The indestructible phone case sat empty next to the upturned coffee table.

Rage boiled in his veins, turning adrenaline to speed.

Kat's living room led into a narrow hallway with two open doors and an archway at the end. Kitchen counters lined what he could see of the far wall. There was a clear shot to the front door. For the moment, no one watched it.

Hunter replaced his phone and eased the door open wide enough for his frame to fit. He shifted to the far side of the door and leaned in, still keeping his body out of the line of fire. His view of the hallway widened to the edge of the kitchen.

No Kat. No Trey.

He hurried inside and eased the door back to its frame. The desperation in Trey's tone grew louder.

"I will carry on the family name."

"No one says you can't."

A large thunk split the air. Something shattered. Two large hunks skidded across the floor in Hunter's view. Several smaller bits followed. "The man you let escape says I can't. My sources say he's been looking for me."

Hunter would have doubled over from the gut shot his words delivered, but that wouldn't help Kat now. Only his very best work would do. He'd love nothing more than to set up in a tree and blow this guy's brains all over the wall, but that wouldn't help Kat move on with her life. He had to defuse the situation, up close and personal.

"I don't know anything about that." Kat's voice sounded calm and confident.

"Don't lie to me," Trey screamed.

She didn't reply.

That a girl. Don't give him any ammo.

From the living room to the hallway lay a minefield of noisemakers. Hunter grabbed a knitted throw from a chair and dragged it across from one side of the mess to the other. The tiny shards made noise, but nothing the maniac would hear over the sound of his own demanding voice. Hunter tossed the blanket out of sight and eased down the corridor to the first doorway.

The bedroom smelled of Kat. Were there not a madman's heir fighting for his place in the world, Hunter would've sported instant wood. He didn't even have time to admire the large bed and fluffy comforter before he shifted to the next doorway. The bathroom smelled like Kat too.

"I know that you and Tor had a different relationship than he and I did," Kat admitted.

"We did," he agreed boisterously.

"I know, but that doesn't mean everything he told you was the truth," she explained.

"What are you trying to say?" A loud bang, like a fist on a table, sailed out of the kitchen and ricocheted into the bathroom.

"Did you know Tor wasn't my real father?" Kat asked.

"Who told you that?"

It was a wonder no one had called the cops yet. Trey's questions and accusations turned to extreme outbursts.

Unflappable, Kat continued. "He stole me when I was a baby."

"No. No. No," Trey's denial grew quieter with each disagreement.

Footsteps squeaked across the floor.

"You may have a family out there, Trey."

"No," he whispered.

Hunter didn't like the change in the guy's tone. Loud he could deal with. Quiet? Quiet meant thinking, plotting, planning. None of Trey's plans would end well for Kat.

"Trey, do you remember when we first met?"

"Of course."

"We went to the hospital, and the doctor set your broken arm."

"So?"

"That's the reason I wanted to become a doctor. I saw how that doctor helped you, and I wanted to help people."

"Well, glad I could help."

"Trey?" There was silence for three long heartbeats.

"What?"

"Did Tor break your arm?"

Trey hollered. There was a loud thud and scuffle. Caution be damned, Hunter rounded the corner.

A rectangular dining table hit the floor, legs up. Trey wrenched Kat from the chair by her neck. She didn't fight but held Trey's arm with one hand. The other she kept loose at her side.

When her eyes collided with Hunter's, she didn't flinch. It was almost as though she'd expected him to pop around the corner.

"You!" Trey yanked Kat more fully in front of his body, forcing her to become a human shield.

"Me." Hunter nodded. "I'm the one who killed your uncle. I'm the one who killed your father."

The handsome man snarled, revealing the hideous beast that lurked beneath the surface. He edged toward the counter. A knife block sat full and too close for Hunter's comfort. If Trey reached the knives before Hunter could get a shot, things wouldn't go well. In real life, there were no duck and shoot signals between hostages and soldiers. He could take a shot, but he couldn't force himself to shoot Kat, even if it was to save her life.

"Here." Hunter dropped his gun on the ground and kicked it down the hallway.

"No." Kat's eyes bulged as Trey clamped down on her throat, choking off her plea.

The only thing Hunter could do was get his attention. "I'm unarmed and one legged. Let her go and come and get the one you really want."

Tears filled Kat's eyes.

If Hunter could get his hands on that little shit, he could end this in seconds. He just had to entice Trey. "Tor was a real sicko. I honestly wouldn't be surprised if he beat you into submission since you were too little to know any different."

"Shut up," Trey screamed.

"I really don't want to know if he visited your room at night." Hunter shook his head. "I can't even let my mind go there. But there are some sickos in the world."

Trey threw Kat to the side. She landed on the table between him and the crazy man.

"Kat, run and don't stop." Hunter ordered.

"She's not going anywhere. Neither are you." Trey reached behind his back and pulled a shiny silver pistol from his waistband. He leveled the barrel at Kat. His sick, dark eyes remained fixed on Hunter. A wretched smile spread across his face.

At that moment, Hunter knew two things. One, Trey Royan was Tor's biological son, and two, he was about to die, saving the woman he loved.

Hunter launched himself through the air.

Two shots filled the room.

This time, just like the last, he didn't feel much. Then he collided with Royan. They crashed to the ground. Hunter wrestled the gun from his fingers and slid it toward Kat. If she needed to, she could defend herself. Blood pooled on the floor, but until the last drop left his body, Hunter would maim this bastard.

"Hunter." Kat called his name.

He reared back to elbow Royan in the face but found it listing to the side. The man's dark eyes stared into the distance that was far beyond this plane.

Hunter eased back. Two bullet holes centered Trey Royan's chest. He turned to Kat.

She dropped the pistol he'd given her at the lake house next to her thigh. The gun he'd ripped from Trey's fingers lay on the floor between them. "Is he dead?"

With two fingers, he checked for a pulse and then scrambled off the corpse and over to Kat. He pulled her into his arms and crushed her to his chest. He rocked her for a long time in the quiet. Finally, he sat back. Her warm cheeks cupped in his hands; he studied her face. "I'm so sorry."

"I'm not." Kat's head shook as much as his hands would allow.

"I never wanted to put you in that position."

"You didn't. He did." Her lips pressed against the edge of his hand. "I tried to talk him down. You tried to end it without killing him."

"My fucking bad," Hunter growled.

"You didn't know he had the gun." She hugged him close. "And if I'm telling the truth, I'm glad to know it's over. He's the last Royan I'll ever have to worry about."

Chapter Twenty Eight

"All right, Doctor." The detective closed his notebook that contained her answers to the forty thousand questions he'd asked. At least this time she was able to answer them on the pillowy softness of her own couch as opposed to the unforgiving metal chairs at the Base Branch Headquarters. He leaned in. "We'll need you to come down to the precinct tomorrow and give a formal statement." Well, damn. Back into the hard chair she'd go.

"Yes, sir."

The brawny man stood and adjusted the too small suit over his large frame.

"Detective Kirk?"

He lifted a stubble covered chin in question.

"Hunter Masters, is he still here?"

Kirk scoffed. "Doctor, I thought we were going to have to ring his bell and drag him outside to get him away from you." They could have tried. "If Reno is done questioning him, I'm sure Masters is on the front stoop waiting for the green light to come inside. But I'll check. Are you going to be okay in here by yourself?"

"Yes. Thank you."

Kat looked around her apartment. All the furniture had been set to right minus the smudges of powder from the fingerprinting. The glass and plastic had been swept up and placed in an evidence bag. Most importantly, the dead body had been removed from her kitchen, and all remnants of it had been wiped away. If only she could wipe clean her mind as easily. She'd done the right thing without question. Living with that choice, though...

The door opened, and Hunter stepped inside with a fresh shirt on his chest and concern on his face.

Living with that choice meant living with Hunter. And that she could deal with. She would enjoy living with it with him if he'd have her.

Detective Kirk stepped in behind Hunter. "There's a slew of people out here waiting to see you two. We're wrapping it up on our end, but we'll keep the crime scene tape up for a few minutes. I expect y'all want some quiet time before the onslaught."

"Thanks, Detective." Hunter waved.

The man nodded and closed the door behind him.

Who all was out there? Hunter's people? Kat didn't have people...but now she did.

"Patrick and Trish are out there." Hunter nodded to her unvoiced question.

"Oh. Are they okay?"

"I talked to them. They know what happened, and that you're not hurt. They'll be better once they see you for themselves."

She bet they were worried sick when she didn't show up at their house. Lord. That in and of itself was enough to give Patrick a heart attack. She needed to get him lined up with a good heart doctor and get him exercising with Trish. They had to be around for forever.

"I know you're worried about them, but they're strong. They've been through a ton and have come out the other side of it an impenetrable unit because they lean on each other and lift each other up."

Hunter stepped closer and knelt in front of her. Kat grabbed his face in her hands and eased her cheek to his. Warmth radiated through them. Moving back and forth, one to the other, they shared the burden, the sorrow, the immense joy, and the excitement of things to come. She pulled back and crushed their mouths together. Her hands ran over his neck and chest and then down his arms with the need to feel he was whole and there for her. It was only then she noticed one of his hands hidden behind his back.

"Not so fast, Doc. You're going to make me skip over things."

"Things?"

His smile brightened the room that dimmed with the waning daylight. "I had time to think while we were apart."

"You had time to find my family." Tears slipped down Kat's cheeks even though she'd bargained with herself about not crying again today. "I'll never be able to thank you enough for that. Never."

"The look on your face is enough for me." He smoothed the hair from her cheek, grabbed it at her nape, and pulled her close. "But I do recall an enticing message about using your body to thank me. I'm not opposed to that." His grin melted her heart. He chuckled and released her.

"I had a lot of time to think about me and my issues; lack of commitment for fear of investing and losing, the future of my career. I'm not fired from Base Branch, and I even got a shiny medal for saving Ollie's tail."

"Oh, my goodness. That's amazing."

"It is pretty nice." He grabbed her hand and smoothed his finger over her knuckles. The contact sent a wave of tingles rolling across her skin. "How are you doing with your issues?" His lips pressed against her knuckles. "I'm not trying to pry, but I need to know where you arc in that pretty head of yours."

"I called you."

He offered an excessive grin. "I needed you to meet your parents before you dealt with me."

"Several times," she continued, "to tell you that I have a therapist, and I'm mulling through all my stuff. I feel like me but better than I've ever been."

"Was that all you wanted to tell me?"

"If you'd answered or called me back, you'd know. Wouldn't you?" She poked him in the ribs they'd nursed back to health.

"Hey, I showed up today for a very important reason that had nothing to do with Trey. And fuck, Kat, I'm glad I did."

She nodded and pulled him to her until they were chest to chest. To hell with the surprise flowers behind his back. She'd smelled them soon after he'd knelt. Her fingers hit something hard. Intrigue snared her, and her fingers explored the object. It was big.

"You little sneak." He set her back on the couch and straightened only the second button-down shirt she'd ever seen him wear—the first having been covered in blood. "I've never been a romantic, so I got a little help with these and a candle lit dinner we probably won't get to tonight." Hunter handed over the most beautiful bouquet of red, pink, yellow, white, and orange roses. "They all mean something different. Of course, right now I can only remember pink because I admire the hell out of you, Doc. And I remember red because I love you like nothing else."

Kat hugged him so hard she squealed.

"As I said, I had help with those, but this..." He handed over a stunning leather-bound dictionary with gold embossing that read *American Dictionary of the English Language*. A white square of paper had been taped over the bottom portion of the front cover and yellow and pink tabs stuck out on the top from the gold-edged papers. They were all numbered. Yellow was one through three. Pink was one through four. "This I did all by myself."

"What's all this?" Kat hugged the sturdy book to her chest and stared at the tabs and then at Hunter's wide, excited eyes.

"Look at the yellow tabs first."

"Okay." Kat's cheeks hurt from smiling so much, which she never expected to happen after their morning, but this was what Hunter did to her. He made her face her troubles so she could release them and enjoy life.

She set the book in her lap and pulled open the page with the first yellow tab. On the hyperirritability through hypochondrium page, *hypernova* was highlighted yellow. "Oh, my..." Kat covered her mouth with one hand. With the other, she flipped to the second word *hypocaust*, and then the next word *desire*. "Hunter." Her finger sank into the collar of his shirt and held tight to this man who got her when no one else in the world did. "I love it so much. I can't even find a word to define how much I love it."

"We're not done yet." He smiled, took both her hands, rubbed the tears off them onto his shirt, released her, and motioned for her to grab the book.

Impossibly, she loved him more for protecting the thin pages from her tears.

"Now pink, in order, and you have to read the highlighted definitions."

"Okay." Her head bobbed, and her fingers flew over the silky soft pages.

Her fingers landed on the page with definitions from wild-eyed to wimple. She had no idea what wimple meant, but that wasn't the point of this exercise. Not that she had a clue what the exercise was, but she was dying to figure it out. Her fingers scrolled down. Found it.

"Will - Third definition. Expressing a request." She looked at him for a signal to what it all meant. He shooed her on to the next tab.

Yokel through yuck. "You - First definition. Used to refer to the person or people who the speaker is addressing."

These were all easy words. She'd known their definitions since she was a little girl. Her fingers flipped to the next tab.

Marquess through marvel. "Marry—"

Kat's mouth fell open. She looked at Hunter. His gaze was narrow; his mouth clamped between his teeth. Had she ever seen him—the man who was down a leg and still launched himself at people trying to hurt her—nervous?

She swallowed, licked her lips, and started again. "Marry - Definitions one and two. Join in marriage." Her fingers tingled on the page. "Cause to meet or fit together; combine." Her fingers flipped furiously to the final tab. It wasn't far away.

"Me - used by a speaker to refer to himself or herself as the object of a verb or preposition." Her tears fell in earnest.

Hunter took the book and set it beside her. He cradled her hands in his rough ones. "I'm no woman's hero, Kat, but I want to be yours."

"You already are mine." She squeezed his hands.

"Says the woman who's saved me twice." He held her chin and leaned close. "Kat, I love you. I admire you." He pulled the white rectangle of paper from the front cover. The gold embossing read Kat Masters. "I want to spend the rest of my life leaning on you and holding you up. Will you marry me?"

Epilogue

"Who'd have thought the three of you would get married?" Khani Slaughter stalked forward—because she walked that way—with Street. Their former leader and her man looked smoother than a Calvin Klein ad in matching black outfits. Khani's sleek dress hugging a lot closer than Street's suit.

"Not to each other is the surprising part, I think." Oliver poked the pin through the collection of tiny roses on Hunter's lapel and clapped him on the back.

"I'm not hitched." Tyler threw up his hand.

"That's only because Cara doesn't believe in marriage," Hunter offered.

Tyler rolled his eyes. "Women. I thought they all wanted to get married, and I fall in love with the one who doesn't."

"Not all." King stopped in front of them and held his arm out for Khani. "If I've learned anything over the past two years, it's that women are complex, strong creatures who'll keep you on your toes better than any adversary."

"Hey, I'm not hitched either, so let's get this show on the road." Hunter kissed Khani's cheek, shook Street's thick hand, and opened the door to the ballroom of the historical manor for them to head inside. He didn't look into the room where Base Branch soldiers and staffers from all over the country and the world gathered along with Kat's family and friends to witness his and Kat's marriage.

"I see Zeke and Greer," Khani whispered to her lover, and he closed the door behind them.

The back door opened nearly in sync with his closing of the other one. Magdalena stepped inside and stopped cold. Someone bumped into her back. Mags braced both hands on either side of the opening and barred their entrance. "You bloody fools." She waved one hand, swishing them wildly toward the front of the building. "You're supposed to go around the front. The bride comes in the back."

"Wow! Your accent is thick when you're bossing people around," Oliver poked.

"Law would say that's all the time." Hunter should have kept his mouth shut. He knew Mags better than the two friends with whom he stood. Since he and Kat had stayed in her childhood home for almost two months, the two women had become best friends, inseparable even by the thousands of miles between them.

Mags hiked the gray dress that revealed no hint to the fact that she had a six-month-old baby. Well, her boobs were bigger, but he wasn't supposed to notice things like that anymore. Old habits.

"Hunter Masters, so help me. If you see Kat before she comes walking down the aisle, I'll steal your leg and give it to the girls," Mags threatened.

Behind him, the guys erupted in laughter. The girls were being raised by the best operatives in Base Branch history. His friends didn't realize how illusive Sloan and Baine's operatives in training were.

Mags didn't realize how badly he wanted to see Kat. He walked toward the door, and the woman's eyes bulged. Her cheeks bloomed with red. "Don't you dare come over here. You can't break tradition."

"Look around, Mags." He gestured to the grand colonial manor. "If we weren't breaking tradition, I'd be in the back working the fields."

"Match point, Masters." Magdalena nodded.

"Hunter?" Kat's voice curved around the door and arrowed straight to his heart. "I didn't even think about that when Mom and Dad set up the venue."

"Because it doesn't matter. I like what it represents; the past and you're my future." He reached his hand around the door but kept his face back to keep Mags from stabbing him with her stiletto. Her fingers intertwined with his, and he couldn't fight the smile that stretched his mouth. "I'm so ready to marry you."

"I'm ready to marry you." Kat giggled.

"Then go on." Mags shooed them.

"See you soon, Doc." He let go and headed down the hallway that ran the length of the ballroom.

The guys followed. Midway down the hall, a side door opened so quickly he couldn't duck. The thick wood smacked into his shoulder and sent him crashing to the ground. He was up and ready for the attack in seconds.

A red-faced and cutely pregnant Piper Noble gasped in the doorway. "Ay! Dios!" The Base Branch operative shook her hand as though it hurt, but Hunter soon realized it was one of her expressive gestures. "I'm so sorry. It took us forever to find the bathroom, and I was worried we'd miss the ceremony."

"There won't be one if we take out the groom." Her husband, Ryan Noble, held her close and smoothed a reassuring hand down her bare shoulder.

"Hush now. He's tough. I'm sure he's fine," Piper chided. Her gaze found his. "Are you okay?"

"You're just making sure I don't lose my edge," Hunter assured.

"Like any of you could." She grabbed her husband's tie and pulled him through the doorway and across the hall to the ballroom's side entrance.

"What exactly were y'all doing in the bathroom?" Tyler readjusted the cowboy hat he'd shined up especially for the occasion.

"Not your business, Tyler Grace." Ryan ushered his wife inside and headed for their seat.

When Hunter and his two groomsmen stepped into the room, all eyes followed them to the front of the room to Law, who'd agreed to officiate the ceremony.

"Ready for this?" Law asked.

"More than." Hunter shook his hand, hugged his best men, and then turned toward the back of the room.

Several minutes later, the music started. The back doors opened, and no eyes were on him any longer. They watched a sweet and sunshiny Magdalena walk regally down the aisle. "She's got them all fooled," Hunter whispered to her husband.

"Not the ones who matter." Law chuckled and waved to his baby who was in the first row in Sloan's arms and oblivious to his fatherly attempts at communication.

Next, Trish Austen preceded her daughter, walked to the front, and stood as her matron of honor with the biggest smile on her face he'd ever seen...until the doors opened wide.

Kat and a slimmer Patrick Austen beamed so hard their smiles alone might light the place. The two walked arm in arm up the aisle.

His wife to be rocked his world yet again. She wore a sheer cream-colored gown that hugged her to the hips and then cascaded down in wavy layers. The delicate embroidery on the top added the perfect touch, accentuating her femininity along with her loose flowing locks. He couldn't wait to touch her.

When Pat kissed his daughter's cheek, tears glittered in his eyes. He turned and offered Hunter his hand. He took it. The man squeezed harder than he remembered. "I wouldn't trust my daughter to anyone except you, Hunter. May you love each other as completely as Trish and I do."

"Thank you, sir. I know we do." Hunter took his soon-to-be wife's hand, kissed it, and took just a moment to stare in wonder at the beauty about to promise to love and cherish him forever. "I'm one lucky bastard."

"You're my lucky bastard." Kat kissed his hand.

Together, they turned toward Law who welcomed their dearest friends and family, defined love and marriage per Kat's dictionary obsession, and then got to the goods. "Are you ready to state your vows in front of your chosen witnesses?"

"We are," they agreed.

"I, Hunter Masters, choose you, Katherine Austen, to be my wife. I promise to trust and respect you, to honor and adore you, to lean on you in times of sorrow, and lift you up when you need my strength. I love you always."

Trish sniffled.

Kat beamed. She squished his hands in hers. "I, Katherine Austen, take you, Hunter Masters, to be my husband. I promise to trust and respect you, to honor and adore you, to lean on you in times of sorrow, and lift you up when you need my strength. I love you always."

"The rings." Law signaled to Oliver and Trish.

He and Kat grabbed them and turned to each other. Kat's feet danced under her long lace gown. It forced a laugh from his throat that wasn't accustomed at the wedding, but then again, he wasn't accustomed at weddings. When she joined in, nothing mattered except them.

Hunter took her hand in his and eased on the double X banded rose gold ring with its hexagonal framed slice of translucent moonstone. "This ring is a symbol of my heart."

Kat smiled, but a well of tears formed in her eyes. "I love you."

"I love you, Doc."

She took his hand and slid on the thick gray tungsten carbide band with its sliver of rose gold curved through the center. "This ring is a symbol of my heart."

"By the power vested in me by the state of Virginia, I pronounce you husband and wife." Law looked at Kat and jutted his chin Hunter's way. "Kat, you may kiss your husband but remember small children and your parents are watching."

"Which means you'd better kiss him good," Trish whispered.

Kat handed back her bouquet and rubbed her hands together.

"Looks like I'm in for a wild ride." Hunter laughed.

"Looks like we both are." Kat grabbed him by both lapels and gave him a hint of their wonderful life to come.

ENEMY MINE
A BASE BRANCH NOVEL

When friends become enemies and enemies become lovers.

Born in the blood of Sierra Leone's Civil War, enslaved, then sold to the US as an orphan, Base Branch operative Sloan Harris is emotionally dead and driven by vengeance. With no soul to give, her body becomes the bargaining chip to infiltrate a warlord's inner circle. The man called The Devil killed her family and helped destroy a region.

As son of the warlord, Baine Kendrick will happily use Sloan's body if it expedites his father's demise. Yet, he is wholly unprepared for the possessive and protective emotions she provokes. Maybe it's the flashes of memory ... two forgotten children drawing in the dirt beneath the boabab tree... But he fears there is more at stake than his life.

In the Devil's den with Baine by her side, Sloan braves certain death and discovers a spirit for living.

FOR ALL TO SEE
A BUREAU NOVEL

Pristine waters and purified evil.

Two by two, dark-haired beauties vanish only to reappear as hanging, plundered corpses. The Virgin Islands boast diamond-white beaches, lush green mountains, a rich cultural heritage—and a brutal killer.

Three years on the "Field-Dresser" case and Special Agent Nathan Brewer is days away from catching the bastard—if he can convince a certain brunette to trust him. Only the woman is more likely to take a casual stroll on the surface of the sun.

After fleeing her troubles in the United States for the quiet life of a school teacher on the island of Tortola, Madelyn Garrett never imagined she'd be fixated upon by pure evil.

In a fight for her life—with a dwindling number of friends—she must rely on her cunning and Nathan's skills for survival.

Megan Mitcham is a *USA Today* bestselling author who has penned more than 15 sizzling suspense novels. Her work is said to whisk you across the globe, wedge your heart in your throat, make your hands sweat and your skin tingle. Check out Megan's special forces heroes in the Base Branch Series. If you like the darker side of suspense, try her Bureau Series. She is a Mississippi native, living and loving it in the natural state.

For information on releases and giveaways subscribe at meganmitcham.com!

Facebook: AuthorMeganMitcham
Twitter: @MeganMMMitcham
Pinterest: MeganMitcham5
Goodreads: Megan_Mitcham
Website: www.meganmitcham.com

FOR INFORMATION ON NEW RELEASES &
GIVEAWAYS, SIGN UP FOR MEGAN'S
NEWSLETTER AT WWW.MEGANMITCHAM.COM.